LIKE

MOTHER,

LIKE

DAUGHTER

LIKE
MOTHER,
LIKE
DAUGHTER

***

KIMBERLY
McCREIGHT

ALFRED A. KNOPF

NEW YORK

2024

THIS IS A BORZOI BOOK PUBLISHED
BY ALFRED A. KNOPF

Knopf, Borzoi Books, and the colophon are registered trademarks
of Penguin Random House LLC.

ISBN 9780593536421

Jacket artwork by Evan Sklar
Jacket design by Jenny Carrow

Manufactured in the United States of America

For Harper & Emerson—

What a gift it is to know you.

What an honor to be your mother.

Once she was born I was never not afraid.

LIKE

MOTHER,

LIKE

DAUGHTER

PROLOGUE

As soon as you begin to show, the lies start. They will be well-meaning, all of them. Friends, family, doctors, total strangers—pretty much anyone who spies your pregnant belly will tell you:

Don't worry, you'll know what to do when the time comes.
Don't worry, your maternal instincts will kick right in.
Don't worry, your body will bounce right back.
Don't worry, you're going to be an amazing mother.
Don't worry, it's not as hard as it looks.
Don't worry, being a mother is the most rewarding job in the world.
Don't worry, you will love them more than you ever thought possible.

The last one is true, if dangerously oversimplified.

It is indeed a ferocious love you feel the second you hold your child, hot and wriggling, against your naked chest. You will die to protect that child. You suspect, uncomfortably, that you could also kill. You have never thought of yourself as this person before—wild, animalistic. It will make you feel both powerful and afraid.

This is your first true introduction to motherhood, this study in contradictions.

And then there is the cost of this boundless love that no one warns you about: the worry and sleepless nights. The fear that they will get sick or grow up sad or be forever lonely. And that it will be your fault. Or that someday they might stop returning your calls. After all, just because you love them without condition does not obligate them to love you back.

Oh, and you will get so much of it wrong. Partly because there *is* no right answer, to any of it. And on that rare occasion when you *do* knock it out of the park? That will only make you believe that other mothers must be doing it right all the time. You will commit to trying harder.

You will try until your eyes burn and your arms ache. Until your heart crumbles to dust.

You will do whatever it takes. Even when you don't know what that is. Especially then. And get ready, because this will be your job forever, this fixing of everything, including the things that cannot be fixed.

For as long as you both shall live.

CLEO

Our brownstone looks beautiful, lit up a warm gold in the fading April light. Homey and pristine Park Slope perfection, thanks to my mom, of course. God forbid anything she does ever be less than perfect. Except here I am, frozen on the corner, half a block from the house where I grew up, consumed by dread. And this is not exactly a new feeling.

I could turn around right now and get on the subway. Head back to NYU, to that party in my dorm that will probably start soon. To Will. But there was something about the way my mom reached out this time. She insisted she needed to talk to me in person, *right now*. That's not new. But then she said that she understood why I wouldn't want to come, that she was asking me, begging me, to please come anyway. And she sounded so . . . sincere—and that *was* new. Of course, it went downhill from there. In the past twenty-four hours, she's fallen back on her tried-and-true method: brute force. Take the messages I got on the train a little while ago—*Are you on your way? Are you on the train? Are you almost here?* Texting with my mom can be like facing a firing squad.

A car horn blasts on Prospect Park West, and I dart across the street. At the top of the steps, I ring the bell and wait. If my mom is in her office at the back, she might not hear it. And of course I've forgotten my keys.

My phone buzzes in my hand: *And?*

Will. My breath catches.

Not sure what time yet. I check my phone. It's already six-thirty. *I'll text on my way back?*

We're hanging out, that's all. Hooking up. Simple.

OFC, he replies after a beat. And there is that flutter in my chest again. Okay, so maybe it is a little more than hooking up.

I ring the bell again and again. Still nothing.

I send a text: *HELLO? Been here for 15 minutes.*

It's only been five minutes, but seeing as my mom got me back to Brooklyn under duress—emotional extortion—the least she could do is answer the door. Also, I'm freezing here on the stoop in my white ribbed tank top and low-rise jeans. Of course, that'll be a whole thing—*Where's your jacket? Where are the rest of your clothes?* Forget about it when she spots my new eyebrow piercing.

I pound on the door, which pops open the second my knuckles meet the wood.

"Mom?" I call, stepping inside the big open space. Living room and dining room to the left, kitchen to the right. "You left the door—"

Something's burning. A saucepan is on the stove, the front burner blazing, the outside of the pot blackened from the flame. I rush over to turn it off, grab a dish towel to toss the pot into the sink, and turn on the faucet. A cloud of steam rises as tap water sizzles into the now-empty pot.

There's an open box of couscous on the counter, next to a neat pile of chopped green beans. A half-empty glass of water on the island. "Mom!" I shout.

Popping and hissing noises are coming from the oven. When I open the door, I'm blasted by a wall of heat and gray smoke. The baking pan I yank out is filled with blackened rocks that I'm guessing used to be chicken.

"The food is burning!" The smoke alarm starts to screech. "Shit."

I'm about to climb up on a stool to shut it off, when I hear a loud noise—*thump, thump, thump*. It's coming from the direction of my mom's office. *Shit.*

"Mom!"

The thumping stops.

I press my body against the wall as I make my way down the hall. But when I poke my head into the office doorway, it's empty. My mom's laptop, I think her work one, is on the floor near the door, which is weird. But otherwise, it's immaculate as always.

The thumping starts up again. I realize it's coming through the wall, from the adjacent brownstone. George and Geraldine's house—or just George's now, since Geraldine died. George was once a famous doctor, a neurosurgeon, but he has Alzheimer's now. My mom tries to keep an eye on him, brings him groceries sometimes, that kind of thing. For sure, George does some weird stuff over in that house all alone. Right now, it sounds like he's pounding on the walls. He used to do that sometimes when I was in high school and he wanted me and my friends to keep it down.

The smoke alarm is still going off. That's probably it.

I return to the kitchen, jump up on the stool to hit the reset button. The alarm finally stops. A second later, so does George's pounding.

I look past the kitchen island to the long dining room table, the living room beyond. Spotless.

"What the hell is going on?" I whisper. My mom is many aggravating things, but she's not the kind of person to disappear.

I spy something under the sofa, then jump down from the stool for a closer look. It's one of my mom's standard-issue light gray canvas flats—very plain, very expensive. When I pull it out, I see that the side of the shoe is smeared with a reddish brown streak, a few fingers wide. Turning back toward the kitchen, I notice the broken glass on the floor, the shards fanned out, glittering in a pool of what looks to be water. There's also another shiny circle on the hardwood floor. Closer to the end of the island, it's about the size of a dinner plate, the liquid a thicker consistency than what's under the glass. When I head over and crouch down, I can see that it's a similar reddish brown to what's on the shoe. *Oh my God*. It's blood.

I drop the shoe. My hand trembles as I tug my phone out of the back pocket of my jeans.

"Hey!" my dad answers. "Walking off the plane!"

And for a split second I think, *Oh, good, Mom and I won't have to eat alone after all.* Like the world hasn't just exploded. I look over at the puddle again. Blood. That's definitely what that is.

"Dad, I think something's happened to Mom."

A multidistrict litigation was certified today against Darden Pharmaceuticals in the Southern District of New York on behalf of all pregnant patients who took the seizure medication Xytek between the date of its first manufacture, October 25, 2021, and the present. The bellwether complaint was brought on behalf of unnamed plaintiff Jane Doe, who alleges that Darden knew of and disregarded risks to pregnant patients and their unborn children. It is further alleged that the adverse impacts of Xytek in pregnant patients included "serious bodily damage to newborns and, in some instances, death." The bellwether case seeks $20 million in actual damages and $200 million in punitive damages. Given the number of potential plaintiffs, the result could be one of the costliest pharmaceutical litigations in history. With regard to the lawsuit, Darden general counsel Phillip Beaumont said, "Xytek is a drug that has saved tens of thousands of lives and has made meaningful living possible for hundreds of thousands more. The data makes clear Xytek is both incredibly safe and enormously effective at eliminating debilitating, life-threatening seizures. We look forward to our day in court to prove that publicly." Xytek sales in the last year alone topped $2 billion, though many of those who take the drug do so for off-label uses. When reached for comment, plaintiffs' liaison counsel said: "Darden Pharmaceuticals ignored known risks. They prioritized profit over patient safety and hundreds of infants have paid the price. We expect this case to change the way the pharmaceutical industry does business and the way drugs are fast-tracked by the FDA."

KATRINA

I opened my eyes to the glare of sun through the wall of floor-to-ceiling windows. It took me a second to remember where I was, who I was with. Not an unfamiliar sensation these days. The first time it happened I'd panicked, thinking I'd blacked out, had something slipped in my drink. But no, I'd freely chosen to be there, in a strange bed.

Not that Doug was a stranger anymore—half a dozen dates, three nights together. In this brave new world of dating—where I had to google half the abbreviations, ENM, GGG—I think that counted as married. So far, it had been a steep learning curve. But I was figuring it out. And I knew that I liked Doug. That this could be the beginning of something.

I listened to him breathing deeply in bed beside me. This was the first time I'd stayed until morning. In fact, it was the first time since my separation four months ago that I'd shared the intimacy of a full night's sleep with any man. And that felt weightier than sex. And so here I was, at long last watching the sun rise with someone other than Aidan next to me. I waited for the guilt to set in. But instead I was overwhelmed with relief at having made it this far.

Doug and I had met at a firm outing, both on the clubhouse porch avoiding the golf course and reading the same book: *Thinking Fast and Slow,* which made him appear thoughtful but, I'd worried, might make me appear cold and unemotional—one of Aidan's routine complaints. But Doug had seemed only charmed by the coincidence. In fact, he seemed charmed by everything about me.

I didn't love that Doug was a senior executive for one of our client companies. A new client, and not one I worked with, but rules were rules, and romantic relationships between employees and clients were strongly discouraged, outright verboten without disclosure. But the thought of sharing details of my newly burgeoning sex life with HR was simply too much to bear. So I'd decided to conveniently forget how we'd met and remember that I was a partner—I was allowed to bend rules. It helped that Doug was also violating Darden Pharmaceuticals' policy against fraternizing. Maybe keeping it a secret even made the whole thing a little more exciting for both of us. And we did honor the confidentialities these rules were trying to protect—neither of us talked about our jobs.

I was just so glad to be dating someone I'd met in real life. Online dating had been mostly a disaster for me. Those dates got high marks if I managed to make it through an entire dinner. I found the whole process utterly alienating: "matching" with strangers; the stilted overly intimate messaging with someone you hadn't even met; the padded profiles that verged on outright lies. It had seemed like a necessary transitional endeavor, though—an ugly, awkward wrecking ball to my old life.

But Doug? He was a genuine possibility. He was funny and kind and incredibly smart. Like me, he'd come from nothing and worked ridiculously hard to get where he was. And, it turned out, we had plenty to talk about besides work. His daughter, Ella, was about Cleo's age, and Doug, a widower, struggled to connect with her in so many of the ways I did with Cleo. Ella was a singer, Doug a scientist turned businessperson. "A story of opposites," he'd said somewhat sadly on our first date. "I think it would bother me less if I wasn't trying so hard to bridge the gap." Doug was quirky and charming, too. He was teaching himself to make fresh pasta from YouTube videos and working his way slowly through the American Film Institute's top one hundred movies of all time. It didn't hurt that he was also extremely attractive, with thick salt-and-pepper hair, bright hazel eyes, and an infectious laugh. Not as gorgeous as Aidan, true—few men were—or as tall. But he wasn't nearly as self-centered, either. Doug was also (a little unexpectedly) excellent at sex, gentle in all the important ways and assertive in the right ones.

"You're awake?" he asked sleepily, turning over and wrapping an arm around my hip, his face still buried in the pillows.

"I'm sorry," I said. "Go back to sleep."

"Mmm, okay," he said, hugging me more tightly. "But only if you do." A second later his breathing had deepened again. Doug was sweet—that was what I liked most about him. Sweet and kind. Sometimes you didn't realize how much you needed something until it was offered to you. Turned out I was absolutely desperate for someone to be gentle with me.

I quietly lifted my phone from the floor. There would be work messages. There were always work messages, even at 9:30 a.m. on a Saturday. But no Cleo—of course not. She and I hadn't exchanged so much as a text in three months. Still, I always felt deflated when I scanned my messages and didn't see her name.

I did have twelve texts from my assistant, Jules, passing on messages from clients, none nearly as pressing as they surely thought. My clients, with their kinds of predicaments, were so fueled by embarrassment and frantic for a quick fix that niceties like respecting weekends went right out the window.

I also had a text from my boss, Mark, asking if I could touch base with Vivienne Voxhall. One of my few female clients, Vivienne was the high-profile CEO of UNow, a new social media platform that was setting the world of college students on fire. UNow was designed to upend the Instagram obsession with likes and curated content. It was also designed to make money, a *lot* of money. Vivienne had run marketing for Spotify and iTunes and Hulu—she was one of the most successful women in the tech world, in part because she was also a coding savant who had street cred with the engineers. But she had an anger-management problem, as well, which most recently had resulted in her threatening to push a middling senior executive's chair "out of a window" if he rocked in it one more time while she was talking. In Vivienne's defense, he was apparently categorically awful to the women who worked for him. Vivienne didn't always have such noble targets for her rage, though. So far, she'd just been lucky enough to keep the stories contained. But now, this executive was threatening to go to the media if he wasn't given a C-suite role at UNow. Impressive chutzpah by any measure. And the timing couldn't be worse, given UNow's impending billion-dollar IPO.

Mark didn't know any of these details, of course. He was the hands-off firm liaison. I was the hands-on fixer. Given Mark's role as managing partner at Blair, Stevenson, it made sense for him to have plausible deniability. And I was to keep even the existence of my role confidential. That this was imperative was clear to me, though it was never stated explicitly. Mark no doubt assumed that I'd told Aidan. Spouses were tacitly exempt from most rules about confidentiality. But notably, it had never occurred to me to trust Aidan in that way, not even ten years ago, when I'd transitioned into the position. Nor had it occurred to me to see that lack of trust as problematic. I was used to secrets.

And so we had a system: Mark would give me the name and phone number of what was usually a high-level employee of an existing corporate client. Mark assured the client—generally the employer of the wrongdoer employee—that I would make the problem go away. I didn't circle back to Mark until the mess was officially cleaned up. What happened in between was my business. But Vivienne wasn't above calling Mark in the middle of the night to get what she wanted when she wanted it. Typical of her to give me only minutes to respond before going over my head.

I spoke to Vivienne late last night, I wrote back to Mark. *It's already sorted.*

Vivienne was losing it over a voice mail from a *New York Times* reporter who was sniffing around. I had assured her, less than eight hours ago, that there was no way the *Times* was going to run a story *about* Vivienne without officially reaching out to her for a comment. One voice mail wouldn't be enough. The story would be on hold, so long as Vivienne didn't answer the phone. Another problem solved, at least temporarily.

My job could be satisfying that way, even if it meant regularly wading into some fairly murky waters. Were all of these wealthy, entitled people—some of whom had done some pretty unsavory stuff—deserving of a second chance? Probably not. But then, maybe I wasn't, either.

Through the vast, sparkling windows, the Hudson River glowed. Doug's view was spectacular, the apartment an impressive loftlike one-bedroom with polished ash floors. But Doug preferred the family house in Bronxville; the pied-à-terre made him feel lonely. Or it had, he said, until I agreed to stay over last night.

I slipped out of bed and tiptoed toward the bathroom, resisting the urge to put on my clothes first. My self-confidence in that particular arena was a work in progress.

When I came back, Doug was awake but distracted. He was sitting up, feet on the floor, eyes locked on his phone.

"Is everything okay?" I asked.

His eyes remained on his phone as he brought his other hand to the back of his neck and shook his head. "I just got the strangest message . . ."

"Work?" I asked as I walked around to the opposite side of the bed and grabbed my bra and shirt from where I'd thrown them the night before.

"No, no," he said, looking up at me. "There's some . . . We used this college counselor for Ella . . ."

I waited for him to finish his thought, but instead he rubbed his forehead. I came back to his side of the bed, tugging on my clothes as I sat down next to him.

"And you're hearing from him now? Wouldn't that have been, like, three years ago?"

"At least," he said, quickly darkening the screen of his phone when I glanced over at it.

"Is there . . . Do you want to talk about it?"

"I don't even remember the guy's name . . . Advantage Consulting was the company." His voice drifted again. "Somebody is demanding money for . . . well, to keep quiet. About something I did *not* do."

I put a hand on his back. "Oh, I'm sorry. That sounds . . . upsetting."

Doug nodded. "Yes, and also . . . odd. We didn't pay for anything illegal. I mean, the guy hinted at options, sure. You know, 'We could do more for a price.' But we *never* took him up on it, obviously." He frowned. "We didn't fire him, either, though. I guess we could have done that. Taken our business elsewhere. That probably would have been the more ethical thing to do."

"The message said they were going to claim you *did* do something illegal if you don't pay?"

Blackmail—now that was something I knew a thing or two about. I glanced down at his still-darkened phone. I wanted him to show me the message, so I could see for myself what he was dealing with. You could tell a lot by the way demands were phrased.

"Yes, that they'd report it to the police. And they said they'd tell Ella I bribed her way into Amherst, which honestly concerns me a lot more. The police will eventually figure out the truth. But Ella? This will be the perfect excuse for her to be done with me."

I knew that feeling, too. My own phone vibrated in my hand then.

Call me ASAP. Aidan, great.

Aidan loved to cryptically demand my immediate attention on weekend mornings when I might be indisposed. He knew it would work because I'd worry it had to do with Cleo. I was still Cleo's official emergency contact. I'd spent twenty years filling out the camp forms, school forms, doctor's forms, emergency forms for programs and classes and school outings that Aidan barely knew existed. So even now, if Cleo was sick or injured or incapacitated, it was my phone that would ring. But if she had some kind of crisis where she was able to pick up the phone herself? She'd call Aidan, no question. They were far closer. That had been true ever since Cleo was a teenager. But it was especially true since the whole Kyle situation.

"Now *you* look worried," Doug said, nodding toward my phone.

"I should probably go outside and take this," I said. "It's Aidan."

This time Doug put his hand on my back. "I'm sorry."

Doug got it, all of it. After only three weeks, I felt like he saw me in a way that Aidan never had.

"Can we get together again soon?" I asked as I stood.

Doug smiled. "I'm counting on it."

I dialed Aidan from the sidewalk on West Street, the memory of Doug's hands on me evaporating quickly in the chilly April air.

"Well, hello." Aidan's tone was sharp, the *It took you long enough* implied. "Sorry to tear you away from . . . whoever."

He did a convincing job of sounding wounded. Technically, it had been my idea to separate, though Aidan had essentially left me no choice. And Aidan did want to "work on things"— meaning he wanted me to forget what had happened and go back to pretending everything was fine.

But it was definitely my idea to keep our separation a secret from Cleo and to wait to do anything official, like divorce, until after NYU let out for the summer. She'd only recently dug herself out of the academic hole she'd fallen into during her time dating Kyle. I didn't want to be responsible for yet another setback. But it was also true that I knew a divorce, even a separation, would probably be the final nail in *my* coffin. Abandoning her beloved dad would be all the proof she needed that I was the awful, unfeeling monster she had cast me as during our most recent face-off.

"What's up, Aidan?" Sirens blared around the corner, one of those never-ending parades of fire trucks headed up the West Side Highway. I pressed a finger to my ear.

"It's about Cleo," he said.

"Really?" It was never *actually* about Cleo. "Tell me."

"Where are you? You sound like you're standing in the middle of the BQE. If this guy has an apartment that close to the highway, I'd get a new boyfriend."

"Aidan, what's the matter with Cleo?"

"Look, I'm handling it," he said.

"Handling what?"

"Don't yell at me."

"I'm not yelling." But he was right: I *was* kind of yelling. "Don't tell me this is about Kyle."

"Kyle? This has nothing to do with him. I think you made sure of that."

"Luckily."

"Not sure Cleo sees it that way."

Of course she didn't. The mess with Kyle had pushed things between Cleo and me from dicey to outright hostile. I'd threatened not to pay for school unless she broke up with him—her deadbeat drug dealer boyfriend. Her *rich* deadbeat drug dealer boyfriend. But every time I thought about how aggressive my threat had sounded, how angry and punitive, I felt worse. In my defense, Kyle had gotten Cleo mixed up in dealing drugs. Not using, luckily, *just* dealing. But still. Kyle, a trust-fund drug dealer, who was probably only doing it in the first place to piss off his rich parents.

Cleo had mentioned casually to Aidan that Kyle was doing "a little dealing" on campus. To Aidan's credit, he'd told me right away. At which point, I'd muscled my way to the bottom of the situation. And I did what I do best: I made the problem go away.

First by forcing Cleo to break it off. Then by going directly to Kyle to drive my point home. Neither Cleo nor Aidan knew about that second piece, of course; nice corporate law partners don't show up with cops, making illegal threats. And the threats I'd made to Cleo herself had given her more than enough reason to stop speaking to me. Still, I'd do it all again if I had to.

"Anyway, it's not Kyle," Aidan went on. "Cleo asked to borrow money."

"Money?"

"She *is* a college kid, remember? Being a little over budget isn't like a shocking turn of events." But I could tell he was holding out on me. There was the tiniest hint of concern in his voice.

"I don't understand. How much money?"

"Well . . . you need to stay calm."

"I *am* calm, Aidan," I said, biting down hard on the inside of my cheek.

"Two thousand dollars."

"Two thousand dollars?" I was officially shouting. "What could possibly require that kind of money? Kyle is involved, obviously."

"That's not obvious at all. Cleo told us she broke that off, and I happen to believe our daughter. Once in a blue moon, you could actually give someone the benefit of the doubt, Kat." Aidan's tone was thick with self-righteousness. "That's always been your problem—you assume the worst about people."

That wasn't even necessarily untrue, but I wasn't the focus of this conversation. "Please tell me you asked Cleo what the money was for."

"No."

"Not even 'Hey, what's the two grand for, considering you used to be a drug runner and all?'"

"I don't believe in shaming people for their mistakes, Kat. I don't think that's love."

Aidan had a terrible way of nailing things even when he was completely in the wrong.

"I'm concerned, Aidan," I said, keeping my tone calm. "I really think this could have to do with Kyle."

"So what if it even does! You can't control everything, Kat— the makeup, the clothes, who she's dating. Fine, maybe she's even making another mistake. She's in college, and that's what college kids do! Anyway, look at where strong-arming her has gotten you. Cleo is a human being. She has feelings."

Aidan's aim was impeccable.

"Yes," I said, gritting my teeth. "I am aware our daughter has feelings. Please go back and tell her you have to know what she needs the money for. Ask her about Kyle specifically. I'm sure she'll tell you the truth, Aidan. She trusts you." Flattery—I knew Aidan's soft spots, too.

He was quiet for a long beat. "Okay . . . I can do that," he said at last. "But first there is something else I need to talk to you about . . . not related to Cleo."

"And what's that?"

"Financially . . . I've, um, run into something of a cash-flow issue with the film."

Now it was my turn to be quiet. Aidan would help with Cleo . . . *if* I gave him a loan? He hadn't said that explicitly, of course. He didn't need to.

"Hello? Kat, are you there?" Aidan asked. "I mean, I don't think I'm being unreasonable asking for a favor, considering we were married for nearly *twenty-two* years. And considering you're the one insisting on breaking up our family. I'm just trying to survive."

"Right," I said quietly.

"Well, are you going to answer me? This is serious."

I cleared my throat. No, he wasn't going to get me to do what he wanted by making me feel like I was a bad person, not anymore. "Yes, Aidan," I said. "I'll answer you about the money for your film. As soon as you find out what the hell is going on with our daughter."

CLEO

"Cleo!" Janine breaks into a huge grin when she opens her front door and sees me standing on her steps. "What are you doing here?"

In a cap-sleeved T-shirt and jeans, her thick dark hair up in a messy bun, she looks like a model. Janine is that mom—cool about everything. But not in an embarrassing way. She's nice, too, always. And so understanding. The one time Annie got in real trouble when she cut school in eighth grade, Janine felt bad *for* her. Back when we were still friends, I was always so jealous of Annie that she got to have Janine for her mom, while I was saddled with Cruella de Vil.

"Cleo, honey—what's wrong?" Janine asks, stepping closer. "You look— Are you okay?"

When I open my mouth, my throat clamps tight. I can't speak. I can barely breathe.

"Whoa, come in, come in." Janine ushers me inside and locks the door. "Are you hurt, Cleo? Did somebody hurt you?"

Annie appears on the stairs, freezes halfway down. Her eyes flash in my direction before she descends the rest of the way without looking at me. Annie and I lost touch when we started high school at Beacon, and she started running with a more, let's say, bookish crowd. And yeah, sure, I was partying a little bit with some of the cool kids. But it wasn't like I was that close with them. They were just fun to hang out with. Annie and I could have stayed friends if she hadn't judged me.

"What's going on?" Janine asks as she guides me to the living room couch. "What's that in your— Whose shoe is that?"

I look down. My mom's shoe is in my hand. I don't remember picking it back up.

Janine's expression is grave. "Cleo, why do you have a shoe?"

I quickly explain what happened back at the house—what I know of what happened—and that my dad is on his way. He was the one who told me to get out of the house, to go across the street to Annie's, where I would be safe. Janine's eyes are wide, her mouth open as I talk. But then she forces a smile. "It's good you came here. Everything is going to be okay." She turns to Annie. "Sweetheart, why don't you get Cleo a glass of water?"

Annie glares at me before heading into the kitchen. Okay, we drifted apart, but that was years ago. We haven't even seen each other for months. Why is she acting so pissed?

"I'm going to call your dad, so he knows you're safe." Janine grabs her phone from the coffee table, then confirms that the front door is locked. She goes to the front windows, too, jerking the curtains closed one by one. Meanwhile, there seems to be an excess of angry slamming from the kitchen.

"Oh, Aidan, I'm so glad I got you." A pause—Janine's hand goes to the back of her neck, her fingertips whitening as she squeezes. "Yes, she's here. And she's fine, just fine. Don't worry." She nods. "Okay. We'll be here. See you soon."

Annie reappears and shoves a glass of water into my hand before flopping down in the chair farthest from the couch.

"Your dad is on his way," Janine says. "And the police should be here any second." Janine's eyes are on the shoe in my hand. "Oh, honey, let me take that." She walks into the kitchen and returns with a plastic shopping bag. "Drop it in here." She averts her gaze from the bag as she knots the handles and places it in the front vestibule.

"I was asking Annie about you the other day, Cleo!" Almost

cheerful. Like there's nothing going on here but old friends catching up. "But she said that you guys never see each other."

"It's a big school, Mom," Annie growls. "Anyway, I didn't say we *never* saw each other."

Janine rolls her big blue eyes good-naturedly. "Oh please, that is *exactly* what you said," she teases Annie.

"I said we weren't *friends*." Annie stands. She's lost her self-conscious slouch, and she looks good with her blond hair pulled back, maybe even a little makeup on. Annie was always way more beautiful than she seemed to realize, but she kind of came into her own at NYU. She's even in one of the big sororities now. A real "popular girl," awash in a sea of mean, generic blondes—each one prettier than the last, but none of them beautiful. "I'm a biology major, and Cleo is English. There's not a lot of overlap, right, Cleo?" she asks, but the way she looks at me is weird, like she means something different entirely.

"What is taking the police so long?" Janine mutters. She's scared—it's obvious, even though she's trying to hide it. "This *is* an actual emergency."

Annie is still staring at me.

"So, what's up?" I ask casually. If I act normal, maybe she'll knock it off.

"You mean in the past six years?"

Jesus.

"Sure, in the past six years," I say flatly. Now I'm starting to get annoyed.

Technically what ended our friendship was Annie talking shit about me in high school. There were all these rumors sophomore year about my sleeping with people's boyfriends, none of which were true. And word was that Annie had started the rumors. She denied it, and I couldn't prove it, but I couldn't ever trust her again, either. I've had a hard time trusting any friends since.

The doorbell rings. "Oh, good. That must be your dad."

"Cleo!" My dad bursts in as soon as Janine opens the door. He rushes over, wrapping me in a bear hug. And for a second it feels so good, like everything is already okay. But as he hugs me, I can feel his back is damp with sweat.

Janine goes to stand at the window, tucked to the side, so she's not visible from the street. "I see lights. That had better be the police. Oh, good, it looks like they're coming here. Finally, for God's sake."

"Are you okay?" my dad asks. He looks stunned.

"Mm-hmm." If I try to speak, I am going to start bawling.

"It's going to be okay, Cleo," he says, kind of robotically. "It's going to be fine."

I point in the direction of the plastic bag. "Do you want to see Mom's shoe?" I ask. He needs to know this isn't an "Everything is going to be fine" kind of situation.

"Uh . . ." My dad rubs a hand across his forehead.

Janine intervenes. "No, no, no. No one needs to look at that shoe again except the police."

"But Mom's okay, right?"

"Of course she is." He sounds calm and confident now. And I really want to believe him.

"I was late, you know?" My voice breaks as the guilt fills my throat. I haven't talked to my mom in months. I've been so angry at her. For good reason, but right now that feels beside the point. "Maybe if I'd been there—"

"Cleo, no." Janine reaches forward to hug me. "Whatever happened doesn't have anything to do with your being late. Your mom would *not* want you blaming yourself. And the last thing she would want is for you to have been in harm's way, too. Not that we know that anything bad happened to her, either, obviously." She pulls back to look me in the eye, gripping my upper arms. "I'm sure she's just fine."

But we all know that's not true. There's blood—on my mom's shoe, in a puddle on the floor. Something has happened to her. Something terrible.

November 1, 1992

Okay, so the writing club was actually kind of cool, even if the whole thing is only Daitch trying to pretend this place isn't a hellhole for the next state inspection.

I'd never written anything "creative" in my whole life. And it was nice not to be me for a little while. The tutor guy was right. Being a character is an escape. We were supposed to write a paragraph inspired by the view out the window, which sounded so dumb to me, until I started. Then I got totally sucked in.

"And I search always for the edges of the sky," that was my last line. The tutor told me on the way out that my paragraph was really good. And then he repeated that line back to me—from memory.

Anyway, it was nice to have a distraction. A whole hour not to think about Silas, who for some reason has gotten fixated on me this week. He searched my room because he said someone reported that I had drugs on me. Took all my underwear out and spread it across the bed. Shaking each pair out while he stared at me with his gross mouth hanging open.

The worst part is that I'm not even mad. All I really feel is scared. And small.

KATRINA

I was fifteen minutes early to meet Doug. Force of habit, the punctuality. Yet another thing about me that started irritating Cleo no end by the time she entered middle school. As if bringing her someplace a few minutes early was something I was doing *to* her. It wasn't cool to be early. Of course, for her entire childhood before that, God forbid we were three seconds late.

When things between us first started going south and I blamed myself, it was my best friend, Lauren, who insisted that Cleo's resenting me was normal, healthy even. It was her way of individuating, and a sign that I had built a safe-enough place for her to do so.

But I had also done things wrong, hadn't I? Things I regretted. And not only with the Kyle situation. My mistakes as a mother had been accruing over time, as Cleo grew from little girl to teen and, increasingly, needed me simply to love her, and not to try and fix everything. But instead, I panicked. Because I was excellent at doing. I wasn't so good at feeling. And I was absolute shit at uncertainty.

I think that's why I made such an issue about the clothes, and the terrible black makeup, and, God, all the piercings: They were one thing I could still control, at least in theory. And, boy, did I try. Aidan was right about that.

But the worst was when Cleo came to me about losing her virginity. It was as if I was following instructions from a *What Not to Do as a Mom* textbook. I said all the wrong things. Actually, I said awful things. The kind a mother should never say to her daughter. It broke something between us—I'd seen it in Cleo's eyes.

"Can I get you another?" the bartender asked, pointing toward my empty wineglass.

She was a very pretty brunette with a nose ring, her left forearm covered in vibrant tattoos. She didn't look much older than Cleo but seemed so much more at ease in her own skin—probably because she had a mom who made her feel loved no matter what she wore or how she chose to express herself.

"Sure, another drink would be great," I said, checking my phone again.

"This one's on the house," the bartender said, winking before putting down the full glass.

My face felt warm. She'd assumed I'd been stood up. At my age, I probably looked like a person that happened to. But Doug had been nothing if not dependable until now, always sending a text if he was running even a few minutes late, calling hours ahead the one time he'd had to cancel.

"Kat?" came a surprised high-pitched female voice behind me.

When I turned, there was Janine, Annie's mom—chic as always in an emerald green jumpsuit, hair piled elegantly on her head, and absurdly tall heels that she wore like flip-flops. Janine was a stay-at-home mom who managed to be fashionable but also approachable and earthy. She was host of the best Park Slope holiday party and had the chicest Halloween décor. Her equally attractive—but, okay, chilly—husband, Liam, was a dashing British architect who, like Aidan, traveled constantly. Annie and Cleo were born only weeks apart, and so Janine and I, already neighbors, had become fast friends in those bleary-eyed baby months.

But with my maternity leave limited to four months, our friendship always felt like it had an expiration date. I'd also always been keenly aware that Janine was much better at being a mother than I was. She handled even those early weeks the way she'd handled everything since—with calm confidence, Pilates abs, and flawless red lipstick. She didn't seem the least bit bothered that Liam wasn't there, maybe because she was a full-time mom. Still, I'd felt intimidated by her ease in those days when neither of us was working. Janine wasn't overwhelmed by taking care of Annie alone. In fact, she seemed . . . delighted. Meanwhile, I'd been an unqualified mess, precisely as I'd anticipated, which was why I'd never planned to have children in the first place.

It was hard to believe in your maternal instincts when you'd never had a mother.

My parents had disappeared when I was four and a half. After that, I'd bounced from foster home to foster home until I was nine. An "unlucky sequence of events," according to one social worker, explaining to yet another prospective family why I still had not been adopted by the age of ten. But no one wanted a tween no matter how innocent the explanation, certainly not one who'd been in the system for years.

As for my mom these days? Anything was possible. Long ago, I'd promised myself that was one door I'd leave forever closed. Maybe she was dead—OD'd, killed in a drug deal gone wrong, a car accident while she was high. Or maybe she'd cleaned up her act and was living a quiet, productive, and happy life without me. Maybe she'd even gone on to have more babies, to be a good mother to a different little girl.

After all, I'd gone on to have a baby despite my doubts. And at only twenty-six no less. I'd gotten swept up in Aidan's conviction that I would be a great mother despite everything, his belief that having a baby would transform me. I'd wanted so badly to believe that was true. In many ways it had been, from the time Cleo was two until she was maybe about twelve—those brief years between the terrifying life-and-death stakes of babyhood and the terrorizing uncertainty of parenting a teen. In those middle years,

I was an excellent mother, consistent and steady and patient. I followed all the schedules, provided the right food, limited screen time, and maximized sleep. But as Cleo got older, it was like my navigation system started faltering, and my doubt quickly fed on itself. Soon I had lost my way entirely, and I was doing the opposite of what all the guides advised: holding on too tightly.

It did not help that I felt so alone.

When Cleo was two weeks old, Aidan had gone to Paris to interview a famous French bioethicist for his first documentary, about shrinking ice sheets. I remember standing in the dark nursery holding a screaming Cleo in my arms, trying to make it through my fifth sleepless night, when Aidan called. I started to cry as soon as I heard his voice.

"You just need to relax, Kat," he'd said, sighing. "She can feel your stress."

"I can't do this, Aidan," I'd whispered, even though what I'd really meant was *I can't do this alone.*

"Of course you can do it," Aidan had said, and went on to describe how beautiful it was outside his hotel window, the sun rising over the Eiffel Tower. "I'm right here to help."

And I'd thought, *What's wrong with me?* I was so lucky—a kind, supportive husband, a beautiful baby, a good job, a gorgeous home, money—things I never dreamed of having back when I was growing up at Haven House or even later, after I'd gone to live with Gladys in her beautiful Victorian home in Greenwich. And yet, there I was with so much to be grateful for, but I felt miserable and terrified all the time. Even a little angry, if I was completely honest—at Aidan, but also at *Cleo,* who was just a tiny, helpless baby.

Aidan was off filming for much of Cleo's early years. He missed her colic and the four times she needed stiches and the months of night terrors and the potty training and the time her impossible third-grade teacher made her cry. He was there, though, for the bright patches in between—the holidays and the parties and the awards. For the part where you say *this* is why people have a family. To run a single finger through the icing on the cake of domesticity that I baked daily from scratch. But I was there for all of it despite my grueling work hours, which required the use of two nannies in separate shifts. Because you could outsource caregiving, but you could never outsource being a mother.

And now here was Janine making a beeline for me, ready to remind me of all the ways I'd screwed up in the end anyway.

"Janine!" I called back, my voice high-pitched and frantic instead of cheerful like I'd intended.

I'd forgotten entirely that I'd actually heard of this restaurant from Janine—I was still on an old group email that occasionally went out, Park Slope moms, pooling recommendations. It had not occurred to me that I might risk running into her here *with* Doug. Of course, Janine didn't know Aidan and I were separated. I couldn't risk Annie finding out and spilling it to Cleo.

"Oh, my goodness, Kat, how are you?" Janine asked with an easy laugh and a wave of her small silver clutch. She looked around. "Is Aidan here?"

"No, I'm meeting a client."

Janine's eyes flicked up mischievously. "A client, huh? This place is awfully cozy for that."

"Is it?" I looked around now myself.

She raised her eyebrows, but I could see her decide not to press.

"Well, a friend of mine from college works at Tom Ford, and *we* had way too much wine at their show. So now we're going to pretend to eat something and try to sober up. Or maybe we'll have more wine." Her cheeks were flushed and her eyes glassy. Then it was like she remembered something. "Oh . . . How is *Cleo,* by the way?"

"Cleo?"

"Oh, sorry. You look like a deer in headlights." Janine barked out a laugh, then leaned in conspiratorially. "I know things have been a little . . . dicey with that, you know, boy situation . . ." She rolled her eyes. "Boys are always the problem."

Were Annie and Cleo back in touch? Or . . . had Cleo reached out to Janine to talk? Cleo had always been enamored with Janine. For an unfortunate second, I pictured the two of them cozying up across the street, having the kind of mother-daughter chats that we hadn't had in *years*.

"Yes, Kyle . . ."

Janine grimaced. "Right. Anyway, I think you did the right thing."

But it sounded like maybe she thought the opposite.

I forced a smile. "Not sure Cleo agrees."

"What do they know?" Janine shrugged. "The real problem is that we agreed to let them go to college so close to home. Annie is back asleep in her childhood bedroom a couple times a week. I mean, I love the kid, but come on. Out of the nest already!"

Of course Annie would be home too *much*. Annie and Janine were always inseparable, having coffee on their stoop on weekends or heading to yoga class, giggling. And this was back when Annie was in high school. What teenager *wants* to hang out with their mom?

"Come on!" Janine's girlfriend called out. "They have our table!"

"Gotta run." She leaned in and pressed her cool, smooth cheek to mine. "You hang in there now. And don't worry about Cleo. They drive *us* insane, but that's so *they* can be fine. It's like the circle of life. Or Darwinism. Or something." She walked a few steps, then turned back. "And, hey, come across the street. Have a glass of wine and vent. It's been too long."

I nodded and smiled. "Sounds great."

My phone buzzed in my bag just as Janine disappeared into the crowd. *Shit.* Vivienne—that was my thought as I groped for it. A couple hours ago, the *New York Times* reporter had left word, officially requesting comment on the story the paper intended to run. The clock was now ticking. We were going to need to respond.

But the text wasn't from Vivienne.

Hi, Kat. It's Jules. Can we talk privately? it read. *Away from the office?*

I stared at the unfamiliar number. Jules and I were in constant contact—we were never really off the clock; even on weekends she fielded my calls. But this number wasn't programmed into my cell, and I had all of hers: home, cell, her sister. I was suspicious, of course. I was always suspicious. Texts, emails—you never really knew who they were from. Say little, assume the worst. That was my policy in general.

New number? I texted back.

Oh, sorry, my work cell is dead. Can we meet?

Sure, I wrote back, still not convinced. *How about tomorrow afternoon? We could step out for coffee?*

This was a surefire double check, since I knew that Tuesdays didn't work for Jules. She was a single mother to a two-and-a-half-year-old daughter with significant developmental delays that required a vast array of therapies: speech, OT, PT. Jules had somehow been able to keep most of the weekly appointments contained to a single afternoon—Tuesdays.

Okay, she wrote back. *That's fine. I can have a friend pick up Daniela and take her to therapy.*

It certainly sounded like Jules.

Or maybe we should talk now on the phone? she added. *I'm a little worried about waiting . . .*

Not wanting to wait until the next day? Talking outside the office? It must be a personal problem.

Please, Kat. It's important; otherwise, I wouldn't ask.

Will call in two seconds. Let me step outside.

* * *

Out on the sidewalk, I texted Doug, in case he somehow arrived without my noticing. *I'm outside on a call. Be done in a minute. You close?* I waited a beat. No reply. Even now, he was only a couple minutes late, but even that wasn't like him. What if he really was standing me up?

Jules answered right away.

"Thank you," she said. "I didn't—I wasn't sure who else to call."

"Jules, what's wrong? Oh, wait, did Vivienne unleash on you? I'm sorry, she can be a lot—"

"It's not Vivienne."

Her voice was quavering.

"Whatever it is, I'll try to help." There was a crackling, tinny sound on the line. "Shoot, Jules, I think you're breaking up."

"I don't hear anything," she said. "You hear something?"

"Oh, maybe it's me. I'm—"

"What do you hear?" Jules demanded. "Exactly."

"Oh, it's just . . . It's gone now. It sounded for a minute like the call was breaking up."

"You know what, Kat—I'm sorry," Jules said. Her voice had turned crisp. "I'm actually okay for now. I think I was overreacting."

"Jules, come on . . . I can tell you're not fine. Talk to me."

"I've got to go. Daniela needs me," she said. "I'm sorry I bothered you, Kat."

And then she was gone. When I called back, it went straight to voice mail.

I heard the ping of a text coming in as I was leaving a message. "Oh, that's probably you texting. Call me back when you can, though? I want us to talk."

I hung up to read the text, also from a number I didn't recognize, an unfamiliar 332 area code.

It's your past calling. Almost all the way caught up to you.

I hit the side button on my phone and closed my eyes as the screen went black. No. I'd misread that. I'd misunderstood. And yet, my mind still flashed to the small pocketknife I carried in my bag all these years later for protection. I resisted the urge to dig it out.

And then I was there again, all those years ago, washing my hands again and again in the icy water in Haven House's downstairs bathroom, trying to scrub clean the beds of my nails. It had been all over my clothes, too, soaked through my gauzy pink shirt. The blood was everywhere.

I bolted awake the next morning at the ping of a text. I was hoping it was Doug, explaining why he'd never shown up, but I was afraid it might be another ominous, anonymous message. Sent from, I'd since figured out, New York's newest area code. Or, more likely, some kind of burner app. I'd seen enough client-related texts to know that the apps generated similarly random numbers, always brand-new area codes.

But it was Lauren. *Call me when you're up.*

I dialed her right back.

"Don't worry, I'm okay now," I said groggily. I'd called her on my way home the night before. I'd ranted for a while about Doug and Janine, leaving out the part about the anonymous message.

"Kat, I have some . . . I think I know why Doug didn't show up last night."

"Because he's a jerk?" I said.

"No. Are you sitting down? It's not good." Lauren's tone was somber.

"What?"

"You can . . . Maybe you should read it for yourself. I'll send you the article."

Three little dots appeared and then a link to the morning's *New York Post:* "Bronxville Pharma Executive Dies in Tragic

Accident." I clicked on it and then cupped my hand to my mouth. Fifty-two-year-old Doug Sinclair's car had smashed into a tree on Midland Avenue near the Yonkers-Bronxville border. His twenty-year-old daughter, Ella, a junior at Amherst, was now an orphan. The pictures of the mangled car were horrifying. And so was the unavoidable truth: Doug was dead.

TRANSCRIPT OF RECORDED SESSION

DR. EVELYN BAUER
SESSION #1

EVELYN BAUER: Do you know why you did it?

CLEO McHUGH: You mean helping Kyle?

EB: Yes—you said that's why you're here. That your mom insisted you start therapy because your boyfriend talked you into helping him sell drugs.

CM: I don't get what part of this she doesn't understand . . . I knew that Kyle was dealing when we got together. It's not like he hides it. And he didn't force me to do anything. Maybe I even kind of liked that he wasn't afraid to break the rules. I'm sure that sounds dumb.

EB: It doesn't sound dumb, Cleo. Listen, I know you feel that your mother has judged you and your choices. But I am not here to judge you. I have no moral stance on this whatsoever. And on a personal level, I understand the appeal of a guy like that. It can be exciting.

CM: Yeah, I guess . . . It can be.

EB: How long into the relationship did he ask you to start working for him?

CM: Again, he didn't ask. I offered. And no, I wasn't using myself.

EB: I didn't—

CM: My mom thought that. She probably still does, even after I passed her stupid drug test. I'm not saying I've *never* tried anything. I've smoked pot and tried cocaine and E. It's just not for me.

EB: Dealing drugs isn't . . . typical for someone in your position, a college student, well-off, lots of choices.

CM: Tell that to Kyle. Anyway, I wasn't exactly dealing drugs. I could have been delivering anything.

EB: That's a pretty fine distinction.

CM: Okay. Maybe I wanted to do something wrong, too. Maybe I was sick of following all my mom's rules.

EB: Maybe?

CM: I was definitely tired of her thinking that I *was* doing bad things even when I wasn't. I was tired of never being good enough.

EB: Does your mom criticize you a lot?

CM: Like it's an Olympic sport. My hair, my clothes, my friends. My taste in music! It's relentless.

EB: That sounds like a lot to take.

CM: And bigger things she tries to control by "worrying" about me. That way, she can feel like a saint and control me at the same time. To be clear, my mom doesn't *really* care that much about the drugs. A little bit, sure. But that's not what really matters to her.

EB: Then what does matter?

CM: She's obsessed with who I'm sleeping with, wanting me not to be having sex with anyone, really. That's the point, and that's always been

true. Way before Kyle. She thinks I'm some kind
of slut, for sure. But sixteen—okay, seventeen—
people is not that many people, right? Most
of those have been while I've been in college
anyway. And that's only because I haven't had a
real boyfriend since Charlie . . . The number
would be lower if I had.

EB: Do you want a boyfriend?

CM: Of course I want a boyfriend! Doesn't everyone
want a boyfriend? Or a girlfriend. Or whatever.

EB: Not necessarily, I don't think.

CM: Well, yes. I do want one. And Kyle doesn't count
because—he doesn't. I never thought we were
going to be a thing.

EB: Tell me about Charlie?

CM: End of seventh grade through the first half of
freshman year in high school. A whole year and
a half. Charlie was so sweet and funny and cute
and we clicked—I could totally be myself around
him. He was my first love. I miss him even now.

EB: So what happened?

CM: My mom. She came along and ruined what Charlie
and I had. She ruins everything.

CLEO

The first time I finally stood up to my mom I was ten. It was the summer before fifth grade, and we were at the beach at Jacob Riis Park. My mom was standing next to me at the water's edge, the sand damp and cool under our feet, my dad back up at the umbrella with Annie and Janine, who'd tagged along with us as usual.

I could swim in a pool fine, but I'd been terrified of the ocean ever since I'd sprinted in headlong when I was little and gotten knocked out by a wave. A lifeguard had performed CPR on me. To this day, I remember it only in flashes—the burn of the water in my lungs, the pain of my skin being torn by shells and stones, the terror.

"How about we try that swim now?" my mom suggested, nudging me for the *second* time that day. For years, she'd been harassing me about swimming in the ocean, basically every time we'd been to the beach since my accident. Of course, she was an annoyingly strong open-water swimmer, and the way she obsessed about the whole thing made me want to scream.

But that day I'd finally had it. "Can you shut the hell up, please, like for once? Shut up and think about what I want? Instead of trying to control everything!"

She looked like I'd slapped her. And I was glad.

"Cleo, that's not—"

"You're supposed to love me no matter what, you know."

And then I stormed off, away from the waves, waiting for guilt that never came. The truth is, I still feel like I was right that day. My mom was always pushing me to be someone different. When all I wanted was for her to love me as I was.

For an hour we've been sitting in the living room, watching the police work. They've looked around, taken pictures, swabbed for DNA, lifted fingerprints—from the front door, from the unbroken glass on the kitchen island. The water in that glass is still cold, a wet ring underneath. No coaster. From the living room couch, I stare at the glass. Whoever left it there, it was definitely *not* my mom. She'd never leave a ring on that Carrara marble.

"We'll run fingerprints and any DNA we've found, but I'm not optimistic," says Detective Wilson, the one in charge. "Thank you for your samples. It will help with exclusion."

She's short and solidly built, neatly dressed in trim navy slacks and a blue button-down, the sleeves cuffed carefully. She's pretty, too, with large, deep-set eyes, dark brown skin, a small tattoo on the inside of her right wrist, another on her left forearm, barely visible beneath her sleeve. She carries a fancy pen and a yellow-lined notebook, spiral-bound at the top, and her hair is in a high ponytail, which highlights a delicate jawline and great cheekbones. She's no bullshit in the way you'd expect from a Brooklyn cop; not especially friendly, either. I like her immediately.

"Not optimistic?" my dad asks. "What does that mean?"

He gestures with his favorite mug. It says *Screams Internally,* with a little cartoon of a howling Earth. My dad ordered a case of them last year to give out to random friends or funders or whoever if conversation turns to his environmental documentaries. Of course, manufacturing and shipping the mugs leaves a larger carbon footprint than gifting one could ever fill. I've never pointed that out, though. My dad is big on heart, light on logic. But he means well.

"I'm sorry—I wasn't referring to your wife's well-being." Wilson shakes her head. "I meant not optimistic with respect to the fingerprints on the door. There's no doubt we'll find dozens. Every delivery guy, service person, family friend who's been here. But we'll have no idea when any of the prints were left, so they're next to useless. Now the glass is a different story . . ." She points at it. "That's got temporal relevance. It was used around the time of whatever happened here. If your wife had a guest and he or she used that glass, that's somebody we want to talk to . . . Of course, that person would also need to have prints or DNA in the system for an ID to be possible. Lots of bad people haven't been caught."

"She could have gone somewhere for work, right?" I ask my dad, but he avoids eye contact. I turn back to Wilson. "My mom works all the time. She's got meetings and calls at all hours. She's a partner at a big law firm. Maybe it was an emergency, and she didn't have time to call anyone."

But even I'm not really buying it.

"I don't think so, Cleo," my dad says, motioning toward the kitchen, the broken glass on the floor, the blood—which is not as much as it seems, apparently, according to one of the techs. "You'd be surprised how much people can bleed from a non-life-threatening injury," he'd said. "Like shocking amounts of blood." This was supposed to make me feel better, I think.

"Something happened here. There's no question about that," the female detective adds, eyeing me firmly. "Now, that doesn't mean we're not going to find your mom, and that she won't be fine. We've got some blood, not a dramatic amount, but enough. Signs of a struggle, burning food, and your mom isn't in any of the area hospitals. You can't reach her, and her phone is off. Her disappearance is suspicious—full stop. But let's take this one step at a time. And the first step is for you two to stay calm and optimistic. I realize that's not easy when you come home to broken glass and your house almost on fire."

At last my dad looks up, forces a smile. "We can definitely stay calm and optimistic, right, Cleo?"

The detective is focused on my dad. The husband, it's always the husband—that's what she's probably thinking. And he sounds stiff and awkward. He's just uncomfortable, but it seems like he's lying. *Don't waste your time,* I want to tell her. *They never even fight.*

"What happens now?" I ask instead. "What are you all going to do?"

"Well, given the suspicious circumstances, this does qualify as an official missing person case, which is helpful because it means we can move forward immediately on all fronts and dedicate maximum resources. We'll get Katrina's description out there, send the relevant alerts, and we're already canvassing the neighborhood. We'll collect camera footage, run her credit cards. We found her laptop on her office floor, and I'll send the techs back to do a forensic analysis on the desktop in there, too, though that might take a day or two. Computer Crimes has been backed up." Then she seems to realize how that sounds, like my mom is an administrative problem. "We will do everything we can to find her as quickly as possible."

She's choosing her words carefully: We will do everything we *can,* not we *will* find her. The blood on the floor, on her shoe—it's sinking in. My mom's blood. *You'd be surprised how much people can bleed.* I look away from the detective when my eyes start to burn.

"Is there something we can do to help?" my dad asks. His hand is shaking as he puts the mug down on the coffee table. He is more freaked-out than he's letting on.

"You just came in on a flight, Mr. McHugh?" The detective is watching his shaking hand. Then she glances around the room. "No bags?"

He shakes his head. "Day trip to Boston. For work."

"I see. What kind of work is it that you do?"

My dad looks up at her, his eyes kind of panicked. I want to nudge him and tell him to pull himself together, but the detective is looking right at us. "I'm a filmmaker. Documentaries."

"What's in Boston?"

My dad smiles sheepishly. "One of those fake sustainability companies," he offers with a shrug. "Working to greenwash City Hall up there. I had a meeting with the mayor's press secretary, Gail Stevens. You can check with her if you want."

"Okay," Detective Wilson says, seeming marginally satisfied by this answer. I can tell she doesn't like my dad, though. He needs to be careful. He's not used to not being liked.

"Honestly, I don't think there's even a story there. It was pretty much a waste of a day."

"Uh-huh," the detective says, looking over at the other officers, who have started to pack up. Detective Wilson chews her lip. The thought of her leaving floods me with unease.

"But—so what's . . . what exactly is next?" I ask. She's an exhausted New York City police detective. She sees some of the worst shit on the planet. This situation, my mom, it's probably another box for her to check. But I need her to care. To really care. "She's my mom." It's all I can think to say.

"I know she is." Her face softens as she meets my eyes. "I know she is."

The detective looks from me to my dad and back again, like she's checking one last time to see if he will spill something incriminating.

"If either of you remember anything else, anything at all you think could be useful, call me immediately. Day or night." She pulls a business card from her pocket and hands it to my dad. "That's my personal cell. If I don't answer, leave a message or send a text. Better yet, do both. I'll get back to you as soon as I can. And if Mrs. McHugh *does* show up or if you hear from her or otherwise learn she's not missing, *please* let me know. People forget—they're so relieved the whole thing is over—and days later we'll still be out there searching for someone who's been found."

"We'll call you, for sure," my dad says, rising to his feet. He seems glad to be getting the detective on her way.

He really is not good with stuff like this. My mom may be controlling and judgy as hell. But, man, is she good at handling shit. She doesn't freak out at the first sign of trouble, but she doesn't just sit back and wait for the other shoe to drop, either. In other words, she is the exact person you want in an emergency. Too bad she's not here. My mom would be so good at finding herself.

"Wait!" I call after the detective as she approaches the front door. My voice is too loud; I'm practically shouting. "Can't we *do* something? I mean, instead of waiting. Like, I don't know, put up signs?"

My dad gives a little laugh. "She's not a cat, honey."

The detective shoots him a look. "Actually, signs aren't a terrible idea, Cleo." She turns back to me. "You can do that. But the absolute most important thing is to talk to anyone you can think of who might know something—friends, colleagues, tennis partners. People we might not come across in a neighborhood canvass but who might know something about some small thing that was going on in your mom's life, some incidental detail. Maybe something or someone will stand out—a petty grievance, someone she was supposed to meet. To be clear, I don't love families getting involved. Even with the best of intentions, it can be easy to corrupt an investigation. But the priority right now is to find your mom. So I'll take all hands on deck." Maybe this detective does care. "But the second, and I mean *the* second, you get any sense you've found something remotely relevant, you need to stop everything and call me. Period." She eyes me and my dad. "Understood?"

"Understood," we both say quietly.

Detective Wilson's eyes narrow. "I'm serious. We could lose valuable time and critical leads if you guys are in there turning up dust. Oh, and do either of you have her passwords for social media? She was logged in to the computer already, so we're okay there, but social media can be the mother lode."

"I'm sorry, I don't," my dad says. "I know Kat has a Facebook account, but I don't know the password. She wasn't big into any of that stuff, though. I can't imagine it would be very helpful."

The detective turns to me before he's even finished. "What about you?"

I shake my head. "I don't know them, either."

She looks from me to my dad like, *What's wrong with you people?* And you know what I think, even now with her missing? *Trust me, my mom's not so easy to live with. You'd give her a wide berth, too.* I regret it immediately. But it's *not* untrue. I cross my arms tight across my chest. It doesn't do anything to stop the burning in my lungs.

"Okay, well, might not matter, as you said, but if you come across the passwords, that would be helpful. Be sure to look around the house again, too. We did our search, but you know her better than anybody." She doesn't actually sound convinced, though. "You might see something important that we overlooked. But *don't* go chasing down leads. You come across *anything* useful, you pick up the phone. Immediately."

"Of course." My dad walks pointedly toward the door. Wilson eyes him but doesn't follow. Instead, she turns to me.

"You can also call me anytime, Cleo. Yourself. For any reason." She holds out one of her business cards and doesn't release it until I meet her eyes and nod. "You okay with that plan?"

I still don't want her to leave. Because the police leaving feels like a door closing, and I'm afraid to be locked outside with my mom still gone.

But I am also pretty sure that begging her to stay will make me feel worse. "Uh, sure." I try to keep my voice steady. "Thanks."

My dad and I stand in silence for a while, staring at the closed front door.

"What a mess, huh?" he says, then drops down onto a kitchen stool. "I'll start calling around. I've got most of your mom's friends and work people in my contacts already. You want to look around upstairs, make sure they didn't miss anything?"

He's got his phone out and seems focused and determined. Could be I'm underestimating him. I hope so. "Yeah, sure."

I stand in the doorway to my parents' room, staring at their sleek low bed with its crisp white bedding, neatly made, as always. The bureau drawers are hanging open, and so are the closet doors and bathroom cabinets. I wonder what the police thought they might find in those drawers. Proof of a robbery or some sign my mom took off on her own? I step forward and look into my mom's side. Her clothes are all there, folded Marie Kondo–style, ready to spark joy. She didn't pack up and run away—of course she didn't. God forbid she do anything that might—

Wow. There I go again, kicking her while she's . . . whatever she is. But if I were the one missing, she'd probably be doing some version of the same thing, thinking about how all of my "reckless choices" had brought on whatever had happened to me. Or at least I think she would.

We are just nothing alike, my mom and I, no matter how clearly I see her face staring back at me every time I look in a mirror. We have the exact same eyes, which shift from blue to gray to green depending on the light, identical jawline and cheekbones, the same long, thick black hair. But that's where any similarities end. To say she's type A is putting it mildly. And it's not only my clothes and makeup she's obsessed with controlling. A single dirty dish in the sink or a stray pile of crumbs on the counter and she freaks out. It's like she can't handle any sign that humans actually live in our home. Once, when I was little, she tried to ban Play-Doh. Even she eventually realized that was over the top. Meanwhile, I love messy things. I *am* a messy thing. Messy and confused and irrational and overemotional. But at least I feel things. I feel everything.

I start with my mom's drawers, run my hands through her clothes, underneath and on the side. Nothing secreted away, of course. No sex toys or weed. Then my eyes snag on my dad's middle drawer of the bureau—it's empty. When I look down, his other drawers are all empty, too. My dad went to Boston for the day. Where the hell are his clothes?

I head over to the walk-in closet, flip on the light, and look around. Sure enough, my mom's clothes are hanging where they should be, but my dad's side is completely bare. Even his tuxedo and premiere-night suits are gone, and every single pair of his shoes.

Okay, something is not right here. My dad needs to explain. I'm almost at the bedroom door when I hear him on the phone downstairs. I can't make out the words, but he sounds worried. He's on with one of my mom's friends, I think. She doesn't have many, but the ones she does have—like Lauren from law school—she's very close to. Way closer than I am with any of my friends. They talk and text constantly.

I creep to the top of the stairs.

"Calm down?" I hear him ask. And he's angry. Really angry. "All I'm saying is that we have a fucking problem. You and I *both*."

A fucking problem? What problem?

I bump into my parents' bed behind me. I didn't even realize I was backing up, away from the anger in my dad's voice. Somebody from his work, it must be. As laid-back as my dad is, he

gets really frustrated with incompetent assistants and annoying bureaucracy, and there's a lot of that when you're making a
movie. But his voice was so . . . I press a hand to my chest, but I
can't get my heartbeat to slow.

I drop down onto the bed and land on something hard. I pull
back the comforter and there it is: my mom's laptop. Her personal laptop. The police must have taken her work one. It looks
like my mom accidentally made the bed over it.

I open the lid and enter my mom's password. I do know the
one to her home computer. It used to come in handy when I
wanted to order stuff on Amazon. When I was little, I'd always
ask first, and my mom would always say yes to that new notebook
or another cool set of gel pens. After Virgingate, I started buying
stuff to piss her off—goth makeup and the teeny-tiniest tops and
that big, blingy jewelry I knew she hated.

When the laptop comes to life, it actually takes me a minute to
figure out what I'm seeing frozen on the screen: photographs of
men lined up in little squares, twelve of them, like playing cards.
"Your matches," it says. I squint at the screen. A dating site?

The profile is definitely my mom's, too, a photo I've never seen
before. Taken outside, with her hair down, her face soft. She
looks almost like another person—younger and more beautiful.
Light and relaxed. Happy—she looks so much happier than I've
ever seen her.

TWO DAYS BEFORE

Why do you need *me* to do it?

> Well, I don't *need* you to do it. I can try to
> do it myself.
> But it would be helpful if you would, yes.
> It'll be a lot easier for you.

And you'd be appreciative?

> Ha. Of course. I'm always appreciative.
> You know that.

Let me think about it.

> Okay—and let me know if there's
> anything I can do to sway you. I can be
> very persuasive.

I'm well aware of that.
It's already gotten me in way too much
trouble.

KATRINA

Caffe Reggio is a New York City institution filled with lots of dark wood and antique framed photographs of Hemingway and Dorothy Parker. At nearly 6:00 p.m. on a Tuesday evening, it was also packed with cranky NYU students waiting for a table, shooting daggers at the middle-aged lady who'd been hogging a table to herself for fifteen minutes.

Aidan was late, as usual. The only real question ever was *how* late he would be. Aidan ignored banal things like time, like these concerns were beneath him. Of course, once you had a child, someone needed to keep an eye on the clock—a child needed to eat at set times, go to school, have a regular bedtime. That someone had always been me. Not that it had curried any lasting favor with Cleo. And fair enough. Just because I'd been denied basic caretaking as a child, providing it for my own daughter didn't make it some kind of prize.

Also, Cleo might have preferred a little more chaos in her childhood in exchange for a mom who was less of a drill sergeant.

Cleo had, of course, taken Aidan's call about the two thousand dollars. According to him, talking in person over coffee about what Cleo had confided would be "more productive." That had ulterior motive written all over it, but what choice did I have?

And so I'd been left to worry all day about Cleo, on top of grappling with my strange and unexpected grief about Doug. It didn't help that I had no one to share it with. I hadn't met Doug's daughter or any of his friends. I knew he had two brothers, one in Chicago who was a doctor, and one in San Francisco who was a teacher. They both had families. But what was I going to do, call them and say, "I dated your brother for three weeks and I was really starting to like him and I'm sad"? Besides, what I felt was mostly loss for what Doug and I might have been someday—not what we had already become.

I couldn't suppress a nagging tug of suspicion about his accident, though. It could have been my overactive work brain, but the timing seemed an odd coincidence given the whole college blackmail situation. Doug had decided to ignore that first text a few days ago, hoping that they—whoever they were—would go away. Not a terrible tactic. More often than not, blackmailers didn't escalate, certainly not to some kind of, what, assassination by automobile only days later? Was that what I was thinking? Not a great strategy to kill people before they paid up, much less so quickly. But, according to Doug, they had made at least two further demands within only a couple days. And criminals didn't always behave in ways that made sense.

I'd already done some poking around through my contacts at the NYPD. I had a Rolodex filled with connections I'd spent years cultivating with favors: free legal advice (real estate, wills, divorce), legal-assistant positions for college-aged children, firm box seats to games, and theater tickets. Among them were therapists, criminal defense attorneys, immigration and licensing officials, people who were good at breaking into places and good at keeping others from doing so. People who could be called upon at a moment's notice to lend a hand. My contacts were loyal. And discreet. I was very attached to some of them.

"Not an accident," Detective Larry Cross of the Bronxville Police Department had said after my old pal Gil Suffern, a lieutenant in the Central Park Precinct, of all places, had convinced him to talk to me. "That's all we know."

I'd felt stunned, even though that was exactly why I'd called—to confirm my suspicion that it hadn't been an accident.

"What do you mean?" I'd asked.

Detective Cross cleared his throat. "Indicators at the scene don't align with an accident. Looks intentional."

"Intentional?" I asked.

"A suicide," he said, like this should have been obvious.

The thought that Doug might have killed himself felt even more absurd than the idea of a blackmailer killing him before he'd paid up. Or was that because I didn't want to think he would have committed suicide when I thought we were falling for each other?

After I ended the call, I'd found myself on the Advantage Consulting website, unsure of exactly what I was looking for beyond proof that I was right. The site was predictably unremarkable, the testimonials about their tutoring and application support glowing, the descriptions of their successes suitably over the top. That said, it all looked very professional and slick. It made no sense that they'd blackmail their own, very lucrative clientele.

But maybe it wasn't people *in* the office itself, but someone associated with the scheme who'd demanded money from Doug. That person could be an amateur, the type who went too far, too fast in applying pressure, and Doug had accidentally ended up dead.

When I called the office, I'd spoken with an assistant who said that Brian Carmichael, president and owner of Advantage Consulting, would call me back. I was still waiting. My plan was to get in there and feel around a bit. If I couldn't grieve for Doug in a way that felt satisfying, I could at least try to get to the bottom of what happened to him.

I'd also had a client emergency crop up, which had been a helpful distraction. Ben Bleyer, the CMO of Play Up, a new, shockingly successful site dedicated to kids' sports, had run afoul of yet another inpatient rehab, this time for trashing his very expensive room. I'd spent two hours on the phone with the director, convincing her to give him another chance. Play Up was about to go through Series C funding. They needed Bleyer at the meetings, and they needed him clean. He could not seem to stay sober, but he was *very* good at his job. Lucky for Play Up, so was I. Because it had been one of those exhausting situations where the director was simply a good person, trying to do the right thing for all her patients, which meant my only choice was to muster up the emotional energy to convince her not only that I—Ben's best friend from parochial school in Kansas—was also a good person but that deep down Ben was, too. In reality, he'd seemed like a childish prick the one time I'd met him.

I scanned the sidewalk through Caffe Reggio's front window. Aidan was now nearly forty-five minutes late. The irony, of course, was that it was Aidan's confidence that had drawn me to him. He was ten years older than me, with a failed acting career behind him and a new, just-as-uncertain career ahead as a documentary producer when we met. And yet he'd been so self-assured. In retrospect, there had been something a little entitled about it, but Aidan was also infectiously charming, which made that easy to overlook. And what a relief it was to be with someone who moved through the world sure that everything would work out fine. Especially when he was also sure about me.

We'd actually met in a café similar to Caffe Reggio, way uptown, near Columbia. I'd been studying for law school exams when Aidan had appeared at my table.

He was very good-looking and tall, with an electrifying smile.

"Hey," he'd said. "I couldn't stop thinking about you, so I came back."

"Oh," I said, resisting the urge to look around and confirm he wasn't talking to someone else.

"You didn't notice I left before, did you?"

"I didn't notice you at all." It was true, but it had come out harsher than I'd intended. A bad habit.

But Aidan had only laughed, unfazed. "There's this thing you do when you're concentrating—you stick your tongue out a tiny bit," he said, almost like a question, but not quite.

"What?" I could feel myself flushing. "I do not."

At least, I hadn't *thought* I did anymore. I'd trained myself out of it at Haven House.

"Anyway, it's adorable," Aidan said. And I'd thought, *It's nice, someone seeing me differently than I see myself.* "Wanted you to know."

I nodded. "Oh . . . thanks?"

"Let me take you out to dinner?" Aidan had added. "I promise not to mention your tongue again, which I realize now was probably inappropriate."

By the end of that first dinner, I'd been totally smitten. Aidan wasn't put off by my wary nature the way so many men were. And he wasn't afraid to pursue me, and pursue me hard. He was that sure of himself. He was also openly emotional in a way that I could never imagine being myself, probably because of his warm, caring parents and the older brother he was very close to and the beautiful house he'd grown up in. It was disarming. Even my posture had loosened by the time our pastas were delivered.

"I love your laugh," Aidan commented at one point, a compliment I had never received before. Probably because I didn't often laugh so loudly, or freely.

Aidan's family's money was largely gone by then, thanks to his father's compulsive spending and some unfortunate late-in-life investments. But the money had never been what made his childhood special, Aidan insisted; it was the love and security, which did indeed sound enviable. In fact, it sounded like exactly what I'd been longing for my entire isolated life.

It wasn't until we had been dating seriously for a while that I explained how I actually did have money. Thanks to Gladys Greene, who had been old enough to be my grandmother when she'd whisked me away from Haven House at the age of fourteen. Gladys donated money over the years and had been a regular volunteer at the home, but she hadn't ever been considered a candidate to adopt. And rightly so. Gladys's age and noticeable dementia clearly made her unqualified. Of course, I'd skipped all of that when I explained my adoption to Aidan, including the reason Gladys's unfitness had suddenly ceased to matter.

I'd also left out the part about having murdered someone.

Standing in the bathroom of Haven House that night all those years ago in the oversize gray sweatshirt Director Daitch had thrown at me after he'd summoned a staff member to dispose of my bloody top, I had felt absurdly grateful. And so when he told me that leaving with Gladys would keep what had happened a secret and keep me out of jail for murder, I jumped at the chance. I would leave and Daitch would erase me; that was the deal.

It was weeks before the bloodstains beneath my cuticles disappeared completely.

The entire time I lived with her, Gladys thought I was her younger sister, who'd died when she was a girl. And I probably did a lot more caring for her—cooking and cleaning and sometimes bathing—than she ever did for me. Still, those were some of the happiest years of my life. Because even if Gladys's love for me had really been for her sister, it was still love. She'd died in her sleep shortly after I'd gone to college, so sad to be alone again maybe. The real surprise was that she'd left me a large chunk of her estate, nearly four million dollars. Three and a half million of which I still had. I didn't want to spend it. I earned a good living, and I preferred knowing we had the safety net. Also, Gladys's cousins had sued—a lawsuit that stretched on until after I was married, and I was still worried that someone else might show up someday, staking a claim to the money.

When my phone rang, the two students at the table to my right shot me annoyed looks. Aidan telling me he was running even later, no doubt. I accepted the call before it could ring again.

"Hold on one second," I said quietly as I headed toward the

door. "Where are you?" I snapped once I was on the sidewalk. I was not in the mood to listen to his excuses.

"Oh, hello there!" boomed a male voice. "Ms. Thompson?"

Karen Thompson: my go-to pseudonym. It was impossible to verify anything about someone with such a common name; all searches led to an avalanche of results. I'd used my Thompson alias in the message I'd left with Advantage Consulting.

"I'm sorry, who's this?" I asked, playing dumb.

"Brian Carmichael."

I stayed quiet another beat.

"Advantage Consulting?" He sounded vaguely irked, like he was a celebrity giving a dim-witted person a moment to acknowledge his importance. "Sorry to call so late, but the day got away from me."

"Oh, yes, of course, Brian. I'm so sorry!" I exclaimed. "Thank you so much for returning my call. I feel so overwhelmed these days, it's hard to remember whether I'm coming or going."

"No problem!" he said. "I have two kids of my own. Believe me, I understand how stressful this can be."

"As I mentioned in my message, it's about my daughter Sophia," I began. "We were hoping we could get some help with her transferring. She's at Columbia right now, and she's really not happy."

"Well, first off, congratulations on Columbia. That's a terrific school. Just wonderful." I moved the phone away from my ear; his voice was so loud. "Doesn't mean that it's the right place for her, of course. And transferring can be complicated, it goes without saying, but the good news is that you're starting from a strong place."

"Great," I said, clearing my throat. "Your assistant said the next step was to set up an in-person consultation?"

"Yes, an in-person consultation, exactly," Brian went on. "I like to establish a personal *rapport* with a family before we go any further. We'll sit down with Sophia, talk about her objectives, her likes and dislikes, and life goals. Every family is different. Every child is different. Every school is different. We're looking to assemble a complex puzzle, and this process works best when we all work together to align our objectives."

"A consultation would be great," I said. "We'd like to move quickly, though. Sophia would like to transfer as soon as possible. Ideally to Amherst."

Couldn't hurt to zero in on the same school Doug's daughter had gone to, if my plan was to eventually ask about him.

"Not a problem, Ms. Thompson," Carmichael said, using precisely the extra-gentle voice I reserved for clients who were permanently fucked. "I understand that completely. We can expedite as necessary, I assure you. I'll have my assistant reach out to schedule ASAP."

"Oh, how wonderful," I said, making sure to sound relieved. "Thank you. This has been very stressful."

"We will get Sophia where she needs to be, Ms. Thompson," Brian said. "You're in excellent hands, I assure you."

As I dropped my phone in my bag, I saw Aidan closing in on the sidewalk, hands jammed in his pockets. He'd aged well into that "hot dad" thing, looking easily the same age as me now, instead of a decade older. I could only imagine the women he had to chase off, who surely mistook him—as I had—for a security blanket.

But at least I didn't feel angry at the sight of him. All I felt was relieved. Because Aidan wasn't my problem anymore, thanks to those texts from *Her*. Literally—that was how she appeared in his contacts. They were from Bella, Aidan's assistant. I'd known it instantly. I'd been suspicious as soon as he'd hired her, a former student from the New School program where he'd been an adjunct. She was twenty-six and gorgeous and worshipful. Aidan always lit up around Bella, basking in her admiration as he dismissed my suspicions as paranoid and delusional.

Aidan had gotten good at weaponizing what he knew of my

troubled history when it suited him—the subtle suggestions, the gaslighting. After initially denying it, he did eventually admit *Her* was Bella. He fired her immediately in an attempt to make amends. Though it was already far too late for that.

"Hey?" Aidan asked now, ducking his head to meet my eyes. "Everything okay?"

"Sorry, I was on a work call," I said reflexively, then immediately regretted apologizing.

Aidan had never bothered to hide his contempt for my "soulless" corporate legal work. As though we didn't live off my income. I could only imagine what he'd have said if he knew how I actually spent my days.

"Don't let Mark run you so hard on that hamster wheel," Aidan said. "You look tired. Great, too. But tired."

"Well, one of us does need to earn a living." It just popped out.

"Nice, Kat, really nice."

"I'm sorry," I said. Bickering with Aidan wasn't helpful now. "Can we just— What did Cleo tell you, Aidan?"

He opened the door and made a show of ushering me in. "Getting right down to business, huh? Can we at least sit down inside like actual humans who made *another* human together?"

"Listen, Aidan," I went on more gently once we were finally sitting in a booth against the wall. "I'm grateful you went back to Cleo, really. That you're *able* to talk to her at all. But I'm also worried, so if you could get to the point."

"Sure, but can we first finish our conversation about division of the inheritance?"

Division. Last time hadn't he described it as a loan?

"*Before* you tell me about our daughter you want to talk about money *you* need?"

"Well, Kat, it's a little hard not to feel used right now. I've done what you asked with Cleo, even though it wouldn't necessarily have been my way of doing things. And yet you won't answer a very simple, very reasonable question. In light of our twenty-two years of marriage, and co-parenting of Cleo, asking if you can advance me my portion of the inheritance doesn't seem so unreasonable. I mean, the money will be half mine once the divorce is finalized, and it's your idea to wait on that. By the way, it was also your idea to break up our family."

"*You* had sex with your assistant," I snapped.

"And I've apologized for that. Countless times," Aidan said very slowly and condescendingly. "I wanted to work on our marriage. You're the one who's not willing. And listen, I know it's hard for you to trust people given where you—"

"You had *sex* with your *assistant,*" I repeated.

"And I'm sorry. I really am. But people do make mistakes! I still love you, Kat. I have always loved you." Aidan paused for a moment and cocked his head; someone was playing saxophone on the sidewalk outside. I took a breath and tried to calm down. Nothing good ever came of me losing it with Aidan. "Hey, you remember that first apartment we had? When you hadn't started work yet and Gladys's money was still in probate?"

"You mean the one with the water bugs?" I shuddered. "Impossible to forget."

"Remember when our neighbor took up the violin? How we were freaking out about the walls being thin? We were awake half the night after we saw him bring it home. You were so determined to be nice about it."

"And you were plotting to break in and steal it." I laughed a little. "And then he was so—"

"Good!" We said it at the same time.

"It was like a free concert every night," I said.

"Which was lucky, because that was all we could afford," Aidan added. The saxophonist appeared to have moved down the street. He sighed. "Kat, I want to save our relationship. I've said that countless times. These things do take work. You know that. Or maybe you don't. Or maybe you don't care. Sometimes I have no idea."

Even now, Aidan could still make me feel like he was speaking down from some moral high ground. A place only people who came from nice families in Westchester could occupy.

But no matter how irritated I was now, those early days with Aidan had bright spots. He was warm and funny and full of life. He was great at playing with Cleo when she was little—Twister for hours was his specialty. And when she was a preteen, he always seemed to be able to get her out of a bad mood by being silly— ridiculous faces and bad jokes galore. Truthfully, he'd gotten me to lighten up, too, ignoring my defenses and demanding that I join in the fun. It was a breath of fresh air, for a time. But that window it had briefly opened inside me had eventually closed amid all our other problems.

"What are you asking for, exactly, Aidan?"

"It's . . . I'm stressed," he went on, his entire demeanor shifting. His eyes were soft, imploring now. "The new movie—we've had a couple significant setbacks. And we're already so far in the hole financially. If we don't try to see it through and claw the invest- ment back with a sale to a distributor, it will be . . . disastrous. The company will go under. I—I need some help right now to bridge the gap. That's all, Kat."

And what kind of person didn't respond to a genuine plea for help, especially from someone with whom they'd shared more than twenty years of marriage and a child? Only a bad one, obviously. And the thing was, I did have the money. More than three million dollars still in a separate account, the exact amount Gladys's cousins had sued for. We'd used some of it over the years, but I'd always replaced it over time with my bonuses.

"Call it a *loan* if you want, for now. I don't even care. But it is money I'm entitled to." He gave his head an indignant shake.

"Entitled?" I asked. Because that exactly did sum up so much. "It's money *I* inherited."

"And then put it into an account with my name on it," he said. "You squirreling away the account numbers and passwords doesn't change that fact."

It was true. I had put Aidan's name on the account. But only because I'd known he'd be mortally wounded otherwise. I deliberately hadn't researched the legal implications. I'd had a bad feeling what they might be. In my defense, I hadn't thought we'd ever get divorced. But now the money really might end up half his. How could I have been so stupid?

"How much money do you need this time?"

Now his eyes turned down to the table. "It's a lot. I'm acknowledging that right off the—"

"How much, Aidan?"

"Two million dollars," he said, then took a sharp breath. "Well, really two point seven five. I obviously wouldn't ask if it wasn't really important, Kat. This movie—it really has the potential to change things. To have a real impact."

I willed myself to stay calm. "I hear you, Aidan, and I understand. We can absolutely discuss it. *After* we discuss Cleo, which was why I thought we were here. What did you find out?"

He squinted at me for a long moment. This was a game of chicken now.

"We don't need to worry," he said finally. "That's the bottom line."

"Okay, and what did Cleo say?"

"That we don't need to worry."

"That's it? Aidan, you asked specifically about Kyle, right?"

"Of course I did. And she's not seeing him. Like I said. Which was my point about not worrying. My point exactly."

"Then what was the money for?" I asked.

"I don't know . . . *specifically*," he said. "But Cleo assured me that she is okay and otherwise asked that I respect her privacy."

You can't be that stupid.

But had I actually expected that he'd get her to admit that she was back with Kyle, even if he'd asked? Cleo had gotten pretty good at lying right to our faces.

"Well, at least she doesn't have the money," I said, mostly to myself. Because quite genuinely it was the only comforting thing I could think of.

"What do you mean?" Aidan looked confused. "Yes, she does."

"What are you talking about? I didn't see any transfer."

"I wired it from my work account." His "work account" being a business credit card on which I eventually paid the balance.

"Aidan, you didn't."

He shook his head. "I know how much you like to control everything and everyone, but I don't need your permission to do what I know is best for our daughter. And that's *trusting* her. She's not a child anymore. She's practically—she *is* a grown woman. She's allowed to have secrets."

"She was *just* dating a drug dealer! He got her to work for him. She almost failed out of school!"

"That's a bit dramatic, don't you think?"

"It's accurate!" I gritted my teeth. I needed to calm down. "Aidan, get the money back from Cleo. *Please.*"

"I'm not going to do that, Kat. Our relationship is based on mutual trust and respect."

"You mean that you're her friend and not her father?"

"Throw all the stones you want, Kat, because your relationship with Cleo is going swimmingly, right?"

"Fuck you, Aidan."

Aidan closed his eyes and stayed quiet for a minute.

"Listen, I'm sorry, Kat," he said. "You know I didn't mean that. I'm having a hard time. That's all." He gestured with a hand in my direction—me, the separation. "With all of this."

I stood up. I'd had enough manipulation for one day.

"Get Cleo to tell you what's going on. We need proof this time—actual evidence of where that money went," I said, driving my finger into the tabletop. "I don't care what you have to do to get it. But if you don't, I am not giving you a dime."

As I walked toward the West Fourth Street station, the anxiety came in waves. I couldn't leave this in Aidan's hands, couldn't just go home to stew. And so I decided instead to do what I would have done if Cleo were a client's child mixed up in something: investigate. Want to know what someone is really up to? Watch them. Of course, when it was client-related, I never felt guilty doing it.

From a bench in Washington Square Park, I could barely make out the entrance to Cleo's dorm. I had no idea if she was in there or not. I felt so relieved when I finally saw the light go on in what I knew was Cleo's third-floor window. I'd counted the balconies on move-in day.

My phone buzzed then with a text.

I know everything. And it's about time the rest of the world does, too.

My anonymous friend, again. I was gripping my phone so tightly, my fingers were burning. I considered telling whoever it was to go ahead and set a price. I was willing to pay quite a lot for this person to go away. But offering money *before* someone demanded it significantly weakened your negotiating position. Pushing back hard, on the other hand, was always a safe place to start.

Fuck off, I replied.

When I glanced up, Cleo was on the sidewalk in front of her dorm—*very* short skirt, *very* tall boots. She was with two girls I didn't recognize. One of the other girls was a brunette, the other a blonde, neither half as striking as Cleo. She was a standout kind of beauty. I'd told her this once, but she took it as an insult. I still didn't understand why. But your kids didn't give you points for intent, only for how you made them feel.

I was relieved as I watched the girls start off together, arm in arm. Good normal fun, a regular night out. But then Cleo peeled off suddenly and headed the other way. Alone. *Shit.*

Without thinking, I was on my feet, following her carefully—at a safe distance, on the opposite side of the street. When Cleo's stride turned quick and purposeful, a determined march more than a walk, I almost had to jog to keep up. She looked like she was off to do something she'd talked herself into, and all I kept thinking was *Don't do it. Don't do it.*

I followed as she continued deep into the West Village on Christopher Street, pausing in front of a building with a crystal shop on the ground floor and a basement store of some kind, lit up and cheerful enough, though I couldn't make out the sign from across the street. Cleo drew her shoulders back. Like she was steeling herself. *Don't do it.*

She retrieved an envelope from her bag before descending the stairs. I thought about running across the street, dragging her back up the steps, away from whatever lay at the bottom. But of course I could not. Soon a woman in expensive-looking athleisure descended the same steps, talking on the phone. After her came a young, attractive banker type in a very expensive suit. At least these people did not look associated with anything criminal. And it appeared to be a safe, public space.

I jumped when my phone rang, the volume up too loud. Another unknown number.

"Hello?" I answered tentatively.

"Are you fucking kidding me?" I jerked the phone away from my ear. "You have to stop avoiding me!"

Vivienne. Perfect.

"Do *not* yell at me, Vivienne," I said calmly.

"I've called you ten times today and nothing." She was still shouting. "But I call from my husband's phone and you pick right up? What kind of lawyer screens their clients' calls?"

"Vivienne?"

"Yes?"

"I'm hanging up now."

"You can't do that." Her tone was more plaintive now. Vivienne's belligerent bark was, I'd learned, rather easily disarmed with nonreactivity.

"I can. And if you want my help, which believe me you *do,* I suggest you go for a walk, get yourself calmed down." My tone was icy but not angry. "Then *wait* for me to call you back, which I will. As soon as I have a suitable opportunity. Now, good-bye."

"You can't just—"

I hung up just as Cleo reemerged at the top of the steps. Hardly down there for two seconds. And she looked . . . happy. She was beaming, in fact, as she paused to look down at her phone, typed out a quick text. When she'd tucked her phone back into her jacket pocket, she started down Christopher Street in the direction of her dorm, still smiling. I watched until she was gone, swallowed by the distance and the crowded sidewalk. While there I sat, alone in the gathering dark.

UNITED STATES DISTRICT COURT
FOR THE DISTRICT OF NEW YORK

IN RE XYTEK MARKETING, SALES PRACTICE AND PRODUCT LIABILITY LITIGATION, MDL NO. 4236	MASTER LONG FORM COMPLAINT & JURY DEMAND

COMES NOW Plaintiffs in this consolidated action, collectively, and by and through the Plaintiffs' Liaison Counsel, who file this Master Long Form Complaint and Jury Demand ("Master Complaint") against Defendants as an administrative device to set forth potential claims Plaintiffs, on their own behalf and/or on behalf of the estates of deceased persons and their beneficiaries, may assert against Defendants in this litigation. Plaintiffs in MDL No. 4236 bring and/or adopt this Master Complaint, and complain and allege on personal knowledge as to themselves, and on information and belief as to all other matters, as follows:

GENERAL ALLEGATIONS 1. This Master Complaint sets forth facts and allegations common to those Plaintiffs whose claims relating to Xytek products have been filed in this multidistrict litigation. Plaintiffs seek compensatory and punitive damages, monetary restitution, and all other available remedies as a result of injuries caused by Defendants' defective Xytek products. Plaintiffs claim and allege that their damages and injuries, specifically to their infants in gestation, are a direct and proximate result of Defendants' negligent, intentional, and wrongful acts, omissions, and conduct regarding Defendants' design, development, formulation, manufacture, testing, packaging, labeling, promotion of Xytek for use in pregnant patients.

CLEO

My hands are shaking as I scroll through my mom's online dating profile, unable to process what I'm seeing. *My* mom. *These* men. There are chats on one side of the screen—with twelve different guys. *Twelve.* Peter, Matt, Oscar, the list goes on. Without opening them, I can see the beginnings of the conversations.

"Hi, how have you . . ."

"Hi! How's your week?"

"So great to meet you. So you're a lawyer . . ."

"Coffee was fun yesterday. Would love to do it again."

Again? My mom has *met* some of these people? My dad might stray . . . I could see that. He's distractible that way, and a guy. Not that that would make it okay, obviously. But my mom would never cede an inch of her moral high ground by cheating. And now she's hooking up with random strangers from the—now she's hooking up? I try to process this, but I really can't imagine it. She's so . . . not sexual.

Except there it is, in black and white. Her words. Those random men. It's like the opposite of her. She'd had the audacity to judge *me* when I told her I had sex with Charlie? Is she seriously this much of a hypocrite?

I click the first chat at the top. There are a handful of messages back and forth with this Oscar guy, beginning with my mom's opening line: *Is that picture from Iceland? I recognize that—Vik*

Beach. I was eleven when we traveled to Iceland. My dad was filming there on the black sand. I feel a pang of betrayal, like my mom had handed this rando a piece of my childhood.

It is Vik!!

I click on his profile: *42. Leo. Active. Lawyer.* The profile image is of a dark-haired man with intense deep-set eyes, looking back over his shoulder as he heads toward the setting sun, a surfboard under his arm. Not bad. I click on the next picture—the Oscar guy is now in a suit, cheek-to-cheek with a little girl in a frilly dress at a wedding or something. Except her face is blacked out, scribbled over as if with a marker. It's creepy as hell. The one after that is of him shirtless in front of a barbecue, holding tongs in one hand and a beer in the other, decent arms but a noticeable hint of a belly. Hard to believe it's the same guy with the surfboard.

This is my cell. Would it be better to text? is the last chat message from my mom.

She must have decided to give him the benefit of the doubt— more surfboard than scratched-out kid and potbellied tongs in real life. *Ugh.*

My phone vibrates in my back pocket. *Not looking good for tonight, huh?*

Will. I was supposed to have texted him hours ago.

Sorry. Something happened with my mom.

Is everything okay?

Not really. She's missing.

Seriously?

Yeah. It's bad. The police just left.

Holy shit. What happened?

No one knows. I'm kind of freaking out.

Do you want me to come?

Yes, that's what I want to say. *Come hold my hand.* I don't write that, though. Nothing with Will and me is that simple.

Not right now. I'm with my dad. But thank you.

Okay. Here if you need to talk.

"You find something?"

When I look up from my phone, my dad is in the doorway, looking like his usual warm and friendly, NPR-listening self—someone who definitely doesn't troll for women on a disgusting sex app while pretending he's some kind of monk. I slam the laptop shut.

"Where are your clothes?" I ask. No better defense than a good offense.

"What do you mean?" he asks, eyes wide and innocent.

I walk past him and open the drawers on his side of the bureau. "Your stuff is all gone."

My dad scrunches his face as he stares at the drawers. "Oh," he says, kind of dumbly.

"Please don't lie to me, Dad. I really can't—I need to know what the hell is going on here," I say. My dad is the king of the white lie: *Be right there . . . I'm about to do it . . . Of course I remember.* Usually, it's harmless, his way of keeping everybody happy. It's my go-to tactic, also. And one thing I've always known for sure: We've got each other's backs.

He shakes his head. "I told your mom this was a terrible idea."

"*What* was a terrible idea?"

"Not telling you." He drops down onto the bed, right next to my mom's incriminating laptop.

"Dad, what is going on? Where is Mom?"

"You think *I* know, Cleo? And what, I'm keeping it to myself? Why would I do that?"

"I don't know. But nothing here is making any sense." I gesture toward the laptop and regret it immediately as I register his confused look. He doesn't know.

"Wait, what did you find on here?" He reaches over to open her computer.

Be locked. Be locked. But then the screen lights right back up, and all of it is there—the little pictures of the men, the chats. My dad's expression is unreadable. He closes the laptop and runs a hand over the top. He for sure does not look shocked.

"You knew?" Relief and anger collide in my chest.

"I knew that it was a possibility," he says, scrubbing his hands up and down his face. "Your mom wasn't doing anything wrong. She was allowed to be dating people."

"Allowed?"

"Your mom and I have been separated for the past four months. I don't know the details of what she's been doing." He gestures toward the computer again. "And it's not what I wanted. But . . ." He looks up at me intently. "Your mother has been through a lot in her life. She's a good person, though. I think you know that. Whatever she's been doing—"

"A good person who took off with some new boyfriend?" I ask. "Is that what's going on here?"

"Come on, Cleo. She didn't take off, obviously," he says. "She'd never do that to you. And, what, left a bloody shoe to throw us off the trail?"

My brain is slowly piecing together how big this lie really is. My dad and I talk all the time, and, yeah, sometimes he's traveling. But apart from the occasional work trip, he's been acting like he was home the past four months.

"Where have you been staying, then?"

My dad winces, stares down at his shoes. His whole parenting brand has been *I'll always give it to you straight*. He's told me about his mistakes and his bad decisions, the time he almost failed out of college, all the drugs he did, how he once stole a hundred dollars from his best friend to go to a concert. How he's never been a hundred percent sure of anything because uncertainty is a part of life. It gave me permission not to be perfect every second of every day like my mom expected. And I've been so grateful for that. But being a straight-up liar? That's something else entirely.

"I've been staying at Dan's place in SoHo." He looks down at his hands. He's still wearing his wedding ring. "He's out of town on location."

"And you were never going to tell me?"

"I know it sounds bad," he says. When he looks up at me, his eyes are shiny. "Honestly, it was kind of a no-win situation. Your mom thought that . . ."

"Oh, so this was Mom's idea?" That's kind of hard to believe when the whole situation screams impulsive and immature.

He shakes his head. "No, no, that's not what I meant. Obviously, I'm an adult. I could have refused to go along with it. It was a joint decision. We're both responsible. But your mom, in particular, did think it would be better to wait until the end of the school year to tell you. After everything last semester with Kyle. You have your grades up now. She didn't want this to derail you."

I was on academic probation in the fall. But my mom was wrong about Kyle being the cause. It was a hard first semester, that's all. I had all my science and math requirements to fulfill. When I met Kyle, I was already drowning. I mean, did things eventually become bad between Kyle and me, really bad? Yes, in the end. But my mom was freaking out way before that.

"So you're saying you lied because of me?" I ask.

"Of course not, Cleo." He closes his eyes again. "There's no right answer here. Believe me. And your mom really thought—"

"Whose idea was it to separate?"

"I don't think it matters who—"

"Whose idea?"

My dad is starting to look a little pissed now.

"Your mom suggested the separation."

"I don't believe you."

"It's true, Cleo," he says. "You can ask her. When we find her, which we will, she'll tell you. You know as well as I do that she won't lie. She's incapable of it." This sounds like a criticism.

"Did you cheat on her?" That's the only possible scenario I can imagine that would lead to this.

"No one cheated on anybody. God no," my dad says quickly. I don't know if I believe him. "Of course not. Your mom wasn't happy. With me—*I* wasn't making her happy. And I don't like saying it that way because it sounds like I'm making it her fault. And it's not her fault. It's reality." He's quiet for a moment. "Your mom and I *are* really different. Like opposites. I'm creative, and she's . . . you know, she's analytical. She lives in her head. That kind of difference can be exciting for a while. But maybe it's not sustainable. Nothing is set in stone anyway. We aren't divorced yet. We're just taking some time."

"Right." But if my mom is already seeing other people, it seems like her mind is pretty made up. "Did you find out anything on the phone?"

"About what?"

"About *Mom*? Come on, Dad, focus. Weren't you talking to her office?"

"Oh, right, sorry. This whole situation is . . . it's so shocking. Anyway, Jules doesn't know anything. They spoke around the time you were supposed to get here. Your mom mentioned you were on the way, that she was looking forward to seeing you. She had a call scheduled later with a client, some Vivienne something. She didn't pick up," he says.

"And who was the other person you were talking to?" I want to know about the angry call. I want to know about this "fucking problem." I want to know everything, not just the stuff he thinks I can handle.

"Oh, right," he says, making a face like he's only now remembered. "Lauren."

My mom's best friend from law school. That wasn't who he spoke angrily to, though. Not a chance. My dad was careful around Lauren; he'd never talk to her that way. She already didn't like him. It was an out-in-the-open joke between them— except that it obviously wasn't a joke.

"Did Lauren know anything?"

He shakes his head. "No, unfortunately. She's shocked and confused, like us. She said she'd make some calls, mutual friends, that kind of thing. She's going to check back in later."

"And who was the other person you talked to?" I ask. "Besides Lauren and Jules."

"What?"

"I heard you on a call with a third person. Somebody from work?"

His face freezes for a second. Then he blinks and the look is gone.

"From work?" he asks.

"I don't know, but 'We have a fucking problem. You and I both,'" I say, repeating his words. "You sounded pretty pissed."

"Oh, right, that . . . I, uh, am upset." He seems thrown or embarrassed or something. "Dealing with location permits at a time like this for a movie that will probably lose financing and never start shooting anyway? It feels very . . . wrong. But I had to deal with it—so I lost my patience."

"Right," I say.

"God, Cleo. Please stop looking at me like that. Lying about the separation was a mistake and I am sorry," he says. "So, so sorry. But it was to protect you. You're the most important thing in the world to me. I hope you know that."

"Right," I say again. But the word sounds hollow even to me.

I grab my mom's laptop off the bed and head for the door.

"Cleo!" he calls after me. "You can't take that." When I whip around, he looks as worried as he sounds. "We need to give that to the police."

"I will—first thing in the morning," I say, moving toward the stairs.

"Cleo!" My name comes out like a reprimand.

I turn to face him again. "You heard what the detective said. If we give it to them now, it's going to sit there until the tech guys have time. I'm not going to mess with anything. I just want to see if there's anything important on there. That way, I can be sure they know. Either way, I'll give it to them tomorrow."

"That isn't a good idea." He sounds even more nervous. "We're not supposed to get in the way—"

"I'm not going to get in the way. But I'm also not going to sit here and do nothing because someone tells me to," I say. "I'm going to do what Mom would do if I were missing. I'm going to help find her."

I stop at the bottom of the steps to grab my tote bag off the floor. I think of my mom's other computer so out of place on her office floor. Maybe I should check that room myself. After all, the police missed her personal laptop upstairs. Not exactly in plain sight, but still.

The drawers and cabinets in her office are all gaping open from the police search. It looks so chaotic, so messy. So not my mom. And just like that, there are tears in my eyes, and a sudden terrible wheezy feeling in my chest. I take a couple deep breaths until it starts to pass.

Opposite the desk is "the tiny bathroom"—that's what we've always called it. Only a toilet and a small sink. One of those old brownstone quirks, some illegal addition made before we ever lived there. It even has a lock with a little ancient key on the outside instead of within. Probably back from a time when it was only a closet. The lock works, too. I know that firsthand.

I'd just turned fourteen when I locked my mom inside.

I wanted to go with my friends to Gov Ball, the music festival on Governors Island, and she said I was only allowed to go if she came, too. She promised to remain out of sight so that no one would even know she was there. She just wanted to make sure I stayed safe. Not because she didn't trust me, she claimed, but because she didn't trust the world. And so she was going to hover,

I don't know, in the bushes, *watching me?* None of my friends' parents felt the need to do this.

"It's humiliating!" I can remember shouting after I'd already been at it for at least half an hour, following her from the bedroom to the living room to the kitchen. Even now the memory is so close—I can feel the way my heart was pounding as I chased her around.

"Enough, Cleo!" my mom had shouted that day, really angry, which wasn't like her, either. "I'm going to walk away now."

"So you get to decide we're done!" I shouted, still following her down the hall.

"Yes, I do get to decide," she called without turning around. "One of the very few things I get to do as a parent is decide when a conversation is over."

Then she disappeared into her office. I don't know if she had planned to go into the tiny bathroom or if she was trying to get away from me. But when I raced after her and she closed the bathroom door between us, I started to scream, "Mom! You can't do this to me! Mom!" And at that moment I hated her so much. It was like my skin was on fire.

I don't remember deciding to lock the bathroom door. But I do remember doing it. Turning that key so hard and fast, it left my fingers throbbing. And I remember staring at the door after it was done, breathless and scared but maybe also a little thrilled. Then the sound of my mom's voice calling through the door, trying to hide how nervous she was: "Cleo, please unlock this door. Unlock it right now."

She went so fast from calm to mad, then really mad, then frantic and, finally, terrified. Her voice cracked as she started to beg. I remember knowing that my dad wouldn't be home for at least two weeks. That she didn't have her cell phone in there. That I had all the power. In the end, I only let her out for totally selfish reasons. I needed money to meet my friends at the tarot card reader on Fourteenth Street. Otherwise, I can't say for sure what would have happened.

Another person might have removed the key permanently from the bathroom after that. Not my mom. Maybe she left it in the lock because she wanted me to know that she still trusted me. But every time I saw that key it always felt like she wanted me to remember what I'd done. That she was shaming me. And yet, somehow, I never really felt that terrible about the whole thing. Even now it feels . . . complicated. The way everything always is with my mom.

I turn my attention to a cabinet, filled, it turns out, with neat rows of law school textbooks. Another cabinet has files with labels like *Tax Returns* and *Medical Records,* with different years. Cabinet after cabinet of boring, responsible, predictable nothing—nothing that could explain where my mom went. It isn't until I reach the tall cabinet in the corner that I find anything even remotely interesting, a box labeled *Haven House.*

It's heavier than I expect when I pull it out and set it on the floor. Inside are some school papers (all As) and some notebooks and a few photos of my mom as a kid, looking so much like me at that age, it's creepy. I've seen some of these pictures before, when I asked to see my mom's childhood photos. I remember my mom explaining why she was with so many other kids in every picture; she'd lived in a group home for a bit before she was adopted by Gladys, who maybe had some issues but also sounded like a total character, warm and kind and silly. So not a normal childhood, but not horrible, either. But I've never seen these pictures before. She's so much younger in them. She was a *little,* little kid, at Haven House, and she stayed all the way until she was a teenager? She lived there a lot longer than I realized.

At the bottom of the box is also Walt Whitman's *Leaves of Grass*—I've never known my mom to read poetry in her life. There's even an inscription on the first page: *Promise me you'll be a writer, Katrina. God gives the gift to few. xx Reed*

A writer? And my mom never thought to mention that when all I've ever talked about is wanting to be a writer myself? Classic.

Under the book, I find what looks to be a journal. My mother's journal. I stare at it for a minute, feeling a mix of intrigue and dread. I smooth my hand over the cover a couple times before I flip it open to the middle and begin to read.

Olivia took my soap and my towel and then she called me a fucking cunt. Because that makes sense. It's not even like she kept them for herself. She threw them in the garbage AFTER putting them in the toilet. She put my washcloth in the toilet, too. Then tried to shove it in my mouth. I got away, though. I really thought about telling on her this time, but to who? Silas? Anyway, she has that broken spoon.

I snap the journal closed. *A broken spoon?*

"You're still here?" My dad's voice in the doorway. "I thought you were— Did you find something?"

He comes closer, looks over my shoulder into the box. I tuck the journal into my bag. I'm not sure why I don't want him to see it, only that I don't.

"How long was Mom at Haven House? I thought she was adopted by that woman Gladys?"

He shakes his head. "But not until she was a teenager—she was at Haven House for *years* before that. Longer than most kids. There were issues in her earlier foster homes. Bad luck mostly." I can see the lightbulb go on. "Wait, you don't think . . ."

"Don't think what?"

"Well, I guess, I'm just saying . . . that kind of childhood. Maybe your mom was struggling more than we realized."

"So now you're saying she *did* leave?"

"No, no, of course not. I'm saying . . . Your mom's had a hard life. Maybe all of this is related somehow. I don't know."

But I don't want to think about that. I only want to think about her coming home.

"Listen, I'm tired. I need to go." I stand up and walk toward the door. The journal and computer feel so heavy in my bag.

"Are you going to be okay?" he calls after me.

"Yeah," I say. "As soon as we know where Mom is."

KATRINA

Advantage Consulting's waiting room was lovely. In fact, the entire building was stunning, a converted nineteenth-century limestone mansion on East Eighty-sixth, right off the park. The upper edge of the Metropolitan Museum was barely visible through the huge windows. There were two bold abstracts on the wall opposite the couch, nearby an artful black-and-white photo—dark skies over the western plains, a single horse off center in the distance. Brian Carmichael had been raised in rural Montana, or so his bio claimed, before finding his way to the Ivy League. This cast him perfectly in the role of an earthy, wholesome, erudite man who understood how to navigate success without losing sight of his moral compass. Surely the wealthy parents who hired him felt much less terrible by association. Actually, they probably didn't feel terrible at all.

Looking around the room, it was again hard to fathom that Brian Carmichael would spend years establishing a well-run, moneymaking machine only to risk it all by blackmailing someone like Doug, then staging an accident when he didn't immediately pay up. But even those adept at criminal operations made mistakes. That's how they got caught.

But even if it was a dead end, at least meeting with Carmichael was a distraction from thinking about whether the blissed-out look on Cleo's face had had to do with Kyle.

I'd known the second I laid eyes on Kyle that he would be

a real problem. The way he'd barely nodded at Aidan and me before sauntering out of Cleo's room seconds after we arrived. I'd been glaring at him so hard, I was surprised he didn't combust. And Cleo had been on me like a hawk.

"Mom, stop," she'd said before I even uttered a word. "I like him. I'm not doing this."

"Doing what? I didn't say anything."

By that point, I was on high alert; Cleo had already made some bad choices in the boy department. She was together in so many aspects of her life, but she had terrible taste in boys. Not Charlie, her one real boyfriend. He'd been very sweet, despite the whole Virgingate debacle. But Lance, Hunter, Aaron? They'd all been jerks who didn't treat Cleo remotely the way she should have been treated. She was a knockout and that was all they saw. They didn't appreciate her brilliance or her sensitivity or her humor. Or how she could be shy sometimes. They didn't really *see* her at all.

But my feelings about Cleo's earlier boyfriends paled in comparison with my virulent reaction to Kyle and the entitled, obnoxious way he had about him. And I hadn't even suspected he was an actual drug dealer at the time. Hadn't known he would enlist Cleo's help. Couldn't have imagined she'd go along with it. And so I'd kept my mouth shut about him even when Cleo's grades dropped. But when Aidan said that Cleo had told him about Kyle being a dealer, I'd jumped into action. It didn't take much digging to figure out it was way more than a little dealing. Kyle was *the* biggest dealer at NYU, pills mostly—Adderall, Xanax, Oxy.

Cleo had been surprisingly good at covering her own tracks, though. I couldn't confirm that she was actually involved until I got my hands on her unlocked phone at Thanksgiving and quickly scanned her texts. A violation of her privacy, sure. But a justifiable one. By then she and Kyle had been together a few months and it was clear from the texts that she was working for him. There were only carefully worded check-ins and oblique instructions, but it was enough.

I confronted her, even though it meant revealing that I'd been snooping. After railing against me for invading her privacy, Cleo had insisted she didn't use herself. A fact confirmed when, in a rage, she'd taken the drug test I already had on hand. All she'd been doing for Kyle, she'd said, besides being his devoted girl-friend, which might have been the worst part, was dropping off pills and picking up cash.

"It's like a paper route!" Cleo had squeaked, her voice as a little girl popping through her bravado.

She also refused to stop.

And so a couple weeks later I threatened to stop paying her tuition unless she cut off all contact with Kyle and started seeing a therapist. I wasn't proud of making threats, but it wasn't like I'd had a lot of options. Of course, the most questionable call of all was my decision to then pay a surreptitious visit to Kyle myself. But that *had* worked. Or so I had thought until last night, when I'd seen Cleo emerge from the store on Christopher *without* the envelope she'd entered with. Sure looked like a drop for Kyle; maybe he had even been the one at the bottom of those steps.

At least I did know she was seeing the therapist. That was one good thing about paying the bills.

The phone on Advantage Consulting's elegant mid-century modern reception desk chirped discreetly and the receptionist answered in a hushed tone. When she hung up, she turned to me and smiled. "Brian will be right out."

I returned her smile tightly, like I was a woman unaccustomed to being kept waiting. Willing to suffer it only for her child. These kinds of details were essential in establishing my credibil-ity as a potential client: the expression of poised irritation, the camel Agnès B sweater, the way I had myself perched on the edge of the couch, like I was not quite convinced of its cleanliness.

"Ms. Thompson?" When I looked up, there, in all his glory, was Brian Carmichael—chiseled features, gray eyes, thick sil-very hair. Very confident. He indeed looked like he belonged fly-fishing knee-deep in an icy Montana stream. He strode across the room with an outstretched hand. "It's nice to meet you."

I forced another stiff smile and shook his hand, a bit awkwardly because I didn't get up. But the woman I was pretending to be would make Carmichael lean in. She would wait for an official invitation before she stood.

"I'm sorry again about the delay," he said. "I have this one student, incredibly bright and thoughtful, not to mention an Olympic-caliber swimmer. Great, great kid. But, wow, is he disorganized. He was supposed to have gotten me a draft of his Common App essay two weeks ago. Harvard wants him on the swim team, but there are some basic requirements. Let's face it: Harvard is Harvard no matter how fast you can swim the butterfly." He gave a rueful shake of his head.

"Of course. And you would know, right? I mean, you did go there," I said smoothly, obediently taking the bait—the Harvard alum reminder, the evidence of his personal dedication to his students, his fundamental integrity. It was impressive how much Brian had packed into so few words.

"Let's head back to my office, where we can chat," he said.

As he turned, I set my phone to record and dropped it in my purse. Who knew what Brian Carmichael might admit, or how I might want to use it against him later? It was best to be very prepared, and extremely patient. This was always true. If only I could have exercised that kind of discipline when it came to Cleo.

Carmichael's office was well designed and very expensive—all tufted leather chairs and curated objets d'art. Aggressively devoid of personality, though. He took a seat behind his desk and flipped through the documents in a folder there—presumably the doctored ones I'd supplied. Then he closed the folder.

"So, Sophia isn't happy at Columbia?" he asked.

"No, she's not," I said. "The creative writing department isn't what she'd hoped."

"Columbia has a world-class writing program." Brian raised his eyebrows. "Are you sure that's the problem?"

"Does the real reason she wants to transfer even matter?" I looked down at my lap, sighed—the fragile, upset mother. "Sophia and I don't have the closest relationship, unfortunately, which is why she isn't here," I went on. "So, quite honestly, I can't be sure why she wants to transfer to Amherst. She said it's the writing program, but it could be something else. Regardless, I want to help her find a place where she can be happy." My voice cracked, and I could feel my cheeks flush. That last part, at least, was true.

"You're right," Brian said gently. "The exact reason Sophia wants to transfer doesn't matter, not unless it affects which new school she should head to."

"She wants Amherst," I said. "She's done her own research and she's quite sure."

Brian rubbed his hands together. "Okay, then, let's get down to work, shall we?"

"That would be great," I said.

"We *are* going to need Sophia's help with this process, though," Brian went on. "You'd be surprised how many parents think they can do this all on their own, without the student's participation."

"Really?" I asked.

"Really," he said with a small laugh. "I had one guy—an actual count from Spain—who wanted me to write everything, all the essays, personal statements. Apparently, his son was too busy selecting a suitable wife. He offered to pay quadruple the ordinary rate." Brian paused, as though leaving time for this to sink in.

"I guess if you're a count, you're used to being able to bribe your way into most things."

"No one is bribing anyone," Carmichael said. He leaned back in his chair and crossed his arms.

"Of course not," I said, maintaining eye contact. "I just meant—"

"In an ideal world, every student would be evaluated properly. But the reality is that we live in a world of limited resources. Universities are making their best guess based on a fraction of the relevant data. Every child who goes on to be admitted with our assistance is always fully qualified. What we do is simply ensure a fair outcome."

"Exactly, and that's all we want for Sophia," I said earnestly. "Fairness."

But I could tell from the look on Carmichael's face that his antennae were up. "How did you say you heard about us again?"

Giving him an answer that would claw back my credibility was the only option.

"Doug Sinclair," I said.

His face lit up, no sign of the guilty conscience that might be brought on by, say, masterminding blackmail or murder.

"Are you and Doug close?" he asked.

"Acquaintances through work," I said.

"Of course, well, yes, Ella. Now this makes sense. We were so glad to be able to help her with Amherst." He uncrossed his arms and leaned forward. "That was a situation that did require a significant additional investment. But all's well that ends well. Ella is now at Amherst and, as evidenced by his referral, Doug was satisfied with the way the process played out."

A significant additional investment. Had Doug lied to me about making a payoff? I felt stupidly blindsided.

"Yes, and that's why I came to you," I managed, hoping the dismay didn't register on my face. I had been so sure my instincts about Doug were right.

Brian Carmichael smiled as he rose to his feet. My allotted time was up. But he seemed completely at ease now. "Let's take this one step at a time," he offered. "I can put out some feelers at Amherst, see how many transfer spots they expect." He smiled at me. "The most important thing is that Sophia is happy. That's all any of us want for our kids, right—that they stay happy and safe?"

November 16, 1992

*We wrote our first story today. The tutor guy said to base it on a mem-
ory from when we were little. All I kept thinking was: I don't have
any memories. It's like my brain has decided I'm better off not remembering. Besides, in this shithole I've got to stay focused on the here and
now. Eyes open, ready to jump.*

*But then, wham—one detail came to me. The sharp edges of the
mail slot.*

*I'd been home alone for three days. I was four and a half. My par-
ents had left me with a gallon of water and a loaf of Wonder bread. To
this day I've got no clue if they planned to come back. The mailman
found me when I heard him on the other side of the door and forced
my hand through that sharp, narrow slot. So tight my fingers were left
bleeding.*

*When I wrote the story, I made it about a seven-year-old boy. It felt
more believable that way. And maybe less terrible, too.*

*The tutor even wrote a note at the bottom that said it was one of the
best things he'd ever read. Afterward I was actually happy for a whole
thirty seconds, until I walked out of class and Silas snatched the story
out of my hands as he passed by in the hall. Dangled it in the air and
made me jump for it. Watching my boobs the whole time.*

*I have never hated someone more in my entire life. I hate him so
much that sometimes it scares me.*

CLEO

SEVEN HOURS GONE

I sit cross-legged on my bed, chewing on my cuticle as I stare at my mom's closed laptop. I felt so determined leaving the house with the computer in my bag. But as I rode the F train back to Manhattan, the fear crept back in. The blood, the broken glass— what, exactly, do I hope to find on her laptop that would make that any better? I think about the dating that I know nothing about, the profile picture that looks like a version of my mom I've never met. And behind it all, this new hideous stuff about her life at that hellhole Haven House . . . Was it really just bad luck that she'd been so old when Gladys adopted her?

With the clock closing in on 1:00 a.m., the laptop feels like it's dragging me down to a dark place rooted in one awful truth: that whatever I find will inevitably lead to proof that she might already be—that the worst has happened. And so I'm left hoping that I *will* find something on my mom's computer and hoping that I will not.

Turns out my mom's Facebook log-in is saved in this computer's browser, no need for that password. I feel a little twinge of guilt: Detective Wilson wants the social media passwords. But what I said to my dad is true: I'll turn the laptop over as soon as I'm sure there's not something important on there.

My mom's Facebook profile isn't exactly a treasure trove of information anyway. Barely active, she has only 196 friends.

Those 196 "friends" include the moms of *my* friends and *my* coaches and people at *my* old dance school. And my dad's family. So, it's a padded 196. I have four thousand Instagram followers, almost all of whom I consider friends. Not good friends, of course not. Okay, maybe *friends* is even the wrong word. But I do know all of them. Who knows only two hundred people?

But all my mom does is work. She's always been totally obsessed with her job, which is one of the things I actually respect about her. And when she's not working . . . well, I've never really thought about it. She hangs out around the house, I guess. She's always been kind of an introvert, a few-close-friends kind of person.

I study my mom's Facebook profile picture. Mainly it's of me at five or six, riding piggyback on her in Cape Cod. I'm looking at the camera, laughing with my mouth open, but her face is barely visible under a big sun hat. Like I was the most important part of her.

I look away from the picture and swallow a burn that blazes up the back of my throat as I start scanning her page. Maybe she was selling something and someone came to pick it up? Although that sounds like the last thing in the world my mom would have time to do. And anyway, she hasn't posted to her account in almost a year, and before that it was only requests for renovation recommendations—contractors, flooring, electricians. All the posts start with *Hi, everyone!* as if she's writing a letter. *Oh, Mom, so cringe.*

Scrolling back even further, I spot some posts about me and college—looking for a college counselor, essay help, SAT tutoring. Back even earlier—way earlier, but it doesn't take much to get there because my mom hardly posts—there's a message saying a "friend" is looking for a therapist who specializes in sex and relationship education for teens. I check the date. Sure enough, it was right after I told her I'd had sex with Charlie. My cheeks flame. But I'm not embarrassed—I'm mad. No, not mad. Mad would be easier. I'm hurt. That my mom saw me as a problem to solve.

At least she hadn't returned to the Facebook well more recently to ask for drug counselor recs. Of course, when it came to Kyle, she was way more right than wrong in the end. Not right to threaten me; that was out of control. But right about how dangerous Kyle was. Dangerous enough that I need to face the possibility that he's responsible for what has happened to my mom. Like he did something to her as some kind of sick way to get back at me. Except why now? It wouldn't make any sense.

I should tell Detective Wilson about Kyle, just in case. I will, too. But I am afraid of admitting out loud that my own stupid choices might have something to do with this. Unless it was her bad choices. *Online dating?*

"Where are you, Mom?" I whisper, staring at the screen. "Where the hell are you?"

I close the Facebook window and switch back to the dating site, which I've been careful to leave open in the browser. And there, once again, are all the little pictures, all those chats with random men, all so pathetic. So beneath my mom.

The second chat at the top, below the surfer Oscar, is with someone named Peter. My mom opened with a "Hi!" And he responded with a "Hiya, how are you today?"

The exchange goes on, awkwardly, and yet my mom, for some psychotic reason, hands over her number at the end. There are no further messages between her and Peter after that. They ended about a month ago. All the dating exchanges did. Maybe some had turned to texting. I don't have any way to know. We don't have her phone.

Peter is not objectively unattractive, but he's also not remotely in the same league as my dad—much shorter, much less hair. Glancing at the other profiles, none of the other men can compete, either. My dad really is very good-looking, especially considering he's ten years older than my mom. He's also in great shape. He's got a whole aging Brad Pitt thing going on. Like people have actually said it to him on the street—I've seen it. And yet here my mom was *choosing* these other idiots. Or maybe she wasn't choosing them. Maybe she was choosing *not* to be with my dad.

The next two chats ended without the exchange of a phone number, only with my mom's silence. A small "Your Move" banner encouraging her to reply. A third guy opens with "Hey, Sexy" and a smiley face with hearts for eyes that makes me want to puke. At least my mom didn't answer. Still, I can't stand the sight of that emoji, sitting there assaulting her in-box. I go to tap on "Unmatch," but I stop myself just in time—what if that guy is *the* guy? I shouldn't erase suspects.

I want to do something, though. Maybe I could reach out and say hello. See what happens. If this guy is *the* guy, maybe I'll be able to tell by his response, or by his *not* responding. As my hands move toward the keys, there's a knock at my door. I look up, hoping I imagined it. But then it comes again—pounding now. Jennie from across the hall? Everything with that girl is some kind of emergency.

"Jesus! Hold on!"

I jerk open the door, and Geoff is standing there, shoulders hunched, hair a mess. He looks pissed off, wild-eyed. Not exactly what you want to see in a drug addict.

"There you are!"

"Geoff . . . What are you—what's . . . up?" He doesn't live in my building or particularly near it. "It's, um, one a.m."

"I've been looking everywhere for you."

"Me?"

"Kyle cut me off, because of you."

Shit. This wasn't supposed to be happening anymore. That was the whole point of the two thousand dollars—for Kyle to call off the dogs, also known as my former customers. Or not *my* customers, *Kyle's* customers that I delivered to. Since we broke up, he's been cutting them off and blaming me. His form of entertainment. Most of them have found another dealer. But a few have freaked out and hunted *me* down, demanding explanations I don't have. That's the problem with a trust-fund drug dealer: Kyle doesn't care nearly as much about losing clients or money as he does about his bruised ego. For a second, he'd actually seemed relieved when I broke up with him, but then his natural pettiness had set in. But the two thousand dollars—the completely random figure he decided I "owed" him to make up for his trouble—was supposed to put an end to it, and yet here's Geoff, totally pissed off at me.

I step back and start to close the door a little. "Listen, Geoff, I'm sorry, but—"

He slams a flattened palm against the door, wedging it open wider. Whoa. This is way out of character for a nerdy bio major, even one addicted to Ritalin.

"You need to call Kyle," he says. His eyes are red at the edges. He's coming down hard.

"That won't help your situation any."

"Try," Geoff says, taking a step closer. He's looming over me now. "Get him to change his mind. Like right now."

"I'm sorry, Geoff, really, but I—"

"You're *sorry*?" Spit sprays in my face. "What good does that do me?"

Should I call Kyle? I mean, I could. I can't imagine he'd pick up . . . But no. I'm not getting sucked back in. No matter what Geoff wants.

"I'm sorry, I can't call him."

Geoff's upper lip curls and I think he might launch himself at me. But then, just as quickly, he deflates.

"You really are a selfish bitch, Cleo." He says this flatly, like he's stating a simple fact. "Annie was right."

"Wait—Annie? What are you talking about?"

"Your old friend. Remember?" He laughs meanly. "Wow, does she *not* like you."

"Did you—did Annie tell you where I live? Did you go to my house in Brooklyn, looking for me?" Now it's my turn to step toward him. "Did you see my mom?"

If Geoff came looking for me in this strung-out state, my mom would have guessed right away that it had something to do with Kyle. I can only imagine the things she would have said. She might have even threatened to go to the police.

"Sure, Cleo, your mom and I were hanging out. What the fuck are you talking about?" he says. "Listen, I'll try Kyle again on my own. But if I can't get to him, I'm coming back."

When Geoff takes a step back, I slam and lock the door.

I hesitate a moment before texting Will. The situation with my mom has me up in my head, seeing him through her insanely critical eyes. But I need Will right now. And that says something. *You awake?*

Will replies before my second thoughts have time to take hold. *Any word on your mom?*

I'm about to say some version of *Everything's fine.* But everything is so far from fine. I'm afraid of what's happened to my mom. I'm freaked out that Geoff showed up at my door. I'm scared that the two things are connected. I'm scared even if they're not.

I'm not great, to be honest. No word on my mom.

You want me to come over?

Yes. Come. But we both know it's more complicated than that.

That's okay. Tomorrow night maybe?

Yes. Definitely. And if you change your mind . . .

I add a little heart to his last message. So relieved I kept it together. Nothing reads more desperate than clingy late-night texts.

I reach over and close my mom's laptop. But as my head hits the pillow, I notice her journal sitting on the nightstand alongside my bed. I grab it and flip to a spot after that last awful entry I read earlier.

They're introducing clubs at Haven House!

Clubs. See, like at any other school. There were bound to be some less-than-ideal conditions at a place like Haven House—it wasn't a cushy boarding school. My mom had never hidden that part from me. But there was also no way it was all as terrifying as that one entry. Otherwise, my mom could never be the insane overachiever she is.

Director Daitch introduced the clubs as part of this new "improvement project" he's doing. So Haven House can be less like Rikers Island. There's a rumor that the state has been sniffing around, that somebody who got adopted out made complaints. I hope about Silas. Word is that Director Daitch is also trying to get some fancy new job at a regular school. He wants to show that he can treat us like regular kids. So . . . after-school clubs.

Of course, we'll never be regular kids. No matter how many books we read or how hard we smile. Some damage can't be undone.

I flip ahead to a dog-eared page. It's written in careful script.

She loved him in that way young girls do, utterly senseless and deeply brave.

It takes me a minute to realize it's the opening of a short story my mom wrote. Where did that version of her go? I feel like she and I would have gotten along.

Okay, so fine—I do like the writing club. I like the kid who runs it, even if he has that Ivy League way about him. All the tutors do—I mean, they go to Yale. But this one tutor guy, Reed (?), at least doesn't look at us like we're pathetic animals. He sees us as we are. Just kids.

It's just after six in the morning when Lauren opens her apartment door. I'm gripping my mom's laptop against my chest like a flotation device. I'm running out of time before I'll have to hand it over. I know that. I'll let go of it as soon as I'm a little closer to shore.

Lauren wraps her arms tight around me, pressing the computer between us. She's got her glasses on, hair back in a headband, wearing adorable but stained Alo Yoga pants and a threadbare Columbia Law sweatshirt. Lauren is gorgeous, with amber-flecked eyes and flawless skin. Always so pulled together, too. There's something comforting about her being a little disheveled right now. Like she's as upset as I am.

"Oh my God, sweetheart," she whispers into my hair.

Lauren lives in an apartment in Tribeca with her husband and their twin girls, who are ten or eleven—or at least way younger than I am. *Kid* kids. Behind Lauren, I see her husband, Jake, appear sleepily in the hall.

"Everything okay?" he calls out in a whisper.

"I'm so sorry," I say quietly. "I should have called. Your kids must be asleep."

She waves her husband off. "Don't be silly. I'm so glad you're here. Come in, come in."

The apartment is one of those beautiful old lofts with huge original windows. Tasteful and lovely but not obscenely over-the-top. Her husband is a banker but "not the richest kind," Lauren always jokes. As she ushers me into the living room, I can see a peakaboo view of the Empire State Building, the uptown sky turning a pinkish gray behind it.

"Has there been any word?"

When I shake my head, tears flood my eyes. I press my lips together to stifle the sob I can feel in my throat.

"Hey, hey, let's sit," Lauren says. She takes off her glasses and glances at my mom's computer, which I'm still gripping tightly. She pries it gently from my hands and puts it on the table. "Do you want some water or something?"

"No, I'm okay." I shake my head as I lower myself onto the couch. "I wanted to see—do you know anything about the guys my mom has been dating?"

This is what I've come to ask. I need to know if they could be involved. I need to understand why my mom was doing it in the first place.

"Dating?" Lauren asks with an exaggerated frown. She's a terrible liar. Of course she is. She's a prosecutor. Her whole life is about the truth.

"I know they're separated, Lauren. My dad told me," I say. "And I found the dating site." I nod toward the computer for emphasis. "My mom was messaging with people, going out with them. I want to be sure none of them had anything to do with what's happened to her."

"Somebody she met online?" Lauren asks. "I don't think she took any of that very seriously."

"Maybe that's the problem—she didn't take it seriously enough. I mean, these guys, they're pretty bad. I don't know what she was thinking . . ."

"Whoa, Cleo," Lauren says, sitting down on the couch next to me. "We're not blaming your mom for what happened to her, are we? Because no matter what happened, it's not her fault, right?"

"Um, have you *seen* the guys?" I snap. "I'm sorry, but given that she felt free to have a whole lot of opinions about the guys in my life, it kind of seems—" *Hypocritical.* That's what I would have said if my voice hadn't cracked.

Lauren's eyes flutter shut. When she opens them, she stretches an arm across the back of the couch, fingertips resting gently on my shoulder.

"I'm sorry. I know how upsetting this must be. And I know that lately you and your mom didn't always see eye to eye."

"Lately?" I ask. "Try for the past ten years."

Lauren is quiet for a moment. "Listen, I know better than anybody that your mom is wound tight. You should have seen her law school outlines and all their teeny-tiny type. It was like they were written by the Unabomber. And I know she's gotten fixated on some pretty trivial stuff with you—I told her that. She tried her best to dial it back. But you need to know that everything your mother ever did—it's just because she was trying to protect you. She loves you *so* much."

"That's love, huh?" I mutter.

"Come on, you know it's true." She nudges me. "Your mom worries about you. And by *your* mom, I kind of mean *all* moms." She smiles. "Ask *my* girls. Your mom isn't the only one who can be a little rigid. But with her, sometimes I think what she intends as love doesn't always come across that way. I'm her best friend and I can see that. But I will tell you that your mom loves you more than anything. I think that because of how she grew up . . . she can't help seeing the world as a place so dangerous, it needs to be controlled."

"And how did she grow up, *exactly?*" I ask.

"What do you mean?"

"I found an old journal of hers about that Haven House place," I say. "First of all, she was there for longer than I realized. And it sounded way worse than she ever talked about. I didn't read that much—"

"Good, don't—I mean, it is *her* journal. I'm sure your mom wants that to stay private."

"Right, because she excels at respecting other people's privacy."

Lauren shoots me a look. "Okay, well, number one: not the

same thing. You're the kid; she's the parent. Number two: We've established that your mom isn't so great at boundaries because she worried. Number three, from what I hear, it sounds like she had good reason to be keeping tabs on you."

Of course my mom would have told her about Kyle. I'm annoyed. But also ashamed. For a split second, my mind jumps to Will. My mom's judgment is easier to dismiss than Lauren's.

"Because I was dating somebody who was—fine—a drug dealer, that doesn't mean I don't have any human ri—" My voice cracks again. And then I'm sinking so fast, I can't breathe.

Lauren wraps her arms around me, and I finally lose it. I tug her big sweatshirt into my clenched fists as I sob. It's a big, messy explosion. When it's over, I lean back and wipe at my eyes, embarrassed.

"I'm sorry."

Lauren squeezes my hand. "You have nothing to apologize for."

"I just want to—I need to do something to help find her," I say.

"Do you think the police aren't on top of it? Because I might be able to make some calls through the U.S. attorney's office and push things along on that front."

"I think they're on top of it. I mean, I guess. There is this Detective Wilson, who seems okay. But if you could double-check, that would be good. I can't sit around and wait for them to find something, though. I think this dating thing . . . It's—it doesn't seem like her."

"For the record, I was the one who encouraged her to do that," Lauren admits. "I wanted her to realize how great she is."

I make a face and gesture at the computer. "Again, have you seen these people?"

Lauren grimaces. "I'm not saying it was my best idea. Anyway, I really don't think what happened has to do with anyone she dated online. As far as I know, she stopped talking to all of them after she met this guy Doug, whom she really liked. She met him through work. She had been seeing a lot of him lately . . ."

"And?"

She sighs. "He was killed in a car accident. They'd only known each other a few weeks, but I felt bad for your mom. She was starting to really have feelings for him. And he had a daughter your age."

"That's terrible," I say.

"It was. And for your mom, especially after everything she's been through."

"Was it really *that* bad?"

She nods. "Worse. Did she tell you about her parents?"

"She said they left when she was a kid; that's it. And that she didn't know where they went."

"They left her. Four years old. They locked her in the house with some water and a loaf of bread. The mailman found her days later."

"That's—that's terrible," I say again, and I feel like an idiot.

"Extra hard to be a mom when your own mom did that," Lauren says quietly.

I put a hand on my hot neck. "Yeah. Why didn't she tell me?"

"I think maybe she didn't want the bad things that had happened to her to become part of your story. She wanted you to have a 'normal' mom—whatever that means. A good childhood." Lauren leans back and crosses her arms. "So, what is your dad saying?"

"You talked to him. What did he say to you?"

"I didn't talk to him." Lauren shakes her head. "Detective Wilson called me. Your dad must have given her my information, but he never called me himself."

"Oh, I thought . . . I must have misunderstood." But I didn't. My dad lied about talking to Lauren.

"But he told you about the separation?" she asks.

I nod. "He said, 'No one did anything wrong. We can't be married anymore. But it's all fine and good.' Even though none of it makes any sense."

Lauren studies her hands. "Well . . . your dad—" she starts.

"What about him?"

Lauren looks up at me like I know full well what she means. "Listen, you know there's no love lost between us. Is he being . . . helpful?"

"I think so, yes," I say quickly. I know how Lauren feels about my dad. And I'm not feeling great about him right now, either. "I mean, he's not so good with . . . executing."

Lauren smiles ruefully. "That's one way of putting it . . ." She's quiet again, traces a line in the couch with her fingernail.

"What?"

"No, nothing."

"Lauren, I can tell there's something else."

"I don't want to talk out of turn about your dad."

"Please. I want to know. I need to."

"I know he and your mom had also been arguing a bit lately about . . . money."

"Money?"

"Your dad apparently wanted a loan for his latest project? I guess he ran into some financing problems. It was a *lot* of money. From her inheritance. It would have been nearly all of it. And you know how she feels about touching that money."

Maybe my dad didn't feel like this was relevant. But still I hear my mom's voice in my ear: *A lie of omission is a lie all the same.*

"I'm sure that was a hard no."

"Last I heard. And your dad was really not happy about that."

"I can imagine," I say.

"There is something else that I think you should know . . . But it's *really* not good. It might upset you. Actually, it will definitely upset you."

"Tell me," I say. "If you think I should know—I trust you."

"It makes your dad look . . . bad," she says, eyeing me pointedly. It's a warning—my last one. "I also don't think—I'm not saying—I'm sure it's not relevant to what's happening with your mom right now. But it also doesn't seem *ir*relevant." She's stalling.

"Lauren . . ."

"Fine, fine—your dad is having an affair, or at least *was,*" Lauren blurts out like she's ripping off a Band-Aid.

My pulse is throbbing in my temples. It feels like my head is going to explode. "What?"

"Well, I guess technically it wouldn't be an affair anymore. But it was with one of his students. Okay, *former* student—she's his assistant now—but still. Bella?"

I press a fist against my stomach. *I don't believe you.* But Lauren has no reason to lie. And this is obviously not something she even *wants* to be telling me. Also, it rings true. I've always had a bad feeling about Bella. She was patronizing and arrogant, but it didn't occur to me in a million years that she was sleeping with my dad. It probably should have.

"Oh." My voice is very quiet.

"That's why your mom asked for the separation. If you ask me, she had plenty of good reasons before. But she would have overlooked those—she *was* overlooking them. And then she saw some texts Bella sent. Once she realized your dad was having an affair, that was finally the last straw."

If this is true—and I don't have any reason to think it's not—my dad lied. Right to my face and quite convincingly. I wait for the wave of anger to hit, the outrage. But I feel only hollow, gutted.

"Cleo?" Lauren asks. "You look . . . Are you okay? I'm sorry, I didn't want to upset you . . ."

I'm standing. I don't remember standing up.

"It's okay. But I should, um, go." I start for the door, feeling wobbly. I want to get out of here before I lose it again. I need to keep moving.

"Cleo," Lauren calls after me. "It doesn't mean— I'm sure your dad is as worried as we are."

"I'm sure," I say.

"Hey, Cleo, really . . ." Lauren catches up to me, places a hand on my forearm. "She's going to be okay anyway. Your mom knows how to take care of herself."

"Yeah, sounds like it," I say as I open the apartment door. "It also sounds like there was a lot I didn't know."

TRANSCRIPT OF RECORDED SESSION

DR. EVELYN BAUER
SESSION #2

CLEO McHUGH: Can I ask you something?

EVELYN BAUER: Of course, Cleo.

CM: Do you think seventeen people is a lot for
someone my age to have slept with?

EB: Does it matter what I think?

CM: No. But I want to know. When I said it last
week, you had no reaction.

EB: Did you expect a reaction? Is that why you
told me?

CM: I don't know . . . maybe. Even kids my age act
shocked sometimes. So I don't usually go around
telling people. But you were like a sphinx. I
figured you were hiding a reaction, you know,
because you're supposed to.

EB: I'm not supposed to do anything, Cleo. But no,
I didn't feel shocked. It didn't sound like an
especially low number, either. That is also
true. But the much more important thing is how
you feel about it.

CM: I feel . . . numb. Like I'm talking about
someone else.

EB: Are there boys you wish you hadn't had sex with?

CM: A couple maybe . . . But not even really. It's

more like they, in specific, weren't even the point. I liked how their wanting me made me feel.

EB: And what way was that?

CM: Better . . . Like I mattered. Like I was okay exactly the way I am. And it's not like all of a sudden I'd end up falling in love with them and get my feelings hurt. Afterward I still wouldn't really care.

EB: I understand. These were only hookups or one-night kind of things?

CM: Sometimes. Other times it would be more like friends with benefits. A couple times we were kind of dating, like the guy I'm seeing now.

EB: It sounds like you cared about Charlie years ago, too? You said that your mom ended that?

CM: I told her after we had sex for the first time and she completely freaked out.

EB: Oh, that must have been very difficult.

CM: It was, especially because we had been really close. But by high school, we started to fight—anytime I wasn't being exactly the person my mom wanted me to be.

EB: And that was different from the way things had been?

CM: When I was little we were . . . I remember loving my mom so, so much. And she always made me feel like I was the greatest thing on the planet. She was my everything.

EB: What changed?

CM: I don't know. I think it started in middle school, after I got in a little bit of trouble. Like my mom found a vape pen in my backpack, and I got a detention at school once for letting

someone cheat off me. None of it was that big.
But my mom—you would have thought I'd murdered
someone.

EB: That must have been very hurtful, if the two of
you had been so close.

CM: It was . . . But I still kept trying to give her
a chance. I thought maybe she was stressed about
work and that she would go back to being her old
self. And then Charlie happened. I know I was
kind of young, but we'd been dating for a year
and a half and we really loved each other.

EB: You don't have to justify it to me, Cleo.

CM: It feels like I do. What's sad is that my mom
was the only person I wanted to tell at the
time. As soon as the words were out of my mouth,
there was this look on her face. Disgust. Like I
was disgusting. "You're fourteen years old!" She
kept saying that over and over. "Only fourteen."
As if I'd committed a crime. And then she
said . . .

EB: You don't have to tell me if it's upsetting.

CM: No, I want to. I feel like I need to . . .
She said, "I can't believe you have so little
self-respect."

EB: I'm sorry. That's very mean. What did you say?

CM: I called her a bitch.

EB: And that was the end of it?

CM: No . . . Then she said, "I can't believe you're
my daughter."

KATRINA

The building that housed Aidan's Veritas Productions had always been way too nice for a company that had never come close to turning a profit. Even the huge freight elevator screamed bohemian chic.

Every time I came here, the unearned luxury of it got under my skin. I was the one paying the inflated bills, after all. The office was so Aidan: all that surface charm—never mind the reality that his movies *cost* us money. And *Veritas*? So grandiose. Aidan had chosen the name in all seriousness, too. He saw himself as some great hero. In the meantime, his movies had only been sold to the most obscure streaming services. The last one lost its distribution partner altogether after some of its representations had been "called into question." Turned out people who made documentaries needed to be good with things like verifying sources and checking facts. Details. Aidan was terrible at details. *Veritas,* indeed.

But I was relieved that Aidan had texted back after I'd left Advantage Consulting. *Okay. I do have some real intel on Cleo and the money. Meet at my office at noon?* I assumed he wanted another in-person meeting in order to bring up the loan again—or rather, my inheritance, which he now seemed intent on claiming.

Over my dead body was I giving him that money without a fight. I wanted to be sure it was there for Cleo someday. I would respond calmly and politely—matter-of-factly. I might even lie and agree to give him the money in order to get him to tell me what was going on with Cleo. But it was time for me to stop feeling responsible for solving problems of Aidan's own making. In fact, it was time for me to start seeing Aidan as the problem. And solving problems was something I was very, very good at.

The elevator chimed as the doors opened onto Aidan's floor. The funky earth-toned wallpaper in the hall looked more expensive than what we had in our home. Maybe once we moved on to actual divorce proceedings, I'd make Aidan leave this ridiculous office for something more affordable. After all, I did pay his company's bills. I could draw all sorts of new lines.

As I approached Aidan's office, I noticed that the lights were off. I checked the time: 11:45 a.m.—I was early again. God only knew how long I might be waiting. Flipping the switch as I stepped inside, I found myself facing Bella's empty desk. Aidan had fired her right after I saw the texts. It had been a lucky accident, too. I'd been prepping dinner when Aidan asked me to hand him his phone. It was on the kitchen counter and her text lit up the screen as I reached for it. *Can't stop thinking about what your mouth feels like on me.*

I hadn't suspected a thing, either. I'd been too busy doing what I had done for the past twenty-odd years—taking care of everything—when Aidan's affair jumped up and hit me square in the face.

As I'd crossed the room that night and handed the phone to Aidan, prone on the couch, I braced myself for an emotional fallout that never came. Even in the days and weeks that followed, what I'd felt most was relieved. Like the texts had blown my cage apart, leaving me no choice but to make my escape.

But I did know that a divorce court wouldn't care about his infidelity. It certainly wouldn't care that Aidan had used my past to manipulate and take advantage of me. The only thing that would matter to the court would be when and by what means our joint assets were acquired.

"Aidan!" I called down the hall toward the conference room at the back.

When there was no answer, I pulled my phone out as I made my way over to his private office—door open, light off. Standing in the doorway, I looked over at his absurd Roche Bobois desk. "Melt"—that was the name of the style, and it did indeed look like molten wood and steel had been poured to form the rounded abstract edges. Hideous, if you asked me, especially for the insane $13,585.00 it had cost. I remembered the figure exactly. It was the kind of thing that stuck when you were footing the bill.

I'm here?

The ellipses appeared instantaneously. *Oh, you're early . . . Got stuck at a meeting with HBO I forgot I had on the calendar. But I'm right around the corner. Be there in a second.*

A meeting with HBO? I wasn't buying it. And so there I stood alone in Aidan's empty office, his desktop computer only steps away. Booted up and locked, but I knew Aidan's password—it was always the same. His birthday. Sure enough, the computer opened right up. Emails and texts right there within reach.

I started with the messages. *Her* was up at the top, under the message I'd just sent. Couldn't he at least have had the courtesy to change it back to Bella? There was something so insulting about the pseudonym.

She really cannot leave that kid alone, can she? Doesn't she realize she's in college!!!

                    I know. That's what I said!

Kat is the one who needs a good therapist.

                    Agreed. But it's not like I can suggest that!

You can't let her push you around, Aidan.

I'm only trying to stay out of harm's way!

I took a step back from the computer, hand to my chest as if to physically shield myself. It was so much worse than I'd expected. I hadn't imagined they'd be talking about *me*. And as if I was a regular topic of conversation. But there was no way I was going to confront Aidan about the messages. They were too humiliating.

My phone vibrated in my bag. I stood, closed out his messages, and sent the computer screen to sleep before digging for it.

Did you really think you'd get away with it? That you'd get to keep all that money? That no one would find out about the blood on your hands?

I dropped down onto the couch. No, I hadn't thought I'd get away with it. But I also hadn't intended to kill him.

"So sorry!"

Aidan rushed into the office, coffee in hand, sunglasses still on. His hair was messy and he was unshaven. I stared at him. He laughed in a burst as he put his things down on his desk, took off his sunglasses. He seemed nervous.

He sat down on the other end of the couch, took a long sip of his coffee.

"Cleo," I said.

Aiden nodded. "Oh, she's trying to have a positive impact. That's the good news."

"I don't understand."

"The money was for an environmental activism group she's a part of," Aidan said with a dismissive wave of his hand.

"Environmental activism?" I asked, not trying to hide my skepticism. "Seriously?"

"Yep." Aidan seemed pleased with himself—I couldn't tell if that was because he'd gotten answers or because the explanation

dovetailed with his own work. "Cleo's trying to make a difference. And I think she wants to do it on her own."

"Why would being a part of an environmental group *cost* her
two thousand dollars?"

"Come on, Kat, activism isn't free." He leaned back a bit and
crossed his arms. "You should know that by now."

I thought about the stairs I'd seen Cleo descend. Was it possible there'd been some kind of environmental meeting going on
down there?

"It doesn't seem at all suspicious to you that out of the blue
Cleo suddenly happens to be involved in an *environmental* group?"

"Suspicious?" he asked. "What, because it's something *I* care
about? Kat, seriously, that's . . ." He shook his head. "You honestly think Cleo is *that* calculating?"

"She was *dealing* drugs, Aidan."

He sighed dramatically. "I'm sorry, Kat, but I really think this
is sad. That you have so little faith in your own daughter. I mean,
given where you came from, it's understandable you have trust
issues. But have you ever thought about maybe seeing someone
yourself? I mean, we sent Cleo to a therapist . . ."

My hands were balled into fists so tight, I was sure my fin-
gernails were going to draw blood. Wordlessly, I rose from the
couch.

"Where are you going?" Aidan asked.

"I'm leaving."

"You can't leave. We need to talk about the money."

"No," I said, calmly. "*We* don't need to talk about money. You
want to talk about the money, and I need to leave."

"I've spoken to a lawyer, Kat," Aidan said as I reached for the
doorknob. "I'm going to file."

Bastard. I turned back. "We're waiting until the end of the
school year. It's only another month. We agreed."

"No," he said. His tone was icy now. "You *decreed.* And I've
been reasonable. The least you can do is treat me fairly. I don't

want to have our lives ripped apart in court, Kat. But I'm also not going to sit by while you take advantage of me."

"Don't do this," I said, struggling to keep my tone even. "Don't." It sounded like a threat. It felt like one.

"Or what, Kat?" he asked with an angry laugh. "Or what? You've already left me."

Or I'll kill you. It was just in my head.

"Don't do it, Aidan," I said one last time before opening the door. "Or you'll regret it."

As I reached the top of the West Village stairs I'd seen Cleo descend on Christopher Street a day ago, my mind was still racing. What if my past was unearthed in the midst of some lengthy divorce proceeding? Aidan's lawyer would surely try to dig up all the dirt he could on me, and with enough effort, he could strike gold. The more I'd thought about it, the clearer it seemed that my mystery texter had to be the person who had helped Daitch the night of the murder. Male, I was pretty sure, remembering the way Daitch spoke to that person, and I had my theories about who it was, of course. It would simply be a matter of Aidan's lawyer tracking him down and finding out his price, and I'd be done for.

My phone rang and the sight of Mark's name on my caller ID jolted me back to the here and now. I had a job. A consuming one, with lots of clients clamoring for my attention. I'd been juggling calls and buying myself time for the last twenty-four hours. Mark had left a message early this morning, before I'd visited Advantage's office—I'd been so distracted that I hadn't even listened to it yet. I thought about sending the new call to voice mail, but it wasn't like Mark to hound me without a good reason.

"Sorry, I've been tied up on another matter," I lied. One advantage of my "don't ask, don't tell" arrangement with Mark was that he really never knew how I made use of my time. Also, almost all of what I did—clandestine interviews, private meetings—was conducted outside the office and far from prying eyes. "If this is about Vivienne, I assure you that I—"

"It's not about Vivienne." Mark sounded uncharacteristically stressed. "Will you be in . . . tonight?"

From his tone, this didn't exactly sound optional.

"I'll be there by five at the latest," I said, as if this had always been my plan. "I'll go straight to your office."

"Thanks, Kat," he said. "And I do apologize for the fire drill. But you know better than anyone how these things can be. Just want to be able to assure the powers that be that we've taken this new matter in hand. And this situation is . . . a bit unusual. You should vet it before we agree."

Mark was always adamant that I had veto power over any of my projects. Naturally, my default position was yes—to keep the clients happy and thereby keep Mark happy. I had refused only once, a situation involving a COO who'd been caught with an underage prostitute. He claimed that he didn't know she was underage, but looking at her, that was hardly believable. I wanted no part of it, and Mark had declined without hesitation. As it happened, the client huffed off, taking his corporate business with him.

"You know I always appreciate that," I said to Mark. "I'll be there as soon as I can."

As I put my phone in my bag, a horn blasted nearby. A huge eighteen-wheeler was trying to squeak past a double-parked black sedan. Squinting at it, I could make out the outlines of two figures inside the car. Figures that could have been looking right at me. When I took a step forward, the engine turned on and the car accelerated past me before I could read the license plate.

Walking down the stairs, I reminded myself that New York was filled with impatient assholes and terrible drivers, not to mention black sedans. The anonymous texts had me jumpy, no doubt, but it was a mistake to get distracted by imaginary threats lurking around every corner. Inevitably, you missed the ones that mattered.

The basement level was occupied by a fancy boutique gym called the Box. The equipment was old-school, rudimentary, but set off by a stark black-and-gray palette, the overall effect was deliberately, expensively retro—simplicity meets edgy high design. The sole color pop came from piles of fluffy lemon yellow towels dotted around the space. The only person exercising was a very tall, very thin supermodel type with a high blond ponytail, stepping up and down on a raised box—like the ones from aerobic step class, except this was an actual wooden box.

"Can I help you?" A petite and very good-looking blond man in his twenties was perched on a round brown leather stool with elaborate stitching behind a sleek ash-wood reception desk. He eyed me up and down and appeared to find me wanting. He turned back to his computer. "Do you have an appointment?" He seemed confident I did not.

"No, I was—my daughter was here last night," I began. "She's at NYU, so I don't think she could afford to belong here."

"I would think not." His eyes were still on his screen.

"You're not affiliated with NYU in any way?"

His eyes flashed up. "Do we look like a student facility?" I gave him a blank stare in response. "Our memberships are by invitation only and start at eight thousand dollars, annually."

For a wooden step?

"Were you working last night? That's when my daughter came in."

"Yes, I was," he singsonged with obvious irritation. "I am *always* working."

I pulled up a picture of Cleo on my phone. "This is my daughter. Did you see her when she came in?"

He glanced at my phone, ready to dismiss me before he'd even looked. But I saw the moment he registered Cleo's face. He definitely recognized her, and he was definitely going to pretend that he didn't.

"Sorry, I can't help you," he said more sharply. He leaned over to smile at the Kendall Jenner look-alike who'd walked in behind me. "Now, if you'll excuse me, I need to get a member checked in." That's when I noticed the slight tremor in his hands, the beads of perspiration on his forehead, the way he kept scratching the inside of his left forearm. Could be he was a client of Kyle's that Cleo had gone down to meet.

I stepped to the side but didn't leave. I waited until he'd swiped the woman through, exchanged effusive hellos, then handed her a bright yellow towel and sent her on her way. When he saw me still standing there, he frowned. I approached the desk again. This time I leaned over forcefully and pushed my face in very close in to his.

"Tell me what my daughter did when she came in here or I'll tell your employer you're a drug addict."

"What the hell are you talking about?" Except there was a nervous twitch to his lip. He was using something for sure.

"They'll be obligated to give you a drug test. All this access to member information, their lockers . . ."

He glared at me.

"I need to know what my daughter was doing here. No one will know you told me anything."

He leaned back and crossed his arms.

"She wanted me to leave a package for a member in his locker," he said finally. "And before you go around threatening to tell my employer that—I called the member and asked first. He said she could leave it. I would never open a client's locker without permission."

"What member?"

"I can't tell—"

"What member?" I leaned closer.

"Kyle Lynch," he said. "I left the package in his locker. Just like he asked me to. And that was it."

ONE DAY BEFORE

Can you tell me again what she said, exactly?

Why?

Because I can't sleep and I'm worried.

She said there were pictures on his phone, that's all.

What kind of pictures? Exactly? Of who?

I don't know.

Can't you find out?

Not easily.

Please ask.

I can try. But also you should stop worrying.

Easy for you to say.

I don't mean it like that. You know I'm here for you.

Then help me. Please.

CLEO

I sit on one of the benches in the little triangle of green across the street from Lauren's building, my brain stuck on a loop: *My dad was having an affair; my dad* is *having an affair; he lied to my face; my mom is missing.* These facts don't line up well, no matter which way I look at them, and I have tried every single angle.

Detective Wilson will certainly think the affair is suspicious. *I* think it is. Do I really believe it's possible that my dad did something to my mom? No. I still do not. But I've entertained the possibility. I've been willing to ask myself the question. And that has torn a hole in something—something delicate and irreplaceable.

And Bella, of all people? My dad's obnoxious assistant who is, what, *five* years older than I am?

I open my mom's computer on my lap. Find a compelling alternative suspect. That's what I need to do.

I head back onto the dating site, to all those little squares of subpar men who probably abduct unsuspecting women all the time. Looking at them makes me feel both better and worse. Better because these guys do seem much more likely than my dad to have done something to my mom. Worse for the exact same reason.

I cut and paste a message into each one of the chats: *Hey! How are you?* I move fast, so I don't second-guess my plan. Moving fast also saves me from having to reread the awkward conversations, to think again about my mom lowering herself to them. But maybe that was what happened to you when your husband cheated with someone half your age. And then your daughter acted like she wished you were dead.

After that, I shoot off a text to my mom's assistant, Jules: *Can you call me? It's about my mom.* It's not even 7:00 a.m., too early to be texting. But Jules will understand. She's a good person, and she loves my mom. She's got to be worried, too.

Cleo, hi! Great to hear from you! Can I call you back in a little bit? xoxo

In a little bit? And *Great to hear from you!* Not exactly the level of care and concern I was expecting.

Sure np, I write back. *Call me when you can.*

"I wouldn't have taken you for such an early bird."

When I look up, Detective Wilson is standing in front of me, eyeing me with a furrowed brow. *Shit.* And my mom's incriminating laptop is right there next to me on the bench, in plain sight. The detective sits down on the other side of it and gazes up Broadway, which T's in front of us at the little green. Instinctively, I shove my phone in the pocket of my hoodie but resist the urge to hide the laptop.

"How would you know if I'm an early bird or not?" It comes out more rudely than I intended. But then, she did just show up out of nowhere. "Were you following me?"

"Mmm," she hums, looking again up Broadway, still nearly empty at that early hour. "I went to your dorm this morning, but it was so early and I didn't want to wake you—thought I'd wait a bit before going up to see you. Then I saw you leave. So, technically, I did follow you here. But it wasn't premeditated."

"Oh, in that case . . ."

"You don't seem happy about it."

"Let's see: My mom is *missing*. There was *blood* on our floor. And now you're following *me* instead of finding her?"

"Fair enough." She smiles slightly. "I wanted to give you the opportunity to speak with me alone. Back there at the house— it seemed like maybe there was something on your mind. But that maybe you weren't comfortable sharing it in front of your dad."

"I'm not sure what you mean."

"If you say so," she says skeptically, eyes still on Broadway.

"Do *you* know *anything* about what happened to my mom?" I ask. "I mean, isn't that the way this is generally supposed to work? You find out things and tell us?"

She nods. "Well, let's see, the blood we found is a match for your mom's type. DNA will take longer. But more than a reasonable likelihood that the blood is hers, as we suspected. And the fingerprints on the glass aren't in the system, unfortunately. I'm not surprised, but you always hope you'll get lucky. We can take comparative fingerprints from anyone we interview who develops into a suspect. They're still running you and your dad's DNA comparison. You know, for completeness." But was there an edge to the way she said that about my dad? I'm not sure. "Your mom's friend here, Lauren Pasternak, tell you anything useful?"

Of course she knows I was there to see Lauren. We're only steps from her apartment, an address the detective has probably already come across in the investigation. Still, I feel unsettled. Maybe she's suspicious of me, too. Confessing about messaging my mom's dates doesn't seem like a great idea now. But there may be a work-around.

"My mom was on some dating site called Hitch. All these guys . . . I mean, who knows who they are?"

"That's unusual for a married couple," she says.

I shrug, but I don't meet her eyes. "I didn't know they were separated. But you must by now. His clothes were all gone."

She nods. "We did notice that. What did your dad tell you?"

"That it was no one's fault. That nothing was set in stone." I turn to look at her now. I want her to know that I'm not an idiot. "He didn't exactly tell me about the separation on his own. He only told me after I asked him directly about his clothes. But it was apparently my mom's idea to keep it secret." I sound like I'm defending him. "She was trying to protect me, I guess, which does sound like something she would do."

Detective Wilson nods again, waits for me to return her gaze. "We can look into the online dating. But with these kinds of . . . It's almost always someone well known to the victim."

"Victim," I repeat, like saying the word aloud might keep it at bay.

"Of something, that's all I mean," she says, more gently now. "Only of something."

She thinks my mom is dead, though—it's the first time it sinks in. But I need her to stay focused on finding my mom *alive*. Because I know she's still out there. And she could be running out of time.

"It does seem like your parents were a little further along the divorce path than maybe your dad told you. According to your neighbor, Janine, your dad has a divorce lawyer who's going after some kind of inheritance."

"What?"

"You're surprised?"

"No, I mean, that's wrong," I say. "I don't know where Janine heard that, but she's wrong. He wants to work things out."

"Your mom told her."

"My mom?" I ask. "They're not even friends anymore."

"According to Janine, your mom was surprised and upset about this lawyer being brought in. Could have been it resulted in some kind of moment of conflict between her and your dad. One thing led to another, things got out of hand."

I blink quickly to head off the tears. My throat already feels scratchy. "I don't think so."

I think of his affair with Bella. I couldn't imagine what Detective Wilson would conclude if she knew about that.

"You should know—your dad did call *me* with some information." Detective Wilson is looking at me now in a way I really don't like. Like she feels sorry for me.

"He did?"

"He told me that *you* and your mom had a bit of a tough relationship. *Volatile,* I believe that's the word he used."

The word rings in my ears. *Volatile?*

"Okay," I say, because it's clear she's waiting for me to respond. Obviously, my dad was not trying to point the finger at me, even if that's exactly what he did. There has to be a reason he told the detective that. Or a context to his comments that she's not sharing.

"He specifically mentioned some recent conflict over a boy," she goes on. "He didn't get into details. That ring any bells?"

I grip the side of the bench. He told a *detective* about *Kyle?* Is he trying to get me arrested?

"What kind of conflict?" I ask, fishing gently. I need to know exactly how much he told her.

"He said your mom didn't approve of this boy you were seeing and it ended in an argument. That you haven't spoken in months. Is that true?"

Well, at least he didn't mention the drugs.

"We got into a big fight a while ago. I went to Park Slope last night for dinner as a kind of peace offering," I say. "My mom— for sure she drives me crazy sometimes. She can be really judgmental." I cross my arms, even as I tell myself not to. "So yeah, we're fighting about things."

The detective nods, her face unreadable. "Mother-daughter

shit is complicated," she says. "I get that. I don't have a daughter myself, no children. Not a life experience I'm particularly interested in, at least at the moment. I have a very immature husband and an exceptionally needy dog. But I do also have a mother. A *very* opinionated one. My mom and I . . ." She brings her fists together like two cars colliding. "Like oil and water. Things can get pretty heated." She looks at me pointedly. "In the heat of the moment, sometimes things happen that you never intended. We're human. We all fuck up."

"Are you asking me if I hurt my mom?"

"*Is* your mom hurt, Cleo?" She turns to me. I can't tell from her expression whether she thinks the answer might be yes—or if she's only asking because it's procedure. Maybe she needs to officially cross this off her list now that my dad added it there.

"I don't know if she's hurt." I stare straight back at her. "Because I wasn't there. But you're the one who said it's her blood on the floor. So sounds like she's probably hurt, right?"

Detective Wilson considers this response.

"Like I said, what mother and daughter aren't at each other's throats? And for the record, I don't think you were involved in this, Cleo," she says. "But I was a little taken aback that your dad volunteered that information. Seeing as how it does kind of put the focus on you. Seemed worth you and me having a conversation about it. Or worth you knowing about it—maybe that's a better way of putting it."

My mouth is so dry. Like my lips are glued shut. "Right." It's not much more than a whisper.

"Anyway." She stands, brushes off the backs of her navy slacks before heading toward Broadway. "We'll keep looking into everything, Cleo, including these guys she was dating. I promise, we are keeping our eyes wide open. But when you've been in this job as long as I have, you come to realize that the simplest explanation is usually the right one."

"And what's the simplest explanation for what happened to my mom?"

"Your dad."

When I get off the elevator, I can see that the door to the Veritas office is slightly open. I stop for a moment in the hall. I'm here for an explanation. But what if my dad has no excuse for throwing me under the bus? For telling a detective that my mom and I have a "volatile" relationship? I can't pretend that won't make him seem more guilty. That it won't also break my heart.

Inside the office, it's quiet and dark. No sign of my dad anywhere. Not in the conference room at the back or in his private office. Bella's desk at the front is bare. I walk over and pull a few of her drawers open. Empty. It looks like she doesn't work there anymore. I wonder if there could be some real connection between them. Would that make it better? You can't help who you connect with—I know that better than anybody.

"Dad!" I call out, staring at the framed posters of his movies on the walls. "Are you here?"

No response.

Where are you? I text him. *I'm at your office. I thought you said you were going to work?*

Oh! I'm at a breakfast with HBO. That is followed by a bunch of emojis—tired ones, exploding brain ones, tongue hanging out ones. Ones that might be cute if my mom wasn't missing or, you know, maybe dead. *Is it an emergency? I can leave if you need me to . . .*

I stare down at his text. I wonder if he and Bella are off having sex somewhere right now. I wish the possibility felt more absurd.

That's okay. We can talk later, I write back—later, as in after I have some kind of evidence that somebody other than him is responsible for my mom's disappearance.

Are you sure?

I've got to go anyway.

And I am about to go. I am. But then I find myself drifting over to his desk. I drop down into his desk chair, my hand taking hold of the mouse. I know I shouldn't. That it's a risk. But I guess I'm hoping that poking around a little will put my mind at ease. The computer comes to life, password-protected—even my not-good-with-details dad isn't that dumb. But I'm guessing his password is going to be obvious. I try his birth month, day, and year. Sure enough, the computer unlocks, email in-box already open on the screen. A subject line catches my eye—*Good News!!!!* I click on the email; it's from Javier Jameson, my dad's coproducer. But it's a reply, I realize, a response to an email my dad sent with that subject line a few hours ago.

What could possibly be good news right now?

I scroll down to my dad's original message at 5:45 a.m.: *Kat came through with the entire thing, 2.75! I knew she would. The cash is in my account as we speak. We are full steam ahead!*

Fifteen minutes later I'm in Hudson River Park, staring down into the steely water, still trembling. First my mom, and now it's like I've lost my dad, too. The world is gray and waterlogged, the humidity pressing in on my skull. I don't even remember walking to the river.

Lauren said my mom wouldn't lend my dad the money and that he was mad. And now she's missing, and he *has* the money he wanted? *That* much money. I'm pretty sure that's the kind of detail that could land him in handcuffs.

I pull out my phone and text Will: *Can you meet?*

A second later he replies: *Sure. Where?*

I respond with my location and *Thank you.*

You okay?

Not really.

OK. Be there soon.

It's only then that I notice the missed call, and the voice mail. A 212 number. I hit the arrow to play it.

"Hi, Cleo, it's Mark Germaine." His voice is deep and warm. Comforting. "Could you call me back when you get a moment? I'd love to see if there's anything we can do to support you." He hesitates, clears his throat. "Ruth and I have been thinking so much about you and your mom . . . I'm sure you know how much she means to us."

I was so busy obsessing that my mom had no Facebook friends, I forgot about all her work friends. She is beloved at her law firm—weddings and baby showers and birthdays, she's included in all of them. And my mom's law firm is one of the biggest and most powerful in the entire world—yes, I want Blair, Stevenson's help, immediately.

When I dial Mark's number, it goes straight to voice mail. "I—It's Cleo McHugh. I do need help finding my mom. Can you call me back? Please."

2/5/2024
The Xytek MDL Action? HELP!

TeresaB.1987
My two-year-old has severe neurologic damage as a result of complications from my taking Xytek while I was pregnant. We have a doctor willing to testify. And I met with a lawyer who said we have a good case. The medication was only supposed to relieve my symptoms. It wasn't even necessary. But my doctor figured, Hey, why not if it's safe? My daughter has had so many problems: asthma, a heart defect, cognitive delays. I know they're from Xytek. I know it. Even if my lawyer says it may be hard to prove. Anyway, I got a call from somebody, somebody anonymous, saying that Darden is threatening people who sue and that I should be careful. My husband thinks it was somebody at Darden. But he also thinks our lawyer is greedy and full of shit and we'd be better off being guaranteed some kind of settlement than joining the MDL. But I'm not even in it for the money. I want justice for my daughter. Anybody out there gotten a similar call? Thanks!

Lenny12654
Listen to your husband. All these lawyers are only in it for themselves.

RebeccaCartwright
I'm not a member of the MDL. Because it was my husband who died taking Xytek and not a baby. He was a marathon runner and a fireman.

He was only thirty-five. I have three kids under five and I have no way to support them. I have a GoFundMe that I'll link to. He had life insurance, but not enough for us to survive on. I don't know about the differences in the amount of money, but I recommend joining the MDL. I sure would if I could. Always better not to have to go it alone.

NYCMaMa

Don't reach out to Darden asking for a settlement. Join the MDL as soon as possible. Going public and staying on the record as a claimant is the only way to be sure that you're safe. Otherwise, they'll have a reason to come after you. These people are dangerous.

TeresaB.1987

Dangerous? Okay, now you're kind of scaring me.

NYCMaMa

You should be scared. We all should be. Darden will stop at nothing to protect itself. Nothing. I've seen it with my own eyes.

KATRINA

FOUR DAYS BEFORE

Chocolate truffles.

I'd gotten them as a gift from a grateful client—back when Vosges opened their first New York store, a client sent me a box of their truffles in an elegant purple box that was fancier than the one my engagement ring had come in. Cleo had been there when I opened the box, oohing and aahing. She was seven at the time and had a major sweet tooth; I'd nicknamed her "Snack Attack," which always made her giggle.

"Can I have them?" she'd asked. And the answer with Cleo was almost always yes—anything she wanted, anything I could give her. Often to make up for the things I worried I wasn't giving her—affection, warmth, hugs.

But I was headed out to a work dinner, already dressed and with my makeup on, and the evening babysitter had already arrived, because Aidan was away. It was late for chocolate, and some of the truffles might have had liquor in them. I didn't have time to check properly. I might not have been a champion cuddler, but I did *always* carefully read labels.

"Not tonight. Tomorrow, sweetheart," I'd said, kissing her head.

When I got home hours later, I went to check in on Cleo. As I stood there in her darkened bedroom, I panicked; my first thought was that the streaks across her face and sheets were blood. But when I flipped on the lights, I quickly realized my mistake: She'd taken the truffles to bed and fallen asleep while eating them. The whole box.

And I'll never forget how I felt: paralyzed.

Cleo was supposed to defy me: She was a child. And yet in that moment, I knew I'd never survive the gray zone of adolescence— the years during which she'd push back against me by doing deliberately bad, dangerous things. In the end, of course, I'd been right. I had not survived. Cleo and I had not.

I stopped walking a few blocks from the Box, dropped down on the stoop of a stately brownstone next to the Waverly Inn.

There was no getting around it now—Cleo and Kyle were mixed up together again, the handoff at the gym probably to avoid her being seen at Kyle's apartment. Despite the fact that I'd personally made it crystal clear to Kyle that he was never to see Cleo again.

I hadn't gone alone when I went to deliver my warning. He would have easily dismissed me as Cleo's annoying but harmless mom. Seargant Mitch McKinney had agreed to stand behind me looking imposing, but not in uniform, of course, when I knocked on Kyle's door. Stand there, but that was it. And only because Cleo might be in danger. Because Sergeant McKinney didn't have probable cause to be threatening Kyle in an official capacity. He didn't even want to know the details, nor was he happy to be there. But I'd written McKinney the recommendation that he credited with getting him into Fordham Law School. His affection for me ran deep. But it was thanks to the hundred-dollar bill I had on me that we sailed past Kyle's doorman in his absurdly fancy building without calling up first.

"Where the fuck have you been, Tebow?" Kyle shouted as he swung open his apartment door. He made a face when he saw us. "Who the hell are—"

"Stay away from Cleo McHugh," I said.

Kyle's expression flipped from confused to dismissive. Then his eyes flicked in McKinney's direction, totally unfazed. "Fuck off."

I stepped closer. "Go anywhere near Cleo again," I said, "and you'll end up in jail."

Kyle squinted, inspecting my face.

"Holy shit, are you her mom?" And then he laughed as he dug in his shirt pocket for a pack of cigarettes. He stuck one in his mouth, lit it, and inhaled.

"Yes, I'm her mom."

"And you actually think Cleo cares what you want?" He exhaled right in my face. "Cleo hates you. She thinks you're a fucking bi—"

In one swift movement, Sergeant McKinney had Kyle by the throat, jacked up against the wall. "Listen, you little shit," I said. "Stay away from her, or we'll come back and see to it you do."

At the time, the threat had appeared to work—Kyle *had* vanished. I'd followed Cleo some and had never seen her go near his apartment again. But it took me a while to shake the look in Kyle's eyes as we were leaving. Like he wanted me dead. Like he'd happily do it himself. I wondered now if I'd underestimated the danger he posed. Maybe he'd been playing some kind of long game and had roped Cleo in again—but this time for revenge.

I was going to have to figure out a way to warn her. I had to try at least. I pulled out my phone.

How's it going? I texted her.

Three little dots appeared. I blinked, but they were still there. Cleo hadn't responded in so long and this time right away?

OK.

Could we meet for coffee? I typed.

Why?

I'd love to see you. You know, casual. Like we hadn't been estranged for months.

There was a long delay. Perhaps that *love* had been too much.

Maybe next week.

Can we do it sooner? There's something I need to tell you.

Tell me now.

In person. I need to tell you in person. This was true. It was too much to explain in a text. It would sound too bad.

Srsly?

I could come to your dorm?

No.

Come to BKLYN?

NO.

Please, Cleo, I really need to talk. I get why you might not want to come home. And that's okay. But can you please come anyway? I won't be annoying, I promise.

Definitely a lie. Cleo being merely annoyed was the best-case scenario.

I don't believe u.

How about cold, hard cash, then? I'm assuming you take Venmo.

A joke and not a joke.

Lemme look at my schedule and get back 2 u.

Okay! Great! Love you!

I was hoping that she'd write something warm in return. I knew better of course. And it didn't matter. My job was to love Cleo no matter what. Cleo didn't have any job except to be herself.

My phone buzzed in my hand again.

If you want me to go away, you're going to have to pay. In more ways than one.

I stared down at the new message from my anonymous friend, debating. Situations like this required a delicate calibration. It generally wasn't a great idea to completely ignore a person once he'd made a concrete demand for money. That demand *was* bribery, which meant that person had already committed one actual crime. Ignoring them often led to further escalation.

Who is this?

Someone who knows what you did, bitch.

Silas used to call all women and girls bitches, didn't he? It was hard to remember. He said and did a lot of things. But, of course, I'd thought of him first. He'd been working that night. He was one of Daitch's right-hand men. It was Silas sending the messages. It had to be. I squared my shoulders before typing my reply.

I don't know what you're talking about.

What would your law firm think? Or the police? You stabbed someone that night and Haven House helped you cover it up. I know all about it.

It was much later than I'd planned when I got to the office. Mark had even checked in again to confirm I was on my way. He was understanding when I'd cited "family issues," but he was still wound up. I'd tried to reach Jules to see if she had any sense of what might be going on. But my call had rolled straight to her voice mail. Not a surprise, given that it was bedtime for her daughter. But as I was listening to her outgoing message, I remembered our strange call from two nights ago. She'd never called me back. Come to think of it, she hadn't been in touch all day.

I'd spent much of the trip uptown wondering if I should reach out to Haven House, see if I could track Silas down. I did know how to make threats of my own. And in my experience, threats were most effective when their location and timing took people by surprise. But I didn't want to risk intentionally putting myself on Haven House's radar after all these years. I wasn't easy to find. I'd been careful to scour the internet over the years for any references to my maiden name—Columbia Law School was a particularly bad serial offender. But it was surprisingly easy to get things taken down when you were sufficiently tenacious.

From the doorway of Mark's office, I could see him at his

desk, reading something on his massive monitor—the one he said helped him pretend he didn't need more powerful reading glasses. At least it went with his massive corner office, the biggest one on the floor. When I knocked, he turned to eye me over the top of his wire-framed glasses. His face softened immediately.

"Oh, Kat, so glad you're here," he said.

"Did you see Jules today?" I turned my head toward the assistants' cluster of desks, which sat between Mark's office and mine, though they were all empty at that hour.

"I think she may have been out," Mark said. "Is something wrong?"

"I'm sure it's fine," I said quickly.

"Well, unfortunately, we've got something of a priority situation on our hands."

Mark stood, which made him look tiny behind his large desk. Notably distinguished but also very short, Mark had been quite the catch in his prime, I suspected. At sixty-five, he was still very charismatic and youthful, jamming upstate with his college band-mates and running daily in the park. His beautiful, kind wife was a poetry professor at Princeton and was struggling with stage IV breast cancer. Now that their three children were grown, the two of them lived alone in a gorgeous Upper West Side brownstone filled with incredible art and beautiful antiques. And love—so much love. It was the kind of life I'd imagined Aidan and I might one day have, back when I still believed what we had was happiness.

Mark motioned toward his pair of Barcelona chairs.

"I'm sorry I've been hard to reach," I said as I sank into the soft leather seat. "I've been dealing with a bit of a situation with Cleo."

Mark nodded. He knew Aidan and I were separated and he knew about the tension between Cleo and me, though I hadn't shared how bad things had gotten lately. He was also gener-

ally incredibly respectful of family matters. One mention of a
sick child or ailing parent or school play that needed attending
and Mark was the first to insist that take priority. But tonight
the mention of Cleo hadn't elicited even a flicker of recognition.
Whatever was going on must be serious.

"This new matter is a little different than what you typically
work on." He fell quiet, like he was waiting for permission to
continue.

"Maybe you can tell me a little more?"

"Right, of course," he said. "A client has a high-profile employee
who the employer suspects was involved in some illegal activity.
Illegal activity that may have impacted his performance at work,
which has potentially exposed the employer to liability."

"That sounds exactly like *every* situation I handle."

Mark smiled. "Fair point," he said. "Except the employee, in
this case, is recently deceased. A death that his employer suspects
may be tied to the personal issues he was having. Drove his car
into a telephone pole. Seems this employee may have been distracted enough beforehand that he made errors while at work.
Errors that may now be linked to product defects, which injured
consumers."

I cleared my throat. Willed myself not to overreact. This was a
coincidence, obviously.

But my hands were trembling as I retrieved a pad and a pen
from my work bag to take notes. "Who is the employer?"

"Darden Pharmaceuticals."

I kept my eyes on the pad.

"And who is the employee?" I asked, hoping the tremor in my
voice wasn't as obvious as it felt.

"Doug Sinclair, VP of Risk Management." Mark sighed,
adjusting his glasses. "Darden doesn't know what his personal
issues were. And they need to in order to respond to this situation
wholeheartedly. That's where you come in."

I should tell Mark about Doug and me, immediately. It would be the ethically responsible thing to do. But then again, what difference could it possibly make now?

"I'm sorry, what is it that Darden wants from us, exactly, with respect to these personal stressors?" I asked, pressing on.

"Tragedy notwithstanding, Darden would simply like the truth on the record. This employee was entrusted with ensuring the safety of a drug that seems to have had . . . issues. Apparently, he was contacted by a doctor—one of a group of OB-GYNs who'd gotten acquainted at a conference. That doctor had noticed a possible connection between cases involving Xytek and bad outcomes in pregnant patients. But Doug Sinclair never made the required adverse event report to the FDA. If he had, given the severity of the allegation, the drug would have been pulled immediately while an investigation was conducted, or at least an appropriate warning issued. If Doug's personal problems were serious enough that he committed suicide . . ." Mark shook his head ruefully. "Perhaps those same issues could have caused him to mishandle reporting the call."

"What about the people actually involved in the drug's manufacture or the approval process? Aren't they the ones who are really at fault?"

"Doug wasn't a chemist, of course. In fact, he joined Darden after the drug was already on the market. But the reality is, complications often surface later with prescription drugs, often in an unforeseen subset of patients. As soon as a company becomes aware, though, it must be reported to the FDA. From there the drug either gets pulled or it gets a black box warning like Xytek now has. That's the best a company can do—respond to known risks. But Doug Sinclair was the only one who knew about these physicians' warnings, because he got the call. And these weren't small problems. There have been infant *fatalities*." Mark caught himself. "Allegedly. That's according to the accusations in the lawsuit. Now that the MDL has been consolidated, we're going to take over the defense, a big upgrade from that small slice of Darden's M and A business we only recently took over. If this litigation goes well, we could be in line to take over as the company's lead outside counsel on all matters. Fiscally speaking, that would be very helpful. As you know, it's been a challenging couple of years for the firm."

Blair, Stevenson had lost two big clients when they'd been bankrupted by the recession. And then J.P. Morgan had taken a huge swath of their business elsewhere because of a petty conflict between their general counsel and our head of M&A. There had even been talk of a merger, or of us being purchased outright—options none of the partners wanted.

"Personal problems—is that really all they know? That seems awfully . . . vague."

"According to Darden's internal investigation, it seems that Sinclair was being blackmailed for his involvement in some college admissions scandal," Mark said. "Word is that he was already estranged from his daughter; his wife is deceased. He was apparently quite depressed in the weeks leading up to the accident. It appears that this threat of blackmail was the straw that broke the camel's back. Darden needs these facts confirmed, that's all."

This was absurd. Even if Doug had, in fact, availed himself of Advantage Consulting's "extra" services. Even if he had lied to me and *had* bribed Amherst, making the blackmail a bigger threat than he'd let on—Doug was *not* depressed.

"So, no one at Darden had any idea about the issues with this drug before this physician called Doug. *That's* Darden's position?" It came out a bit more sharply than I'd intended.

"That doesn't seem plausible to you?"

"Not especially, given what's got to be a very complex process of checks and double checks. From the little I know, this MDL is massive. Thousands of claimants. Seems unlikely that there were no earlier red flags. And not in any testing, either?"

"I personally don't know enough about the drug development process to assess that likelihood." Mark shrugged. Then he looked me in the eye. "And frankly, neither do you."

Ah, now Mark was being sharp. He was right. I wasn't that familiar with the details of Doug's job or the prescription drug manufacturing process, but my gut said this whole thing didn't hold water.

"Regardless, I don't think Darden needs to worry," I said. "I mean, even if these details about Doug's personal life did surface, the public would be unlikely to make the connection between any of that and Xytek. Why not just leave it alone?"

Tell him you knew Doug. It wasn't too late.

"Oh, no, no. I'm sorry. I'm not being clear," Mark went on. "Darden isn't worried about these facts *surfacing*. They *want* Doug Sinclair's personal situation, the truth of it, made public. They want to demonstrate that they would have acted immediately if they had known physicians were detecting a problem."

In other words, Darden wanted Doug—now dead and unable to defend himself—to be the sacrificial lamb. That said, did I know him well enough after three weeks to say for sure he wasn't responsible in some way, for something? No.

But I also knew a smoke screen when I saw one.

"Understood," I said. Mark kept looking at me like it was my turn to talk.

"Is everything okay, Kat?" he asked. He could tell something was up.

"Oh, yes . . . Cleo, you know, the usual. But don't worry. I'm on this."

And I would be, until I could figure out a graceful way not to be.

Mark nodded. "Thank you, Kat. I really appreciate having you at the wheel here," he said. "Obviously, keeping Darden happy is critical. The billables from this lawsuit alone will help keep the lights on, and getting Darden's entire book of business would secure the firm's future for years. But for any of that to happen, we are going to need to sort this Sinclair situation first—Darden's general counsel has made that abundantly clear. On a personal level, Phil Beaumont is also an old friend, and frankly, I've never seen him so upset. He feels genuinely awful about what's happened to the families impacted by this drug; all of Darden's top-level management does. They want to make this right."

"Understood." I nodded, tucked away my notebook, and stood to leave.

"Wait, Kat," Mark said quietly as I headed for the door. "About Cleo. She'll be okay?"

"Presumably, yes. You know Cleo—she's always liked to push the envelope." I wanted so badly in that moment to confide in Mark about Kyle. I wanted to tell him about the anonymous messages I was getting, too. I wanted to tell him everything. But that would also mean telling him what I'd done all those years ago. And even with all the secrets between us, that crossed a whole different kind of line. "In the meantime, hopefully she won't worry me to death."

Mark smiled.

"Cleo is very lucky to have you looking out for her, that's for sure. Eventually, she'll realize that. They always do."

CLEO

"I'm sorry about your mom," Will says after we've walked along the Hudson for a while in silence. His broad shoulders are hunched against the chilly wind. "I know that things with the two of you are not the best. I'm sure that makes it all . . . worse. Or, at least, more complicated. When you have mixed feelings about someone and then something bad happens, you feel . . . guilty, on top of everything else."

Exactly.

Things with Will might not be perfect, but God, can he articulate things in a way that I could never. My feelings have always been this huge, tangled mess. Like my emotions don't always pass through my brain. My therapist, Evie, has helped me see that doesn't mean there is something wrong with me. But it's satisfying also hearing it from someone who isn't on my mom's payroll.

"You're right," I say to him as I move out of the path of a child wobbling on a bike. "It is complicated. I'm really worried but still mad and also confused because I'm not even sure who I'm mad at anymore."

"What do you mean?" Will asks, fixing his bright blue eyes on me. Sometimes those eyes are all I can see.

"I don't know . . . these things I'm learning about her that don't even seem like her."

"Like the dating?"

"And her childhood."

We are quiet for a time. Watching the runners, and the bikers, the families pushing strollers. I like being here with Will. Away from school, away from everything.

"Also, a kidnapping with no ransom demand doesn't exactly make any sense."

"What do the police say?" he asks.

"They think my dad is suspect number one. And maybe me number two."

"That seems like a good use of their time."

"My dad apparently told Detective Wilson about my mom and me arguing about the Kyle situation."

Will raises his eyebrows. "Why would he do that?"

"I don't know." I tense—if I talk too much about my dad betraying me, I may lose it.

"I'm sorry." Will reaches for my hand, wrapping his strong, sure fingers tight around mine. "I'm sorry," he says again. Like it's an action instead of a word.

"There's money stuff with my dad, too."

We've stopped walking at the spot where the Hudson walkway hits City Vineyard, a wine bar. To the left, a pier extends into the water; to the right, the pathway continues along up the river for miles and miles. We step to the left in unison, toward the empty pier. Will leans his body against mine as we make our way down to the end. The warm weight of him makes me feel small, and safe. It's so nice to be walking together, out in the fresh air.

"Money stuff sounds . . . not good."

"Nope." My throat feels raw just thinking about the rest. But I think I need to say it out loud. To admit it to someone. Maybe the words won't feel as heavy once they're outside me. "And my dad's been having an affair with his assistant," I say. "And he lied about it to my face."

Will frowns, but then his face softens.

"Okay . . ." he says finally. *Lots of guys have affairs*—that's what he means.

"Also, he wanted a loan from my mom. That's the money stuff. A loan for one of his movies, like *a lot* of money. And my mom said no." I look at Will pointedly. "And now, he magically *has* the money."

"Oh . . . wow," he says, grimacing. "But that still doesn't necessarily mean that . . ."

"I know. Not *necessarily*. But it doesn't look good."

"No, it doesn't," he agrees as the wind picks up again, tossing his shaggy hair in front of his eyes.

"They definitely don't think she just took off. Because of the"—I can't get out the word *blood*—"scene. Not that she would do that anyway. I don't think."

"A robbery maybe?"

"Nothing was stolen. And there were glasses, like she'd invited somebody in for a drink."

"Somebody she knew?"

"I mean, somebody she knew enough to let inside. She was dating a bunch of random guys she met online," I say. "So there are lots of possibilities."

Will rests his forearms on the railing, turns to look at me. His bright eyes so filled with . . . love? Maybe. "If there's anything I can do to help . . . And I mean that, really. Absolutely anything."

I rest my hand on top of his. "I think maybe walking would be good?"

"Absolutely." Will nods, looping his arm through mine, even though that's the kind of thing we never do.

"I feel so guilty."

"Guilty?"

"I knew about some of these things in my mom's life," I say. "I never bothered to ask about the details. Honestly, I'm not sure I really cared all that much. That makes me a bad person, doesn't it?"

Will shrugs. "I think that makes you a person, with a mom. Mine died of cancer a few years ago."

"Oh, I'm so sorry."

He nods. "Thanks . . . Anyway, for a long time, it seemed like she would be okay. And there was this one huge fight we got into, about me wearing muddy sneakers in the kitchen, of all dumb things. She was screaming at me, probably because she was stressed about her illness. I called her a bitch. Yelled it right in her face. That's when she told me the cancer was back. That it had spread everywhere. She only had weeks left."

"That's awful." I squeeze his arm.

"It was, and I felt so guilty for so long," he says. "But she specifically told me before she died not to hold it against myself, that she understood I didn't mean it. Your mom knows that, too."

"I hope so."

"If she's anywhere near as thoughtful and generous as you, I'm sure of it."

Back in my dorm later, I try to hold the memory of Will's body against mine, my fingers tangled in his hair. For ninety whole minutes I didn't worry about my mom, or my dad, or the police. Even as the glow is wearing off, I feel calmer, my head clearer.

I close my mom's laptop and pick up my phone. It makes no sense that I haven't heard back from Jules. Maybe she's avoiding me; knows something she doesn't want to share—something about my mom and that dating site maybe? In a way, Jules does know more about my mom's life than any other person in the world—all that access to her messages, contacts, her schedule. My mom used to joke that it was like she was really married to Jules.

Now I wonder if that was less of a joke and more the way my mom really felt: alone. My dad *was* having an affair. He was arguing with her about *her* money. And then there was the fact that she'd grown up in that awful place, alone. At least my dad had my grandmother and Uncle Robert and Aunt Alice. My mom didn't have any family. She hardly had any Facebook friends. In the end, she didn't even have me.

I'm sorry to bother you again, Jules. But I really do need to talk.

Three dots flicker across the screen. Thank God.

Sorry, Cleo. Super busy at work. Will call as soon as I can!

Seriously? She's too *busy*?

I wanted to know whether you have ANY idea what might have happened to my mom?

Another set of ellipses appear, and then vanish.

I'm really worried, Jules. Please. I'm headed to the office now. I'll see you there? I promise it will be quick.

I stare down at the phone, willing Jules to respond. A third set of ellipses flashes across the screen and then . . . nothing.

And now I am convinced—Jules knows something.

The lobby of my mom's office building has thirty-foot ceilings, immaculate polished marble floors, and a fancy security desk. It's even nicer than I remember—it's been a few years. When I was little, I always jumped at the chance to go with her to work. And I'd loved every second of being there, watching my mom do her thing. Being with her, period. It's amazing how easily I forget about that. But we *were* that close when I was younger. Sure, my dad was always better at the messy fun and games, even back then, but I adored my mom. She was my person.

"Can I help you?" the security guard behind the desk demands before I've even reached him. He eyeballs me like maybe I'm there to rifle through people's purses.

"My mom is a partner at Blair, Stevenson," I offer.

"And who's your mother?" He looks doubtful I have a mother, much less one who works at such a fancy law firm. He's even picked up the phone in a way that suggests he's literally trying to call my bluff.

"No, no, she's not here. Because she's missing. She's an official missing person. Her name is Katrina McHugh. The police know. It's a serious situation." I'm going for sympathy, which, from his scowl, doesn't exactly seem to be working. "But I need to speak with her assistant. Her name is Jules Kovacis."

"Mmm." He looks down at his old-school watch, then brings the phone to his ear. "Most support staff is at lunch until two."

He twitches a little and leans forward when someone answers right away. "Ah, yes, I have a Cleo McHugh down here. She wants to speak with a Jules Kovacis about a Katrina McHugh." His eyes flick up to mine. "Oh. Well, okay. I'll send her right up, then." He points without looking at me again. "Last elevator on the right. Floor forty-six."

An older woman with an angular face and a silver bob is standing in the hall when the elevator doors open. She is not Jules.

"Cleo?" she asks, as if she's not sure. When I nod, she steps forward and hugs me like we know each other. Her hair smells of lavender and vanilla and her arms are warm. I don't want to let her go. "I'm Diana Perlstein. Head of Human Resources. We're all so sorry about your mom."

"Thanks," I say into her silver hair.

She releases me, hands still on my upper arms as she looks me in the eyes. "Your mom is going to be fine, Cleo. Just fine."

"I know." I press my lips together as that now familiar burn rises in my throat. I really wish people would stop saying shit like that when they have absolutely no idea whether it's true. "Uh, where's Jules?"

"Oh, I'm sorry, Jules isn't here." She smiles, sort of. It's actually more of a grimace.

"Do you know when she'll be back?" I'm trying not to seem annoyed. But the guy downstairs could have told me that and saved me the trip.

Diana Perlstein sucks some air in through her very even, very white teeth. "I'm sorry, but Jules is no longer with the firm."

"She was fired?" I ask. Is that why Jules is being weird?

"Oh, no, no. Nothing like that," she says. "I do know that our managing partner, Mark Germaine, is anxious to meet with you. He was so glad to hear you were in the building. As I'm sure you know, he and your mom are very close. He wants to see what the firm can do to help find her. Can I take you to see him instead?" She gestures down the hall.

"Okay," I say. "That would be good, I guess." As she steps forward, my phone vibrates. "Sorry, hold on a second," I say as I dig it out from my back pocket.

A text from Jules.

If you're at Blair, Stevenson, leave. It's not safe. As I quickly darken the screen, blood rushes to my ears. I don't think Diana was close enough to see the text, but I can't be sure.

"Sorry, that was . . . my dad." To me, it's clear that I'm lying. Hopefully not to this Diana person. "He's outside. Can you tell Mark that I'll come right back or he can, um, call me if there's a specific time that's good?"

She pats my shoulder. "Of course, sweetheart," she says kindly. "You do what you need to do. Whenever you want to come back is fine. I'm sure Mark will make the time."

I ride the packed elevator back to the lobby, staring at the wall of navy and khaki suits in front of me, brain buzzing. I look around to be sure no one is watching me before I respond to Jules.

What is going on? What do you mean, not safe?

Did you leave?

I'm headed down in the elevator.

There are two men outside in a black car. I was there a minute ago. I saw them.

What? Who are they?

Go somewhere safe. Don't let them follow you. There are people watching you, Cleo.

I can't get myself to move when the elevator doors open. People watching? It sounds paranoid. And yet my mom *is* missing. As the doors start to close, I slip out into the lobby and then through the revolving doors and onto the sidewalk. I brace myself. But I don't see any black car with two men in it. There's a box truck, double-parked, cab empty. Lots of parked cars—also all empty.

Jules, there's no one. What's going on?

"Cleo, what's wrong?" When I turn, Mark is heading toward me, face flushed with concern. Relief—the instant I see him. "Why did you rush out? Diana told me that you came looking for Jules. I'm sorry to have to tell you this. But we had to let her go."

Yes, Jules and my mom are close, but so are she and Mark. *I've* known Mark for years. He and his wife, Ruth, have been sending me birthday cards since I was little. They were at my high school graduation party.

"Oh," I say. "That woman said she wasn't fired."

"We've been trying to keep it confidential, for Jules's sake. She's had something of an episode. Manic. Your mother knew. She'd been trying to help. For the sake of the other employees' well-being, we had to let Jules go." He steps closer. "I'm sorry. I know the last thing you need is . . . well, something else."

Jules's texts did sound kind of delusional. And there *aren't* any guys out there waiting for me like she said. Also, she hasn't responded to my last text. I swallow hard. I really do not want to cry, but the longer Mark stares at me, the tighter my throat feels.

He steps forward and wraps an arm kind of awkwardly around my shoulder. "Come back inside, Cleo," he says gently. "We have hot chocolate."

* * *

A few minutes later, I'm sitting in Mark's office as his assistant, Geraldine, hands me a mug of cocoa. I feel like a kid and it's such a relief.

"You sure you don't want anything else, sweetheart?" Geraldine asks. When I shake my head, she, too, puts a hand on my shoulder. "We all adore your mom here. And we're all worried. But she's going to be okay. I know that she is."

For some reason, it finally makes me feel better when Geraldine says it.

Mark takes a seat across from me as she closes the office door behind her. "Have the police turned up anything yet? We at the firm can certainly help in many ways, but I also don't want to interfere with their progress or step on any toes."

"They don't know anything yet," I say, and I sound annoyed. "They're mostly focused on my dad and me."

But I do think Detective Wilson is trying. Maybe I just want some sympathy and comfort right now from a dadlike person who isn't *my* dad. Somebody who might actually step up and help.

"They're focused on you?" Mark laughs.

I shrug. "Because my mom and I argue a lot, I guess," I say. "I don't think they *really* suspect me. I'm not so sure the same is true for my dad . . ." I don't want to air my dad's dirty laundry. On the other hand, I could use some information. "If I tell you something, could it be confidential?"

"Of course. You're family as far as I'm concerned," he says. "Also, I *am* a lawyer. And starting now, you are my client."

"My dad was having some kind of affair. Also, he wanted a loan from my mom. And, well, she said no—but now somehow he has the money." It comes out in a rush.

"I see." Mark looks troubled. "There's an explanation, surely." He hesitates. "I mean, is that what you think—that there's an explanation?"

"I don't know what to think anymore."

"Yes . . ." Mark hesitates. "That's certainly understandable."

"Would it be possible for someone here to find out how he got the money? Maybe my mom decided to give it to him in the end?"

"We can certainly try," Mark says. "I'll reach out to our forensic accountants—they're very, very good. Anything you can give me in terms of your mom's account numbers or bank names would be helpful, though. Or your dad's."

"Okay," I say, though my mom is careful. She wouldn't leave that kind of information lying around. "I'll look."

Mark stands and walks over to open his door. "Geraldine," he calls out to the assistant pool. "Would you give Ross Jenkins at Digitas a call, let him know we'll be needing some help on a rush basis? It's a top priority. I can call Ross myself if necessary."

Geraldine replies, but I can't quite make it out.

"Okay, so we'll get that started while you get me the accounts," Mark says, seeming pleased to be doing something. "What else?"

"My mom wasn't working on anything here that might have been . . . I don't know . . ."

"You mean dangerous?" Mark asks.

"I guess." It sounds ridiculous when he says it out loud.

He makes a face. "Your mom specializes in patent litigation, cases involving big companies that mostly never see the inside of a courtroom. It's not especially sexy. Certainly not dangerous." Mark considers for a moment. "What about that place she grew up in?"

"What do you mean?"

"I don't know specifically. But it always sounded like that home was filled with some real rough characters. Your mom is very successful now. Doesn't seem entirely impossible that someone from her time there might resurface. It's something to consider. Desperate people can have very long memories."

KATRINA

I'd been waiting on the edge of the playground across the street from Kyle's apartment for more than an hour. I'd been compelled there by Mark's offhand parting remark: "Cleo is very lucky to have you looking out for her." But was she really that lucky? What if I'd actually put her in *more* danger by confronting Kyle all those months ago? And so here I was, doing the only thing I could think of: throwing myself back into the fray.

It was nearly midnight when Kyle finally came out of his apartment, stopped to light a cigarette, shook the sandy blond hair from in front of his eyes, then lifted the collar of his puffy white jacket against the evening chill. He was good-looking, in that damaged, James Dean kind of way that inevitably seems to attract girls. But only if you could get past the whole put-on hoodlum shtick. It was especially ridiculous considering the Greenwich hedge-fund mansion where he was raised.

But then Aidan had been obvious, too, I suppose. It wasn't as though he'd hid that he was a ne'er-do-well. It was like Aidan was so assured of his place in the world that he didn't need to bother to try and prove anything. Even before Cleo was born, I'd known that was a problem. But I'd had so many problems of my own, it had been impossible to gauge its importance. And so I'd had a baby with him. And then I'd stayed with him for two decades, even though I was so unhappy—to give Cleo the stable family I'd never had. But maybe in doing so I'd given her some-thing else. A lesson in the worst kind of compromise.

I crossed the street briskly, heading Kyle off at the far end of the block.

"Oh, you got to be fucking kidding me," he said, waving an exasperated hand in my direction. "I talked to my parents' law-yer, you know. We can sue you for harassment."

"You were supposed to stay away from my daughter."

"I haven't fucking seen Cleo in months."

"I don't believe you," I said with a fake smile. "Do you remem-ber what I promised—about sending you to jail if you ever went near her again? Because I meant it."

He looked about to snap back, but instead he smiled smugly, then stepped closer and exhaled a long stream of cigarette smoke directly in my face. "Go ahead, go to the police. But if you do, Cleo is coming down with me." He held up his phone. "I've got photos on here of her buying, selling, *using*. I keep photos of all my runners. Insurance: You never know when you're going to need it. And I've got plenty of customers who'd be willing to testify to her working for me. Whole bunch of them are pretty pissed at her right now." He dropped the cigarette and ground it out with the heel of his Air Jordan. "So I'd stop fucking threaten-ing me if I were you."

And with that, he strutted away, lifting his phone to his ear as he crossed the street.

Lying in bed the next morning, I had to blink a few times to see Mark's text clearly. *Please update me as soon as you have anything on Sinclair. Darden is all over me.*

It was only 7:15 a.m. Mark never applied pressure; and after less than twelve hours? But I wasn't surprised Darden was agitating—and they weren't going to be easy to ignore. They were accustomed to getting what they wanted, when they wanted it. And right now they wanted Doug Sinclair under the Xytek bus. There was only so much stalling I was going to be able to do.

I'm on it. Be back in touch ASAP.

"Hey, have you found Douglas Sinclair's phone yet?" I asked when I called Detective Cross a few minutes later.

"Nope," Cross said. "Scene guys are still searching, but it's not looking good. Must have been thrown in the accident. Could have been broken into pieces and scattered who knows where."

"Have you confirmed that it was a suicide?"

Cross muttered something unintelligible.

"What was that?" I asked.

"A witness has turned up."

"A witness to what?"

"A black sedan was apparently tailing Sinclair shortly before impact. Looks like maybe it wasn't an accident or suicide."

"Meaning what?"

"Homicide."

I walked briskly up Fifth Avenue toward the Advantage Consulting offices, weaving my way in and out of the sidewalk traffic—moms with strollers, well-dressed ladies on their way to overpriced four-course lunches, the late-morning dog walkers.

Looks like maybe not suicide or an accident, I texted Mark. This was at least *an* update, for sure.

What do you mean? came Mark's quick reply.

Bronxville PD says maybe Sinclair's car was driven off the road. Doesn't rule out a possible link to the bribery/blackmail. I'm checking that out now.

It also didn't rule out Darden somehow being involved. After all, they were the ones who seemed so eager to use Doug's death to their advantage. What if they'd been the ones to cause it? It was way too soon to suggest such a thing to Mark. I'd need some evidence first.

Okay, thanks. Good work. I'll let Darden know.

I was a block away from Advantage when my phone rang. Vivienne Voxhall. I couldn't ignore her any longer.

"Hi, Viv—"

"Where the fuck have you been?" she shouted. "Didn't Mark tell you to call me back?"

I'd had enough. "Scream at me one more time and *I'll* fire *you*. Got it?"

She took a loud, huffy breath.

"The situation is being handled," I went on. "I've left word for the *Times* reporter, but we need to tread lightly there. I want some ammunition of our own first. And I've got a couple decent leads on why Anton left his previous job. It appears that numerous women complained he was verbally abusive." Unable to sleep, I'd finally had time to review the investigation file that had come in. "That's not a justification for your having threatened homicide, but it's the start of something that could balance the scales. I need to do some more digging. *That's* why I haven't called you back— because I am working on it. What's important right now is that you stay calm. If you do something rash, it will give Anton even more power than he already has."

"I have power, too." She sounded like a petulant child.

"In this particular situation, you do not, Vivienne. Not with the scrutiny surrounding the IPO—you can't threaten to kill underlings, no matter how awful they are. You call HR and fire them, like a normal person."

"You're the one who's supposed to be making this go away."

"I'm the one helping you *manage* it," I said, correcting her. "To the best of my ability."

"Fix this, Kat," she said, her voice low. "Please."

I breezed past the doorman at the Advantage Consulting building this time with a brisk stride and a confident wave.

I was determined to find out what had happened to Doug; once I had, I could then decide what to do with that information. Maybe that would be sharing it with Darden. Maybe it would be burying it forever. My instinct was still to protect Doug. So what if he'd lied about paying off Advantage? I understood, given his fractured relationship with his daughter, how he could have ended up there. But first I needed to know the truth, all of it.

"Oh!" the Advantage receptionist exclaimed when I burst in. "I'm sorry, you need an appointment."

"I need to see Brian," I said, making a beeline for his office before she could head me off.

"Oh, no you don't!" she called after me. "You can't do that!"

But I was already opening his door. Brian Carmichael was at his desk, on a phone call. He looked up, registering me. There was no warmhearted Montana boy in those cold eyes—the charm was still there in his voice, though, as he wrapped up his call. "Good to talk to you, too, Roger! And be sure to send my best to Lisa."

The contrast was unsettling. I steeled myself as Carmichael hung up, leaned back, and crossed his arms.

"I'm so, so sorry, Brian," the receptionist stuttered as she rushed in behind me. "She raced right past me. There was nothing I could do to stop her." She sounded genuinely terrified.

Brian waved an irritated hand in her direction. "It's fine, Bethany. Leave us and close the door."

The receptionist wasted no time following his instructions. I took her hasty departure as my cue to move fast.

"You were blackmailing Doug Sinclair." I had no illusions that Carmichael would have been doing the dirty work himself, but wild accusations had a way of dislodging useful information. My money was still on an Advantage employee or associate— someone who thought they should be benefiting more from Carmichael's well-oiled machine.

"I've got no idea what you're talking about," he replied easily, chin resting in his hand. He looked bored and kind of annoyed, but not the least bit concerned. "Now, Ms. Thompson, or whatever the hell your name is, I suggest you get the fuck out of my office."

"Or what?" I asked casually. "You'll kill me like you killed Doug Sinclair?"

Carmichael laughed. "What are you talking about?"

"Doug Sinclair is dead," I said. "He was driven off the road."

"And what does that have to do with me?" Carmichael asked dismissively.

"You were blackmailing him. You tried to apply pressure. Things got out of hand."

He leaned back, hands resting casually on the arms of his chair now. "I didn't even know he was dead until right now."

I shrugged. "Pretty big coincidence, though, don't you think?"

"Call it what you want." There was a tightness to his face now. "I didn't have anything to do with any car accident."

"So that's a yes to the blackmail."

Carmichael shook his head, then made a show of considering the accusation.

"Blackmail him with what, exactly?" he asked, folding his hands in his lap.

"You helped him bribe his daughter's way into Amherst."

"I most certainly did not."

"You *told* me you did at our last meeting, remember? Those extra payments? I have a recording."

"Recording." Carmichael smirked. "What you have on tape, then, is the oldest upsell in the book," he said. "I suggest your friend paid for an extra that he didn't pay for in order to convince you that you need to do the same."

"That's convenient."

"Convenient and also true. Go to the police and open up an

investigation into Ella Sinclair's file if you want—all you'll find is a kid who had some help studying for her SATs, revising her résumé, and crafting essays. All well within the bounds of acceptable and entirely *legal* college counseling. There was nothing to blackmail Doug Sinclair with because he didn't do anything remotely wrong." Carmichael stood. "Now, like I said, get the hell out of my office before I call the police myself."

I crossed Fifth Avenue and walked a couple blocks uptown along Central Park, feeling thrown but also relieved. Doug hadn't bribed Amherst—which meant he hadn't lied to me. Still, this wasn't necessarily the answer Darden wanted. Without any wrongdoing involving Advantage, Doug wasn't nearly as convenient a scapegoat. Doug *was* still being blackmailed, though—I knew that firsthand. And it was theoretically possible that the blackmail had distracted Doug at work, that he'd made mistakes. I still found that hard to believe, but it was a compromise I could potentially accept—letting Darden scapegoat Doug, but allowing him to retain his fundamental innocence.

It was warmer now, a hint of spring in the air as I passed a cherry tree beginning to blossom. I dropped down onto a nearby bench. The fountains in front of the Met were rising and falling in a hypnotic rhythm. The water reminded me of that T. S. Eliot poem "The Dry Salvages," which Reed had us discuss during the writing club. " 'Not fare well, / But fare forward, voyagers.' "

"You're voyagers, too." He'd gestured around the drafty, cavernous room with the windows that wouldn't shut all the way even in December. "This place is only where you find yourselves right now." And then he put a hand on my shoulder as he passed—only for a second. "You have limitless potential."

The Met's dancing fountain abruptly dropped then, its cycle complete. And, in the stillness, I had a clear view across the street. To the black sedan, parked alongside the hot dog vendor. Like that car in the Village that had sped away. Maybe like the car that had run Doug Sinclair off the road. And also like a million other cars.

I stood. But as I stepped forward to take a closer look, the car pulled away from the curb. And then, once again, it was gone. As if it had never been there at all.

November 24, 1992

I wrote about a girl in love during the French Revolution. But there was one line in there . . . "She loved him in that way young girls do, utterly senseless and deeply brave."

I was on my way out the door when he handed my story back to me and said, "It is brave. Very brave."

And in that second I felt sure we were talking about the exact same thing. That our story was already written. That it would end exactly the way I'd hoped it would.

Of course, Olivia shoved into me the second I was out in the hall, ruining the whole thing. "Oh look, Katrina thinks she's Shakespeare!" Then she shoved me again, harder the second time. So hard I knocked into the wall. Face-first. Which only made Olivia laugh and laugh. Sometimes I wonder if I would kill her, if I had the chance. If you promised me that no one would ever find out.

Yes. Of course I would. I'd kill Olivia and I'd kill Silas. Two-for-one special. Maybe I'll take Olivia's broken spoon and do it one day. The world would be better off.

CLEO

I take the north exit out of the West Fourth Street subway station, then walk toward Washington Square Park instead of heading back to my dorm. In case someone's following me. I still didn't see any sign of that car or those men outside when I left my mom's law firm the second time, but it didn't exactly calm my nerves that Jules hadn't responded to any of my follow-up texts asking for an explanation. But then again, maybe that's proof that she's having some kind of episode.

I feel a little better inside Caffe Reggio, smooshed safely into the far corner at a tiny round table. I order a cappuccino, waiting for my heart to slow. I give a start when the door opens a second later, but in comes a thin kid with oversize glasses and an overstuffed backpack—cool-nerdy. I jump again when a phone vibrates on a nearby table. I really need to calm down. I stand up and head over to the window, watch the people headed this way and that, minding their own business. No men. No car.

"Excuse me?" The skinny guy is sitting right below me. I've been hovering over his table in the window. "No offense, but could you *not* keep standing there?"

"Oh, sorry."

I make my way back to my little table and sit there staring at my mom's closed laptop. I want to check and see if any of the men she was dating have responded to the messages I definitely shouldn't have sent. But another part of me feels sick at the thought, so I place the laptop on the table and dig out her journal instead, buying myself a little time.

November 28, 1992

Silas put a dead rat in my bed! Stuck to a glue trap, tucked it right in between the sheets. I had to throw out my fucking top sheet because there were RAT GUTS all over it.

December 1, 1992

There are only three of us left who Silas hasn't messed with. We're all thirteen or younger. Maybe thirteen is his cutoff. If so I'm running out of time. My birthday is in two weeks. Sometimes when Silas walks by he whispers in my ear, "Tick tock, tick tock." Maybe it's Silas who I'll kill first.

Did he end up doing something to her? I flip to the end of the book. The last entry.

December 26, 1992

Director Daitch has had me locked in this room for thirty-eight hours—at least I think that's how long it's been. It's hard to keep track when you're stuck in a windowless tile box. I've been in lockdown before, enough times that I've learned a few tricks—like the fact that they walk rounds every thirty minutes, and they serve meals at exactly eight, one, and six. It marks the time. But when it goes past a single day, you still lose the thread.

Of course, those other times I was in here weren't my fault. They were just Silas being the sick jerk he is.

This time, though, I deserve to be locked away.

The cold is making it hard to think. It's always freezing—this dumb old building with steam radiators that hiss and pop and clang so much, I know they're going to explode someday.

But there's no radiator in here. Only me. And I already exploded.

She may have explained more in another entry, but there are about ten pages ripped out after that date, and all the rest are blank. I leaf quickly through the journal and notice that other pages have been torn out throughout the book. Holes in the story. But did my mom tear them out, or did someone else? I snap the journal shut. Press my palms down against it. I can feel my hands trembling.

My mom did tell me some things about Haven House. Stories I could have listened to more closely. Openings for me to ask about her life, her own childhood. And it wasn't that I was scared or freaked-out—the truth was, I didn't really care. I never saw my mom as an actual person separate from me. And now that she's a person who's missing, I may never have the chance.

I close my eyes and I'm back at the beach. That day when my mom said I should *get in the water and stop being such a baby.* But, no, she hadn't actually said that, had she? Those were only the words in my head—me talking to myself—as I stood again at the edge of the ocean later that same day, my skin tight from the sea air, the cold water licking at my toes, hating myself.

"Sorry, we can't all be like fish from birth, like you," I said, shooting her a look when she hadn't even said a word.

I remember the way my mom winced as she looked away and into the sun.

"The first time I saw a pool was in college," she said. "I didn't learn to swim until law school. And it wasn't easy."

I turned then toward the laughter I heard from the beach. Sitting with Janine and my dad in a circle of striped canvas chairs, Annie looked so happy and carefree. She, of course, could swim in the ocean just fine. And the sun was sinking lower now. I was running out of time.

I waded up to my shins. "You'll have to come in with me. And make sure nothing bad happens. The whole time."

"Okay," my mom said without missing a beat. "I will." And the thing is, even as angry and frustrated as I was, I didn't doubt for a second that she would.

My mom held my hand as we marched out and over the waves and then as we treaded water beyond them. My mom made me—helped me—stay out there until I'd calmed down, until I could let go of her hands. Until I stopped begging to return to shore. Until I finally learned how to swim in the ocean. And when we made it back to the beach, I raced away and up the sand without looking back. Because I wanted to tell my dad.

Finally, I open the laptop; there are responses from every one of the men I messaged. *Hey!* And a *Great to hear from you!* And a *Wow! How have you been?* But beneath all those pleasantries there's Randy. And Randy seems pissed.

So I guess you're not dead. I flinch.

I study Randy's profile. A lawyer who lives on the Upper West Side. In the first of his profile pics, he's standing on a boulder at the top of a tree-covered peak. Fit and attractive-ish . . . maybe. Or at least not totally unattractive. It's hard to tell for sure. He's got on a baseball hat and sunglasses. In the second picture, he's still in the hat and glasses, standing on a boat, holding a large fish—that he's . . . caught? In the last photo, he's ditched the hat and sunglasses, a small curly-haired dog next to his completely hairless, cartoonish face. I'm not sure what he's trying to accomplish. I only know that it's *not* working.

Ugh. Mom, you could do so much better than Randy.

Is it possible she doesn't know that? I mean, she's gorgeous. People say we look exactly alike, but that's only from a distance—the same jawline, same facial structure. Up close there's only one truly beautiful one: my mom.

Any chance you could come by Caffe Reggio? In the Village? I ask Randy. *Would love to see you. I'll be here until 6:00 p.m.*

Three dots appear and disappear, then appear again. *As long as you promise to actually be there this time!*

My mom must have ghosted Randy. *Good for you, Mom.*
I'll be here!

Of course, now I realize that I have no strategy planned for once these men show up. Find out if they know anything—that's the point. "People don't have to admit the whole truth to reveal the part that matters," I remember my mom once saying.

I'd rolled my eyes at the time. Everything to her was a teachable moment. "And you're like some kind of expert on this because you're a lawyer?"

I was listening, though. I'd recently learned that Annie was talking about me behind my back at Beacon. She'd denied it, but I had to get to the bottom of it. I was willing to take any tips I could get.

"I guess, in a way," my mom had said.

"Fine, then explain it."

"There are two keys to getting the truth out of someone: the power of silence," my mom said with a knowing smile. "And the art of the open question."

Eventually, she dropped the Yoda act and explained exactly what she meant, even gave examples. And it had worked with Annie. She admitted she had said something mean behind my back. There's a good chance it will work with Randy.

Still, I should have someone else here, for backup. Not Detective Wilson, obviously. I could call Mark and ask him to come sit with me, though, or Lauren. But I'm pretty sure they'd shut the whole thing down, too. Because meeting with strange men who might have hurt your mom *is* a terrible idea.

I wish I could ask Will to come. He'd be able to make me feel safer, without interfering. But I can't ask him to miss his Eliot seminar, which starts in ten minutes. I send a text instead.

I read my mom's journal.

Ellipses right away, and my heart does a stutter step. It still does every time I hear from him.

Did she say something about your dad?

It takes me a moment to realize what he means.

Oh, no, no. It's a journal from when she was a kid. She grew up in a home. There's so much sick stuff in there.

Part of me feels terrible spilling my mother's secrets so casually. But I'm beginning to think maybe she didn't really want them to be kept hidden.

What kinds of stuff?

Rats. Sex abuse. Things I don't even want to think about.

That's terrible.

And I never knew. Because I'm an asshole.

It's not your fault she never told you.

Maybe she tried and I wasn't listening.

You have to stop beating yourself up . . . I'm so sorry, but I have to get to class. Come by later?

That would be great.

Hang in there. xx

I focus back on my mom's computer, on the other men who've replied to my message—William, Jack, and Cory. All pleasantly surprised, polite responses. Within fifteen minutes, I have all four on their way to Caffe Reggio, at appropriately staggered times.

"Hey." When I look up, there's Annie. I slam the laptop closed. "Wow, that was subtle."

"What do you want, Annie?" I snap. I am out of patience with her and whatever this is.

"You need to call my mom," she says. "She's called you and texted, and you haven't responded. And now she's totally worried. It's rude and selfish. You showed up at our house asking for help, remember?"

I look around in an exaggerated fashion. "Did you stalk me here to tell me that?"

Annie snorts. "Actually, I came here with my *boyfriend* to study." It isn't until she motions behind her that I see Geoff at a table by the window. He glances once in our direction, then looks away.

"You're *dating* Geoff?" I ask. With a tone: *Geoff, the drug addict.* I can't help it.

"Like you're one to judge anyone's boyfriends," she says. She must know about Kyle from Geoff. "Anyway, how is it your business?"

"It's my business if you told Geoff I grew up across the street from you. And he went to my house and got into it with my mom."

"Nope," she says. "We both actually have better things to do with our time than deal with the members of your degenerate family."

"My *degenerate family*?"

"Your mom is an okay person, I guess," she says.

"Gee, thanks, I mean considering that she could be bleeding out somewhere, that's awfully generous."

But it's like she's not even listening. "It's the rest of you who go around doing whatever you want. No matter who it hurts."

"Right," I say, because I want Annie to go away.

"Anyway, *my* mom actually, genuinely cares about people. And she's always been nice to you." Not that Annie exactly sounds happy about this. "And here she is checking in on you and being nice and you don't even care that she's worried. You're selfish. And so is your dad."

Annie turns and heads back to her table. I watch her say something to Geoff as she sits down across from him. He leans in, then turns to look over at me. I nod, stupidly. Janine has texted me a few times. I don't know how many. It was rude to ignore her. But she seemed so worried in her messages. I was afraid it would make *me* more worried if I talked to her.

I'm so sorry! I text her now. *I'm fine. Didn't mean to scare you.*

Oh, I'm so glad to hear from you, Cleo! Janine responds instantly. *I've been so worried! I know you have your dad, but some situations call for a mom! Has there been any news?*

Not yet, nothing.

Try not to worry. I know that's probably impossible ... let me know if there's anything I can do. Anything at all.

My cheeks flush. All I need to do is start bawling while Annie is watching from across the room.

I will let you know. XO

The bells on the door tinkle as it swings open. It's a dad-aged guy wearing a baseball hat, T-shirt, and deliberately ugly sneakers. He takes off his aviator shades. *Randy.*

As I raise my hand, he looks around, like he's checking to see if I'm really waving at him. He looks me up and down as he makes his way over to the table, and I'm pretty sure I see a revolting flicker of excitement cross his face.

"Randy?" I ask with a smile, or what I hope is a smile. It may be more a baring of my teeth. "You're here looking for Kat?"

I extend a confident hand and maintain strong eye contact, the way my mom always told me to. I've locked eyes and done that confident handshake countless times. But never before have I thought of her.

"And you are?" he asks as I yank my hand back from his clammy grasp.

"Her daughter," I say, motioning to the chair across from me.

Randy looks perplexed, but still hopeful. "Ah, that explains the similarity," he says slowly. "Am I in trouble? This like the middle-age version of getting a talking-to from somebody's parents? The kid comes instead." He lifts his hands and laughs like a donkey. "Whatever it is, I didn't do it, Officer."

"My mom, Kat, is missing." *Open questions. Only open questions.*

"Missing from where?" he asks.

"From everywhere. She's missing from everywhere."

He frowns. It's a weird answer.

"Interesting," he says eventually. "That seems out of character."

"Out of character how?" Didn't he barely know her?

He shakes his head. "Well, of course, we only met a couple of times, but she just struck me as a responsible person."

"Yeah."

"I mean, maybe not so great setting boundaries with her 'work.'" He hooks the word in air quotes.

"What does 'that' mean?" I mimic his air quotes.

"I don't know—it seemed like something weird was going on with her job," Randy says. "Maybe *weird* is the wrong word. It was intense. She canceled our first date like four times for work reasons. I could never tell if there really were all those emergencies or if she was lying for some reason. I mean, what corporate lawyer has *that* many emergencies? Something didn't add up." *Probably because she couldn't figure out why she was going out with you and had a moment of actual clarity*—though this seems not to have occurred to Randy. "And then when we did meet up," he goes on, "she took a call—said it was a client, but she was pacing outside the restaurant, talking on the phone for like twenty minutes! Your mom is lucky she's a babe!"

I nod. "Right."

Randy chews on the end of his sunglasses, in thoughtful, full sleuthing mode now. "If she really is missing, you might want to look into that woman she was talking to that night. The call seemed pretty . . . heated."

"Did she mention the woman's name?"

"No." He looks away. "But she did leave her phone to go get a glass of water. You know, the place had a setup like that." He motions to the big jug and paper cups on the nearby counter. "Anyway, I inadvertently saw a text come in: *Don't fuck this up or I'll kill you.*" He raises one eyebrow.

"Holy shit," I whisper.

"I know. Nice, huh?"

"Did you see a name, who the text was from?"

"I did, in fact," he says with an impish grin he tries, but fails, to hide. "Vivienne Voxhall. It's not exactly a name you forget."

TRANSCRIPT OF RECORDED SESSION

DR. EVELYN BAUER
SESSION #3

EVELYN BAUER: You look . . . happy today?

CLEO McHUGH: Do I? I am happy, I guess.

EB: Want to talk about it? It can be nice to talk about good things in here, too.

CM: The guy I'm seeing, we . . . He stayed over last night for the first time. And I—I was a little worried that I'd feel the same way I usually do. You know, like I could take him or leave him after that, but—

EB: Sorry, this boy is . . . ?

CM: Um, Will. We've been seeing each other for a few months. I *was* single, though, for like a whole six weeks after Kyle. And he's . . . I really like him.

EB: That hasn't happened since Charlie, right? You must be relieved.

CM: I am. Ever since Charlie, I've spent so much time disappearing into people. But this . . . With Will . . . I can still be me . . .

EB: Wow, that really is something.

CM: But you want to know the sad part?

EB: What's that?

CM: The only person I want to tell is my mom. Even
    though I know she'd make me feel bad about it.

EB: Maybe she wouldn't. You could—

CM: Oh, she would, definitely.

EB: Still, wanting to tell her is a sign there's
    still hope for you and her.

CM: I don't know . . . Maybe. This new situation
    with Will definitely makes it obvious how messed
    up my relationship with Kyle was.

EB: Because of the drugs, you mean?

CM: No. Caring about that was my mom's whole thing.
    But my relationship with Kyle did, um, have
    other problems. Big ones.

EB: Do you want to talk about what those problems
    were?

CM: Not really.

EB: Sometimes being uncomfortable talking about
    something can be a sign that it's exactly what
    you need to talk about.

CM: Yeah . . . I know. It's so obviously bad and
    stupid. I mean, I should have seen it coming.

EB: Sounds like you're being awfully hard on
    yourself. Relationships are complicated. Being a
    person is . . . complicated.

CM: I don't know . . . There were warning signs.
    Things I ignored. Kyle losing his shit about
    stupid crap. He punched a wall once when he got
    pissed at his dad.

EB: Did Kyle ever get physical with you, Cleo? . . .
    This is a safe space. You won't ever be judged.

CM: Um . . . yeah. He, um, hit me in the face. Like,
    actually punched me. Full-on closed fist. We were
    watching one of those cartoons, like the kind

for adults, and I said, "How can you watch this
dumb shit?" It was a joke. The kind you make
with someone you know. Because they'll know
it's a joke. I guess Kyle didn't think it was
funny . . .

EB: I'm so sorry, Cleo. That must have been very
upsetting, and scary. Not to mention painful
physically.

CM: Want to know the worst part?

EB: What's that?

CM: That was weeks before my mom and her whole
ultimatum about me breaking up with him. I
stayed with him after that. And I'm not sure I
would have broken up with him even if he'd done
it again. My mom was right about him all along.
So why am I so mad at her still?

EB: Maybe it's easier to be mad at her than it is to
be mad at yourself.

KATRINA

I sat back down on the bench after the black car pulled away. At least there, in front of the Met, I could keep an eye on my surroundings. And I needed to get my bearings. Did Carmichael have someone following me? Maybe, but Darden was a more likely possibility, trying to monitor me close-up. I'd need to call Mark—he'd put a stop to it.

My phone buzzed then. Lauren.

"Why haven't you answered any of my calls or texts?" She sounded out of breath, like she was walking. "I've been worried about you and this Doug thing. I know it's weird because you guys just started dating. But I also know you really liked him."

"It is weird, you're right. And I'm sorry I've been MIA. But everything kind of exploded at once. Work's been . . . complicated." Of course I couldn't get into any details with Lauren, not about Doug or Darden. I'd never told her about my role at the firm, though I'd always wanted to. But she was a U.S. attorney, a highly ethical one. I didn't want to put her in a bad position of knowing more than she wanted to. "Plus, Aidan's been all over me for another loan."

Lauren was always my very best audience for Aidan complaints.

"Aidan." She huffed predictably. "I hope you told him to fuck off."

"Easier said than done, given the state of affairs between me and Cleo."

"You cannot let him extort you," she said. "It's sick."

"Cleo is seeing Kyle again." It felt even worse than I'd imagined saying it out loud.

"Oh, I'm sorry . . . I'm sure that's . . ." She sounded sympathetic, but I could only imagine her appalled expression. "Well, I'm not sure what that feels like. My girls are ten. But Cleo is twenty and she's making scary choices that you can't control, and that must be so hard. Even though as your friend I know that you've been doing everything you can."

"Have I, though?" I asked. "Everything?"

Lauren didn't know what I really meant. That I could easily have found someone in my bag of tricks capable of taking care of Kyle. I wasn't that person, though. I wasn't. Also, on a practical level, I knew how terribly those kinds of plans could go awry. What if Cleo somehow got hurt? Kyle's phone, on the other hand? I suspected I could do something about that.

"What mother ever feels like they've done *everything*?" Lauren said, just when I'd forgotten I was on the phone with her. "Being a mother is a rigged game, Kat—you know that. There's no way to win. And from what I can tell, it only gets harder the older they get. But I mean, it could be worse: I'm older than you are, and my *fifth-grade* parent-teacher conferences start in ten minutes. What was I thinking? Twins at forty-three. Twins! I *loved* my life, Kat. I was *fulfilled*."

"Come on, you adore the girls," I said. Lauren wasn't pretending to be fed up, though. She was always brutally honest about everything, but especially how hard she found motherhood.

"I do love them, of course I do. But I do also kind of hate being a mom. Why doesn't anyone ever mention that's a possibility! That you can love your kids and still hate the role." She was laughing now even though I could tell she didn't really think it was funny.

Every mother I knew learned how to laugh at so many unfunny things. Like the realization I'd faced as the parent of a teen, and then a young adult: that you were expected to have endless empathy—but no vulnerabilities of your own.

"You're sure you're okay?" Lauren asked. "I feel like there's something you're not telling me, Kat. You know I can't stand it when you get squirrelly like this."

"I'm okay," I said, lying. "I'm trying to figure out when, exactly, my life became this much of a mess."

"Everybody's life is a mess, Kat. Absolutely everybody's," Lauren said softly. "I promise. And you *are* a good mom. No, you're a *great* mom. Especially considering where you came from. I don't say that often because I worry it will make you feel bad. But it *is* true. Not having your own mom must make it even harder to figure out what the hell to do. And yet you're so good at it. Anyway, these kids aren't cakes—you can put in all the right ingredients, watch the timer like a hawk, but all sorts of other shit actually happens *in* the oven. Things over which you have zero control."

This was true; there was only so much control I had over anything to do with Cleo. But this mess with Darden and Doug? This was the kind of situation I could and did fix all the time. But I needed to be methodical about it.

I called Mark as soon as Lauren and I finished talking. "There's a chance I can get Doug Sinclair's phone records, at least from the last few days," I said after I'd given him a quick summary of what I'd learned from Brian Carmichael, that whatever blackmail had been going on was under false pretenses. That Doug hadn't bribed anyone, and that *was* an important point Darden would need to acknowledge. "If I can, I'll go through his texts and see if I can find anything about the blackmail."

"That doesn't sound especially . . ."

"Legal?" I asked. "You really want to get into that discussion?"

This was already more than Mark and I had ever spoken about the unsavory details of my job.

"No," he said quickly. "I do not."

"You do understand this means that Doug Sinclair is a victim here?"

"Perhaps," Mark allowed. "But it also doesn't rule out that being blackmailed—even unjustly—distracted him from his oversight of Xytek."

"It also doesn't rule out that Darden is trying to use him as a distraction." I wasn't letting Mark play this dumb.

"I understand what you're saying. We will have to cross that bridge when we come to it, depending on what you find. You and I both know we are not going to do anything unethical or inappropriate here. But if we can keep Darden happy, at least until we can get a foothold in managing a bigger segment of their billables—that would be ideal. I, for one, do like health insurance."

Ruth. It was easy to think that Mark could afford to lose everything and still be fine. But his wife was dying of cancer and he had a daughter getting married, and he did seem more concerned lately about money than I would have expected.

"Oh, and one last thing. There was a car following me. A black sedan. Like the sedan that was spotted at Doug's accident scene."

"What?" Mark sounded alarmed. "Are you okay?"

"Yes, yes. I'm fine. But I've seen the same car twice now, last night and today."

"Do you want to . . . should we call someone?"

"The car is gone now—so, no, there's no emergency," I reassured him. "But you should confirm it's not Darden. Because that would make me uncomfortable."

"Of course it would. I certainly hope that's not the case." Mark still sounded rattled. "I will speak directly with Phil today and confirm. In the meantime, Kat, please be careful out there."

I placed one last call after Mark and I said our good-byes.

"Ahmed, glad I caught you," I said.

Ahmed was an SVP at Digitas Data, the cyber investigative

firm I relied upon for all back-channel information gathering for my clients. Ahmed was my go-to guy at Digitas. He was excellent—efficient and fast, and I trusted him. I'd helped see to it that he made vice president at Digitas in half the usual time. In return, Ahmed always made sure my projects got priority. He was also willing to cross some lines when I said it mattered.

He sighed, but good-naturedly. "Let me guess . . . You don't have the phone and it's an emergency because why can't anything be easy?"

"Yes, please. All the texts at least and also the call log if possible? He's deceased, if that matters."

"Only matters if it means *I* need to be worried I'll be next." He laughed. I didn't respond. "Wait, I don't need to be worried, do I?"

"I don't think so," I said, which, at that moment, felt like the most I could promise anyone.

"Okay, but without the phone the best I'm ever going to do is messages from the past few days."

"That's all I need."

It wasn't easy to track down Jimmy Ahearn. Or to get him to agree to talk. It took me a good part of the day, the rest of which I spent trying to persuade Dalton not to kick a client's son out for vandalizing the school locker room. I took the teacher who'd caught him out for an endless lunch at Le Bernardin, which was mostly spent making him feel like a good person for taking money instead of reporting the kid. "You don't want to be responsible for derailing this kid's life, do you? People make mistakes." I couldn't count how many times in my life I'd used that line. And, in point of fact, this was a decent kid whose parents refused to treat his anxiety properly. But today, the whole thing made me want to take a shower.

Jimmy and I finally met at 6:00 p.m. on the edge of Chelsea, in what was technically a cop bar—wood-paneled and Irish, with deep, worn booths lining the side of the room. The bar was Jimmy's choice, which made no sense to me, but that didn't matter. He was a sometime confidential informant with a specialty in breaking and entering. Skills he didn't use anymore "except for good," he claimed. Which essentially meant for an exorbitant price—something the police seemed willing to overlook, maybe because they, too, used his services on occasion. And Jimmy was worth the money. Within minutes, he could get in and out of any place undetected and with whatever you needed safely in hand—or left behind. He also had a real aversion to the idea of going to prison, which meant he never took a job unless he was absolutely sure he could pull it off successfully. I'd gotten Jimmy's name years ago through a parole officer I knew. I'd used him a couple times: to retrieve keys in one instance, given— prematurely, it turned out—to a new mistress with a temper, the other time to get drugs out of a dorm room before a search.

As soon as Jimmy sat down, I slid a folded piece of paper with Kyle's address across the table. Maybe I couldn't control Cleo or her choices, but I could limit Kyle's ability to do any more damage.

"I need his phone. His work one. He probably has more than one. He's dealing."

Jimmy frowned. "Getting a phone is like getting a ring off a finger. I don't do close contact."

I gave him a pointed look. "He's got to go to sleep eventually."

Jimmy unfolded the sheet of paper and scanned it quickly. "Who is it?"

"College student, rich kid. Harmless, the dealing is just at NYU."

Jimmy shook his head and slid the paper back my way. "Nah. I'll pass. People like that do crazy shit. He's probably got a gun he doesn't know how to use in his nightstand."

"Please," I said, and it came out exactly as desperate as I felt.

"This is for my daughter. She's—" My voice cracked. "I need that phone."

Jimmy looked uncomfortable with my display of emotion. He made a pensive, pinched face as he looked up at the mirror above the bar, then took another long pull of his beer. He reached forward and snatched the paper, jammed it in the breast pocket of his windbreaker, already sliding out of the booth. "One whiff this thing is going south and I'm out."

To my surprise, Aidan was already at Bar Six when I arrived. Not even a little late. He was sitting at a table in the back with two glasses of red wine, which was . . . weird. This wasn't a date. And he was sitting so upright, like he was on his very best behavior. He waved and smiled brightly when he saw me. The money. He was going to ask about it again; that was for sure.

"Kyle and Cleo are back together," I said, trying to get to the point quickly so Aidan didn't derail us with his own agenda. "I have confirmation."

He shrugged. "I guess we could have seen that coming." As if he hadn't been maintaining I was being paranoid this whole time. It was straight-up gaslighting.

"Anyway, you should know Kyle has evidence on his phone of Cleo selling." It was hard to hear the words out loud, but I forced myself to keep going. "Evidence that he can hand over to the police anytime he wants."

"Really?" Finally a hint of concern in Aidan's eyes.

"I'm handling it," I said.

Aidan made a face. "Handling it how?"

"I'm getting the phone," I said. Which I was hoping was a burner. So that the photos were only there and not already all over the cloud.

"What do you mean?" Aidan gave me a questioning look.

There weren't a lot of legal options for obtaining a phone that didn't belong to you.

"The details don't matter," I said. "But I should have it by the morning. But we still need to get her away from Kyle, permanently, Aidan."

"I'll help in any way I can. I mean that, Kat," he said, and sincerely it seemed. "I know I've been—listen, I'm trying here."

"I know." I stood and took a swig of wine before setting the glass back down. I wanted to get out of there before he started asking for the money again and things turned tense. This had actually been almost pleasant.

"You're not staying?" Aidan looked wounded.

"No," I said. "I have somewhere else I need to be."

Cleo's dot on my phone was heading east across the NYU campus. *Please, don't let her be making another drop.* I didn't think I could handle watching that again. When the dot stopped at the Bobst Library, I slowed my pace down Sixth Avenue and loosened my grip on the phone.

But it wasn't until I spotted Cleo through the library's glass façade that I allowed myself to relax. She was inside with her friend Nadine, both had headphones on, hunched over their books like regular old college kids. Occasionally, they'd look up and exchange some knowing look or point to something on one of their phones. I liked Nadine. She was a good kid, a solid one. The kind I could not imagine would ever date a drug dealer, much less deal drugs herself.

When a boy in a black baseball hat and puffy white jacket appeared at Cleo and Nadine's table, all I could think was *No.* I moved closer. Yes, it was definitely Kyle. He knocked on the table. Cleo looked up in his direction—not surprised or scared. Not pleased, either. More like she had been expecting him. Kyle said something, and then turned to leave. He didn't give a shit how many times I warned him, did he? He was going to keep coming after her, forever.

Cleo returned to her books. Nadine stared at Kyle as he walked away. Once he was out of sight, she leaned in to ask Cleo something. Maybe *What was that about?* But Cleo just shook her head without looking up.

A moment later, the door to the library burst open and there was Kyle sauntering down the steps, pants ridiculously low, baseball cap lopsided on his head. Walking right past me like he didn't have a care in the world. And there I was, following him again. Even though I was angry enough that it was a bad idea. Even though . . . what was it, exactly, that I planned to do?

The knife in my bag. I knew better than to let my mind go there. Except there I was, thinking of it, following Kyle like I had a purpose, an endgame in mind. I picked up my pace when he turned left, heading downtown instead of west toward his apartment. Right on Mercer, deeper into the shadows now. I wondered for a moment if Kyle knew I was behind him. If he was leading me into the darkness on purpose. And then there he was, turning into a building, a dorm on the corner of Third Street and LaGuardia Place. Or he was trying to. I darted across the street and watched him flash his ID, but the security guard shook his head and held up a hand before turning back inside. Rejecting Kyle specifically, or any visitor who didn't live there—it was impossible to tell.

Kyle shook his head, then shouted something after the guy before pulling out his phone to send a text. He seemed to wait for a response, then texted some more. He'd be on the move again soon, disappearing into the darkness of the quiet side streets. I could put an end to this myself, right now, without anyone seeing. The world would be better off without Kyle; there was no doubt about that. But then, what would become of me?

Because this would be so different from that night. Back then, I was only a kid. And I'd been scared and in pain and so confused standing in the bathroom the next morning. When I looked down at the blood on my legs, I thought, *You wanted this.* And then I thought, *No, you didn't.* I didn't even know what *this* was, exactly. There was just him and his threats and me and all that rage. And the knife on the bedside table that he had used to slice a lime.

But this was me calculating. With time to think.

I watched now as Kyle lit a cigarette and propped himself against the building. A moment later, a couple emerged, arms crossed, shivering—the guy scruffily cute, the girl pretty and blond and, oddly, barefoot. It wasn't until the guy fist-bumped Kyle that I recognized the girl: Annie, Janine's daughter? Yes, it was. It was most definitely her. I watched the quick, furtive exchange between her and Kyle, looked again at her bare feet. Annie, buying drugs from Kyle.

Annie was a good kid, though. She was obviously in over her head. I needed to warn her away from Kyle. I could do that one good thing.

The security guard who had rebuffed Kyle so emphatically seemed to perk up when I stepped inside, but then he tried to act casual, like he hadn't even noticed me. Demure damsel in distress—it was the obvious way to go. I smiled tentatively, twisted my hands. "I'm sorry, do you think you could help me with something maybe?"

He didn't hesitate to call up and tell Annie that she needed to come back downstairs, immediately. He even nodded knowingly when I shook my head instead of offering my name—*I got it,* he seemed to say.

"Because there's somebody here who needs to see you," he said curtly. "No, not that guy. This is an *adult.* I suggest you come down here right away, or maybe I'll tell campus security about your last visitor. They love to search rooms."

When he hung up, he tugged his jacket straight and gave me an officious nod. "She's on her way."

"Thank you so much," I said. "I really appreciate your doing that."

"These kids . . . someone needs to teach them a little respect. Their parents sure as hell won't." I smiled but said nothing. Hoped Annie would get down there quickly, before he worked up the nerve to hit on me.

"I'll go stand over there." I pointed to a spot on the opposite wall. "Out of the way."

A moment later, Annie charged off the elevator, looking wired and exhausted. High, maybe. I was hardly an expert in such things. She waved her arms accusatorily in the direction of the guard. "What's the fucking emergency?"

She was so changed from the sweet, quiet girl I remembered. The one who wore pastel sweaters and headbands long after they were in style at school. The girl who'd never seemed to turn dark and angry the way Cleo had. Annie was more striking now, but harder, too. And in a different way than Cleo. Cleo's tough exterior—the black makeup, the many piercings, and the goth clothes—was like a suit of armor she wore. This new hardness in Annie seemed born from the inside out.

"Hey, calm down," the guard admonished, then gestured in my direction.

It took Annie a moment to register who I was. Then she scowled as she walked toward me.

"What are you doing here?"

"Annie, Kyle is not a good person," I said. "I thought you should know."

"Wow, no kidding." Annie's affect was so flat. It was like all the life had been pressed out of her. "Golly, gee."

"No, I mean he keeps pictures of his customers on his phone," I explained. "As insurance. It's . . . risky."

Her scowl deepened. "Risky?"

"Being a customer." Like she really had no clue what I was talking about. Or she didn't care. "He could use the pictures against you."

"Is that seriously why you called me down here? To tell me *that*?"

"I was trying to help." I waited for it to occur to her that I must have been spying on them. But her face betrayed nothing but a vacant kind of anger. "Your mom would want to know if you were in a bad place. She could help. She would. I'm sure."

I'd gone there faster than I'd meant to. It sounded like a threat—tell your mom or I will.

Annie worked her jaw. "My mom stays out of my business because she trusts me," she said. But there was the tiniest flicker of something in her eyes, a hint of shame, possibly. "Anyway, maybe instead of harassing me, you should worry a little more about what your own daughter is up to. Who she's fucking, for instance."

"Excuse me?" I kept my voice calm, but my mind was racing. Cleo was not only dealing for Kyle; she was back *with* him. Of course she was.

From the little smirk on Annie's lips, she could tell she'd gotten to me. "Yup. Saw them with my own eyes. Or saw Cleo. The guy had his back turned. They were mauling each other up against the side of a building where I guess they thought no one could see them. But it was near the bike path on the West Side Highway. It might not be campus, but there are still a million people over there. Yet another brand-new boyfriend who Cleo practically fucks in public. You must be so proud."

CLEO

I dressed the part. Or at least I tried to. I mean, what does one wear to confront a famous CEO who may have attacked your mother? The priority was an outfit nice enough to loiter in front of a fancy doorman building without being shooed away. And I don't really have a lot of options for "respectable Upper West Side young lady," especially because I'm not 100 percent sure it's even a thing. Upper East Side? Definitely. Even I know that's some version of Chanel. But Upper West Side is trickier. It's more down-to-earth than Upper East, but not Brooklyn earthy, which is slightly (and only slightly) cooler. Upper West Side is like *I didn't thrift this, because I'm above that. But I also didn't spend stupid money, because I'm above that, too. I'm rich, but I'm also a good Democrat.* Even my mom follows the NYC neighborhood uniform—she's "working Park Slope mom" through and through. Think Vince sneakers that cost two hundred dollars. Never Gucci, even though she could afford them, because that would be in poor taste. Her Chloé flats are exactly it, the gray canvas ones that she is *always* wearing . . . or was.

So here I am, leaning against the side of the Dakota building on Central Park West in the frilly, not-me yellow Free People sundress my mom insisted I buy for my grandmother Nell's eightieth birthday party. I feel vaguely ridiculous, exactly like I did at the party.

I'm waiting for Vivienne Voxhall—woman of many vivid threats, who looks like a very tall, even thinner Anna Wintour. Luckily, she is easily googleable. Article after article about one high-powered job after the next. She was recently sued by her co-op board for renovations she undertook despite lack of approval. The complaint provided me with her home address—the Dakota, at Seventy-second and Central Park West—as well as allegations of familiar-sounding threats and, in one case, the record of a physical altercation between Vivienne and another board member. It was just a single shove in a fancy elevator, but it's enough to keep Vivienne at the top of my suspect list—that plus the small matter of her death threat.

I stand near enough to the entrance to see people coming and going, but I'm hoping far enough away not to be conspicuous even in my dumb yellow dress. Luckily the sun is going down, and the doorman who came on at 7:00 p.m. seems more interested in sneaking in discreet vaping sessions than in hassling me. I'm watching him pull out his vape pen again when I spot Vivienne Voxhall crossing the street. She's even skinnier than in photos; in her tight black dress, she looks like a huge praying mantis in a tube sock. She has her phone in one hand, earbuds in, and she's shouting at whoever is on the other end.

Get off the phone. Get off the phone. Otherwise, I'll have no choice but to interrupt her, which I'm guessing isn't going to go well. I hear her snap, "I know you heard what I said, Bob. And I *know* you know what's going to happen if you don't listen." Now she's almost at the entrance to the building. "So put on your fucking big-boy pants, tuck your tiny dick up wherever you hide it, and let's get—"

"Excuse me, Vivienne?" I say, bracing for impact as I step into her path. "I'm Kat McHugh's daughter."

Vivienne peers at me like I'm an alien life-form. The corners of her mouth lift, but it's not exactly a smile.

"Bob, you heard me. Now do what I said," she continues, then taps to end the call, eyes still locked on mine as she drops her phone into her purse. "Now . . . *who* are you?"

It feels like a trap.

"I'm Kat McHugh's daughter," I repeat with an unfortunate waver to my voice. "She's a lawyer at—"

"Oh, I know who Kat is," she says. "I just can't believe she sent her daughter here. It's—"

"She didn't send me here. I—"

"*Brave,*" she finishes, eyes widening at my interruption. "Good lord, you do look exactly like her. She mentioned that once." She leans in so close, like she's checking to see how I smell. "Except . . ." She motions dismissively to my dress. "Never pretend to be someone you're not. It's ineffective. And it undermines your credibility."

My eyes start to burn. I'm not even sure exactly why. I blink a few times, but that only seems to make it worse. Vivienne looks away, shifts her weight, then clears her throat.

"Anyway, let me guess. You want an internship?"

"An intern—"

"Your mom shouldn't have sent you here when she knows I'm not happy with her. So don't go around telling people *I'm* mean or unsupportive of young women or a dragon lady." She lifts her chin defiantly. "That's exactly how rumors get started. And your mom *should* be calling me back. I'm her *client*. She can't ignore me because I got a little mad." She shrugs. "I'm entitled to my feelings, just like anyone else."

"You texted that you were going to *kill her.*"

"That was weeks ago. And it's confidential!" Vivienne shouts. "What were you doing reading her texts with clients? Those are all attorney-client-privileged." And then her eyes narrow. "Oh, wait, you're trying to blackmail me, aren't you? Your mom doesn't even know you're here. Are you hooked on Oxy or fentanyl or bath salts or some shit?"

"No!" I shout back, a little more loudly than I intended. I can see the doorman watching us now out of the corner of his eye.

But Vivienne's not even listening. She's digging around in her bag, muttering to herself about fucking lawyers fucking thinking that they know more than everybody else. She stabs at her phone and puts it to her ear. "Your mother better hope that you read those texts *without* her permission, or I swear to God I'll have her disbarred."

"She's not going to answer," I say.

"We'll see about that."

"She's missing. Her phone is off. She *can't* answer."

Vivienne still has the phone to her ear. "What are you talking about? I just spoke to her." The color drains from her face in a way that would be very hard to fake. She didn't know my mom is missing. "Well, not *just*—but like a day ago."

"She disappeared last night. The police are investigating."

"The police?" My mom's outgoing voice mail message is playing on Vivienne's phone. She sounds very small and very far away on the other end. Vivienne ends the call and puts her phone in her bag. "Disappeared? Wait, what happened to her?"

I shrug. "We don't know."

"You don't know?" She sounds annoyed still, but she looks worried. "So far the *Times* hasn't run their article. I haven't even heard from that reporter in like . . . actually, maybe forty-eight hours. Hmm . . . The least your mom could do, though, is call and actually confirm that it's been handled, instead of leaving me wondering." But her heart isn't really in it anymore.

"Did you hear what I said?" I snap. "She's *missing*. There was blood in our house and broken glass. There's a bloody shoe. My mom is *gone*. What is wrong with you?"

She shoots me an angry look, then frowns as she fidgets with her bag. Finally, she looks away. "Well, how was I supposed to know any of that?"

"So *you* don't know anything about what happened to her?"

"You think *I* did something to her?" She laughs—brittle and sharp.

I shrug. "Somebody did . . ."

A storm cloud passes across Vivienne's face. "Fair enough," she says. "If I were you, I'd come for me, too. That's . . . logical. What day did this happen?"

"Yesterday. Around six-thirty p.m."

She pulls her phone out of her bag, consults her calendar. "I was on a Zoom conference call with Sidney then. People actually saw my face, and I was in my office. You can confirm that," she says quite calmly. "And I mean that—you should. I would if I were you. Also, you should know I threaten to kill people all the time. And all of them are still alive. At least as far as I know. Anyway, whatever happened to your mom didn't have anything to do with me. Besides, her vanishing only hurts me. It's not like I can find someone else to do the kind of thing your mom does."

"What does that mean—what kind of thing?"

"You know, clean up," she says, waving an imaginary magic wand.

"Cleanup of patents?"

"Ha. That's funny—patents." She gives another brittle little laugh "My situation was patently something; that's for sure."

"Please, can you—" My voice cracks again. I can't help it. I can't take one more bad surprise. "I don't understand what you're talking about. My mom is a patent attorney at Blair, Stevenson. And I'm not sure why you think this is funny, because none of it is funny to me."

Vivienne searches my face skeptically for a moment.

"Your mother isn't a patent lawyer. She's a fixer," she says, the bite gone entirely from her voice. "She helps with problems that can't be fixed in a court of law. You know, the tawdry kind."

"*My* mom? She wouldn't do anything that's even in, like, a gray zone." But I feel queasy.

"I agree that your mom is buttoned-up. I was actually worried about that when Mark first introduced us," Vivienne says. "I was like, *this* woman is going to sort shit out for me? She looks like she should be heading up the PTA in Greenwich. But Mark assured me there was more to her than met the eye. And if I hadn't seen it myself, I wouldn't have believed it. But she's good. She showed up at this one guy's job to get information we needed. Huge mountain of a guy, worked in construction. Anyway, she scared the shit out of him somehow, and suddenly he would not shut up. Told us everything we wanted to know. She's also not afraid of me—which is extremely aggravating. But I respect her. From what I hear, she's tangled with a lot of powerful people in one way or another, though. You could have a long list of suspects."

"What other people?"

"I don't know *names*. No one wants these kinds of things getting out—sex, drugs, who knows what else." She thinks for a moment. "Your mom is always very discreet. And nonjudgmental. I appreciate that . . . Anyway, I'd find her other clients. I'm not saying any of them are violent, but it's also not impossible. Somebody caught with an underage prostitute or a hit-and-run, for instance . . ."

"She helped people with those things?" I can't believe my mom kept all this a secret. That she did any of it in the first place. I can't decide if I feel impressed or betrayed.

"Again, I don't know what other people did, exactly," Vivienne says. "I'm just saying these are people with money and power and *a lot* to lose."

"Her boss has been really nice. He's trying to help—but he didn't say anything about this. Actually, he kind of lied when I asked about her job. He definitely said it was patents."

"Well, it's not exactly the kind of work they hand out bar association awards for."

"And now her assistant is having some kind of episode and—"

"Episode?" Vivienne makes a face. "You mean Julia? What are you talking about?"

"Jules. Yeah. They had to fire her."

"Huh." Vivienne considers this, looking up toward the sky.

"That doesn't sound right. I talked to Jules like a day ago, and she seemed absolutely fine."

"And now her phone's been shut off. I tried to call her a little while ago. I have no idea how I would even find her."

Vivienne leans toward me. "Now *that* is something I can help with."

I sit on the edge of the tufted eggplant-colored sectional in Vivienne's fun house of a living room—there's a shag-covered armchair and large cushions on the floor, for sitting, apparently, the color the same as the bright orange poppies on the wallpaper between the massive windows overlooking Central Park West. Her fingers have been flying over her keyboard.

Vivienne snorts quietly, shakes her head. "You'd think that law firms would know better. Their personnel files are basically hanging wide open." She writes something down on a piece of paper. "Jules Kovacis. That's her home number and her address."

I take the piece of paper, look down at the address and nod. Washington Heights. "Thanks," I say to Vivienne.

"Listen, I know I haven't always been so easy on your mom. But I've always admired her. She's a fighter. You ask me, not enough women know how to fight." She's quiet for a moment. "Anyway, call me if you need anything else. I am very good at finding a way around almost any firewall."

The beautiful tree-lined block Jules lives on looks a lot like our street in Park Slope. Except up in Washington Heights, everything is on a slightly larger scale—the sidewalks a bit wider, the brownstones, too. It's also *really* quiet. Too quiet. There's not a soul in sight. In New York City, there's nothing good about empty—not empty streets or empty storefronts or empty subway cars.

I'm feeling pretty jumpy by the time I find Jules's building, one of the best maintained on the block. There's a FOR SALE sign out front. *Luxury Two-Bedroom Unit!* it proclaims with a *Please Inquire* and a phone number.

I look up toward the windows as I ring Jules's bell, 3F. No answer. I ring the buzzer again and lean back to see if the lights are on in her unit.

"You missed her." I whirl around, to find a short white man with a very thick mustache and a snug off-white tank top standing behind me. He's holding a broom. Maybe the super.

"Do you know when she'll be back?"

"Few days, maybe a few weeks." He shrugs. "Just left."

"Just?" I ask, looking up toward her dark windows again. "As in suddenly?"

He busies himself with sweeping the sidewalk. "I didn't say that." He sounds wary now.

"But was she . . . scared, do you think?" I ask.

He stops sweeping and looks up at me. "And who are you, exactly?"

There's a jingle when he shifts the broom between his hands— the keys on his hip. He could have the keys to Jules's apartment.

"Babysitter," I say, my voice rising at the end like it's a question, not an answer. *Crap.* "I left a book and I really need it for this big test I have . . . tomorrow."

Even I don't believe me.

"Oh yeah?"

Pivot. I can almost hear my mom's voice in my head. *Pivot.* The truth. It's the only way to go. It's what my mom would do. I feel sure of it.

"Sorry, that's not true. I'm not the babysitter. Jules worked with my mom," I say. "My mom is missing. And I'm so worried, and then Jules texted me about some kind of danger I might be in, people in cars that might be following me. But she didn't get a chance to explain, and I really need her to."

"Who's your mom?" He still sounds skeptical.

"Kat McHugh."

His body uncoils. "Ah. Kat. Yes. She's a good one. Jules always says she'd do anything for Kat." He leans toward me, lowers his voice. "There was a car, *here,* today, with two men asking for Jules. That's why she left."

Suddenly, it's hard to breathe.

"I'm really, really worried about my mom," I choke out. "Can you help me, please?"

A minute later, I'm trudging up the stairs behind him. He unlocks the door to Jules's apartment and steps back.

"Take your time. I will be downstairs with my wife. Knock when you're finished and I'll lock up."

It's a typical railroad-style apartment. The furniture in the living room is mismatched and dated—a bright yellow couch with a crocheted blanket folded across the back, a pair of faded tan Naugahyde wing chairs. It's sweet, though, homey. There are framed photographs on a wall of Jules, her daughter, and people who look like the other members of a very large, warm family—vacations, holidays, lots of hugging and smiling.

In the area Jules uses as a dining room I spot a file box in a corner beneath the tall front windows. It's labeled *Blair, Stevenson.*

I sit on the floor in front of the box and lift the lid.

Inside are manila folders, all labeled with black Sharpie in clean, careful letters and lined up neatly inside hanging folders. *Research, Impact Statements, Expert Reports, Court Filings: Jane Doe et al. vs. Darden Pharmaceuticals.* That last folder contains copies of a complaint in a lawsuit related to some drug. I don't see my mom's name anywhere, and her law firm isn't listed as the defense attorney on the complaint. But then I find a file labeled *MDL Certification.* The new law firm on these documents is Blair, Stevenson.

At the far back of the box there's a correspondence folder. Inside are emails from somebody who worked at Darden, claiming the company knew that there were problems with the drug. Doesn't look good for them—but how is Jules involved?

And then I get to the last email in the folder, addressed to my mom, dated a few weeks ago. More accurately, it's the beginning of an email. *Dear Kat, Where to start . . .* But then that's it. That's the whole message.

There's a loud bang downstairs, maybe the front door. I stand, the box in my hands. I suddenly feel very nervous in here alone.

I step out of Jules's apartment, resting the box against my hip so I can quietly close the door behind me. I stand at the top of the stairs, listening. Silence. Could have been someone heading out instead of coming in.

Still, I start down carefully, one flight, then two. It isn't until I round the last turn that I can see a figure at the bottom, leaning against the wall near the door. Detective Wilson.

And she does *not* look happy. "Care to tell me what the hell you were doing up there?" She eyes the box.

"Not really," I say.

"I bet." She opens the door and motions me outside. "Let's go."

We sit in her unmarked sedan while I explain as much as I can, which is mostly a collection of random facts. A rundown of where I've been is unnecessary because Wilson has apparently been following me since I left my dorm. She watched me outside Vivienne Voxhall's building, managed to track me down in Washington Heights. I'm getting the sense that she's been watching me a lot. I explain what I now know about my mom's job and why I ended up at Jules's.

"I didn't find anything about any of the other people my mom was doing this fixing for. But, like I said, Jules was really freaked-out, and maybe she's just crazy or maybe she's not. I did find a bunch of documents." I gesture to the box in her back seat. "I don't know what they mean."

She glances back at the box. "You found them where?"

"In Jules's apartment."

She holds up a hand. "You stole something?"

"Borrowed. I didn't break in," I said. "The super opened the door."

"Which *he* shouldn't have done." She eyeballs me. "And what did you find?"

"Documents about some lawsuit against a drug manufacturer," I say. "Jules has a whole box of legal documents all about this one lawsuit. My mom's law firm is defending them. And there were emails from an employee threatening to expose the fact that the company lied, and another one from that employee to my mom, but it was only her name; there was no text—which is also weird."

"Fine, I'll take a look. But I want to be sure it's crystal clear that you are not to come close to breaking any laws trying to 'help' here. You'd be surprised what a defense attorney can get excluded, claiming we put you up to it," she says. "What you should have done when you first learned about any of this was call me, Cleo."

"I know, I—"

"No, apparently you *don't* know. You think your biggest problem is that you can't find the person responsible for all this. But you know what'll be a bigger problem? If you *do* find whoever it is." She gestures toward the building. "Up in some apartment alone where no one even knows to look. You do remember the blood on the floor in your home, right? You think this person will be happy if and when you do find them?"

My throat feels raw again. I don't especially care if Wilson sees me crying—it might even make her back off a little. But I am afraid if I start crying now, I might never stop.

"I can't do nothing," I say. "I feel too guilty. I've gotten so much wrong about her . . . and I've been so mean to her for so long. What if . . . what if that's the last thing she remembers about me?"

Wilson sighs heavily. "Your mom knows you love her. From one ungrateful daughter to another—they always know how we feel, even when we don't." She taps the edge of the steering wheel with her index finger. "Listen . . . I came to find you initially because I need you to confirm your timeline for the evening your mom disappeared. You arrived at the house at six-thirty p.m. Is that right?"

"Seriously?" I shoot her a look. "You still think maybe it was me?"

"No. I do not," she says, looking right at me. "I never did. But I do need to know the time you got there."

"Six-thirty, yes. I guess," I say.

"And your dad says that you called him at around six-fifty-five p.m.?" Her tone is very deliberate. "Does that also sound right?"

"I didn't check the clock. But I looked around inside, found the shoe and everything. And I was supposed to get there at six-thirty. I was probably a little late—I usually am. So when all is said and done? Six-fifty-five could be right."

Wilson nods, frowns. "Because we checked with the airline, and it seems your dad's plane actually landed at four-thirty p.m."

It takes me a second to process what she's telling me. Didn't my dad tell me that he'd just walked off a plane when I first called him? Now there's nearly an hour unaccounted for, during which time my mom disappeared.

"Okay," I say carefully. "I don't know the details of his flight times."

"A neighbor says they saw *you* head into your house about five-thirty p.m. Is it possible you somehow got the time wrong?"

"Possible that I was a whole hour *early*? I've never been early for anything in my life, let alone by a full hour," I say. "Who told you that?"

"Older gentleman, lives right next door?" she says. "He says that he saw you going up the steps then. He described the clothes you were wearing."

"Oh, you mean *George*?" I ask. "George has no idea where he is half the time. I mean, I feel bad for him and he's a good person and everything, but he's not exactly on point when it comes to details like time. He always used to yell about the garbage not getting picked up when it had been the day before. My mom said that was how they first picked up on the Alzheimer's. He was losing whole days."

She shrugs. "He wasn't exactly happy being disturbed or letting us sit at his kitchen table. But he seemed lucid enough."

"That's George—he comes and then completely goes. He used to be a kind of famous doctor. But his wife died, and then he got sick. My mom checks in on him most weekends—she isn't bothered by the hostility." Because that's the way she is—kind. Maybe that's the same reason she hovers over me. Maybe it is just her trying to show love. "Anyway, in exchange, George does things like sweep up our yard, like without asking, which is sometimes nice and sometimes kind of . . . aggressive. But his kids have, like, abandoned him . . . Maybe he saw my mom coming home at five-thirty; we do look a lot alike."

She makes a clucking sound. "I suppose that could be. Now is there *anything* else you've left out?"

I try not to squirm under the weight of her stare, knowing I need to come clean. It's not too late to start telling the actual truth for once in my whole stupid life.

"There's this guy, Kyle, I was seeing. He's . . . not the best person. My mom didn't like that we were together. And he knew she was the reason I broke up with him. That was months ago, though. So I really don't think—"

"How many months?"

"Like six?"

"Six months?" She pulls a notebook from her center console. "But you still stay in touch?"

"No."

"You're sure?" she pressed.

"I'm sure." I hate how defensive I sound.

"Mmm. Okay. What's his last name?"

"Lynch."

"And you know this *Kyle Lynch* from where?"

"NYU. He's a student."

"A student, huh?" She sounds skeptical.

"Yeah, but he's . . . he's also into some other stuff."

"What other stuff?"

"He's a dealer. Not big time, only on campus to the other students." I shift uncomfortably in the seat. "I used to help him sometimes."

"I see," Wilson says, raising her eyebrows slightly as she scribbles in her notebook.

"Anyway, you should check him out, but it would be good if he doesn't know it's because of me. It could make my life . . . hard," I say. But I need to get the rest out, to say all of it. "Also, my dad is or was—he's been having an affair."

"I see," she says quietly.

"I still don't think he'd ever hurt my mom, though," I say. That's still true, but it does feel different when I say it this time. Like maybe I believe it just a little less.

"I understand," Detective Wilson says, and I'm pretty sure I hear pity in her voice.

I think back again to the beach, but not to the day when I learned to swim. The time years earlier, when I nearly drowned. I remember it only in flashes: the way the sand burned my feet, the roar of the waves like a train. Then the terror—the world upside down, the burning pain. Water up my nose, the rocks gouging my knees. That horrible snap of whiplash as I was yanked by the water. *This is dead,* I remember thinking. I'd only just learned what the word meant. And it was so much worse than anybody had said.

But I'm thinking now about what I don't remember—anyone trying to stop me from running into the water. No one shouted *Wait!* Or called my name. No one chased after me. It was only me, sprinting headlong into the roiling sea.

A lifeguard pulled me out. His blond hair hanging down in front of my eyes was all I registered when I came to. And the smell of coconut sunscreen. My chest hurt for days from the compressions. Later, my dad leaned in close and made me promise never to tell my mom, like it was a special secret we shared.

"My dad also wanted to borrow money from my mom, for his movie." And there it is, the last of his secrets I've been keeping. "And she said no."

I meet eyes with Detective Wilson and it feels for a moment like she's holding me in midair.

"Except now—my dad somehow has the money. Her money."

"Oh," she says. "Well, isn't that something."

"Yes," I say. "I think it could be."

December 1, 1992

He asked me to take a walk outside after club let out. We're not allowed to leave the building, except at designated times to go specific places. But Haven House isn't a prison; it's a school. He pointed that out—not to pressure me, he said. But because he didn't think it was right.

Outside, it was so cold that our breath hung in heavy white clouds as we headed across the yard toward the trees.

And in that moment, I didn't feel anymore like somebody stuck living at Haven House. I felt like an ordinary girl, taking a walk to nowhere with a boy she liked. Normal—I wasn't sure I'd ever felt that way before.

I thanked Reed for doing that for me. And you know what he said? That I did that for him, *too.*

And then, as we stepped inside the trees, it just happened. He finally kissed me.

KATRINA

TWO DAYS BEFORE

Back in Park Slope, there was an envelope addressed to me, dropped through the mail slot. I locked the front door behind me, then sat down on a stool at the kitchen island to open it.

Inside were Doug's messages, the ones I'd asked Ahmed at Digitas to get his hands on. I hesitated, looking down at the stack of messages, so many and only from the last five days. There would be some from me in there. Was I also a little worried I might find messages to or from other women? Yes, maybe. Doug and I hadn't had any official discussions about being exclusive, but the thought of learning that he hadn't been made me sad.

But it turned out that it was hard to identify who had sent anything. There were only phone numbers associated with the messages, not names. I was able to pick out his daughter's number by the number of messages and the consistently snarky edge to her responses. Snarky, but not unkind. You could sense the love buried underneath—or I could. I don't think Doug had known that, though, which was perhaps the worst thing of all. He died never knowing that he'd had a fighting chance to get his daughter back.

Maybe I still had a chance with Cleo, or at least more of one than I'd thought. I would simply keep trying. But with an open heart and gentleness. And honesty, for once. I needed to tell Cleo that I'd threatened Kyle on more than one occasion. I needed to admit that there was a chance that my actions had put her in *more* danger, not less.

How about dinner? I texted her. I wanted a commitment. *Would you come home? Please.*

An ellipsis appeared almost instantly but then disappeared. I squeezed my phone, waiting. Hoping.

I know you don't want to come, I added. *I understand, Cleo. I've made a lot of mistakes. And I'm not asking you not to be mad at me. Or to forgive me. I'm not trying to tell you how to feel. I'm only asking you to come to dinner. There's something I need to tell you.*

I stared at the phone, and then finally: *Okay. Dinner. Sunday. 6:30. At home.*

My heart surged with relief. But I knew better than to over-react. Or I was at least trying to learn. Aidan was wrong about so much, but he was right that Cleo wasn't a little girl anymore. I couldn't force her to do anything. I never should have tried in the first place.

Great!

I turned back to the printout of Doug's texts. It was a lot to sift through. But I eventually found the one with the threat about Advantage—$500,000 was what they'd asked for, exactly as Doug had said. A stupidly huge amount of money. It was the mark of amateurs. Or . . . people who weren't after money at all. I was relieved to see that Doug's responses to the demands—three in total, of escalating intensity—matched exactly what he'd told me. And all of it within only a few days. The last message he got certainly did seem like a threat: *You have 24 hours to get us the money. This is your last warning.* Doug's car accident was hours later. Was it possible that the timing was a coincidence? Sure. But it didn't seem likely.

And then one of the last texts he received, from a 917 number I had no way of identifying: *Doug, could you come meet me? I know it's late. My apologies. But it's important. We need to talk. You know that.*

And Doug's reply, the last he would ever send: *Where and what time?*

Now would be best. 126 Nepperhan Avenue. 11:00 p.m.

The address in Yonkers belonged to a small, very run-down strip mall—liquor store, nail salon, dry cleaner's, according to Google Maps. All of which would have been closed at that hour. A late-night, last-minute meeting was suspicious under any circumstances, especially given the location and the fact that Doug had died on his way there—a setup, it seemed.

I called Ahmed.

"I'm pretty sure my work here is done," he said good-naturedly.

"I know. Thank you," I said. "I do need one last quick thing. A reverse number lookup. The name associated with a cell number."

"No good deed goes unpunished, huh? Okay, fine. Give me the number."

He texted back a few minutes later, presumably having paid off some cell phone company employee. That was the fastest way to get a number.

Number belongs to a Phil Beaumont, corporate account. Darden Pharmaceuticals.

I texted Mark the next morning after a night of fitful sleep. *We need to talk about Phil.*

My phone rang almost instantly. Good. A call would be more efficient. And I was done splitting hairs.

"What is it?" He sounded very tense, but short of alarmed.

"Doug Sinclair was on his way to meet Phil the night he died." I waited for it to sink in. Surely, Mark would connect the dots on his own.

"And?" he said.

"What do you mean, *and*?" It came out sharper than I'd intended. "You already knew that?"

"I did," he said. "Doug Sinclair was having problems at work, competency issues, as we've discussed."

"So the Darden general counsel asked to meet him in a Yonkers strip mall at eleven o'clock at night?" I asked. "And now he's . . . dead?"

"Apparently," Mark said, a tinge of exasperation in his voice.

"Mark, seriously, what the fuck?" It had popped out. Mark wasn't the delicate type, but I also didn't usually swear at him.

"Listen, it's terrible what happened to this guy. He had a daughter, I know. And Phil feels bad, of course, that the accident happened on his way to that meeting. It's an awful, regrettable tragedy. But Doug Sinclair is not our client, Kat—Darden is. As you are aware, we have a fiduciary obligation to do what is in their best interest."

"Right," I said, because Mark *was* correct, technically. About Darden's being our client. But I wasn't buying that this meeting with Phil and Doug's accident were some sort of coincidence. It was utter bullshit.

"Sounds like you have the phone records now? I'm assuming that's where this new information about Phil came from—is there anything in there about this blackmail situation?"

"Not that I've seen," I said, the lie a reflex. I was beginning to wonder whether Mark's friendship with Phil, or the firm's financial situation, was clouding his judgment. "I need to go through them more closely."

"Great. Come into the office," Mark said. "We can do it together."

I crossed my arms, even though I was alone in my house. Or *was* I even alone? I wondered if there was a black sedan out there, watching me. All of this was suddenly feeling far too close to home.

"Okay," I lied. "I'll be there as soon as I can."

* * *

With a fair amount of I'm-a-worried-mom cajoling, I eventually got the security guard in Cleo's dorm to confirm that she'd swiped in that evening at about 7:00 p.m. and had still not swiped back out an hour later. Now darkness was settling quickly as I sat on a sidewalk bench alongside the quiet end of Washington Square Park, near one of those unexpected New York City honeysuckle bushes, the kind that always made me feel transported to some bucolic upstate town. I was facing Cleo's dorm across the street, watching to make sure she stayed safe and sound and inside. I was also waiting for Janine. She'd called while I was on my way into Manhattan. She wouldn't say why she wanted to talk, only that she was happy to meet by campus—circumventing my excuse for why I couldn't meet right then in Park Slope.

I racked my brain trying to think of what Janine could want. After an exhausting day smoothing the feathers of cranky clients, I wasn't sure I could muster the energy for any more drama. Could it be that she knew about Annie and Kyle? I was agonizing over whether to tell her Annie was using. What if she already knew and had decided she was okay with it? She was the cool mom, after all.

"Kat!" Janine was striding toward me, dressed in jeans and red platform sandals, her hair back in a chic red-and-yellow bohemian head scarf.

"What are you doing over here, looming in the shadows?" Janine laughed when she finally reached me. But then she looked up to where I'd been looking. "Oh, I see," she said. She sat down on the bench, resting her Balenciaga bag on the bench between us, the brand name emblazoned on the side. "I wondered why you wanted to meet by the park. Which window is Cleo's?"

Janine's face had softened. She knew exactly what I was doing: stalking my own daughter.

"Second from the corner."

"At least her light is on," she said. "Do we know whether she's in there?"

We—such a little thing, not to be alone with my worry for that small moment.

I cleared my throat. "I'm pretty sure she's home."

"Well, at least there's that," Janine said, like this entire situation was par for the course. "Eighty percent of what's dangerous is out in the world. Okay, maybe sixty percent." She checked her watch. "I told Annie I'd meet up with her and some friends for dinner. She's dying to take me to this little Thai place she found."

I shook my head. "Cleo would *never* take me out to eat with her friends."

"I *am* picking up the check."

"I think Cleo would pay me *not* to have dinner with her."

"Ha, well, Annie does plenty of mean things to me, too. Don't worry. Every daughter is a monster in her own special way."

Was this a hint about Annie and the drugs? I hoped it wasn't some sort of test to see if I would offer up what I knew, because I was waiting for an actual question.

"You and Annie are like best friends. It's really incredible—I mean that." And I did.

Janine shrugged. "Some people would say that I've crossed all sorts of lines. That I treat Annie too much like a friend and that puts 'inappropriate pressure' on her and that actually makes *me* the worst mother of all."

"Oh, come on," I scoffed. "No one would say that."

"They would and they have!" She laughed. "To my face! Annie's therapist *and* my therapist were especially hard to dismiss."

"Oh," I said, and then we both laughed.

"Anyway," she went on. "The grass is always greener. We're all doing the best we can."

"You've always been so calm about all of it, though," I said. "Even when they were tiny babies. So unflappable."

"Don't confuse the ability to act calm with actually *being* calm. I didn't feel fine in those early weeks. But I also figured that admitting it would only make me feel worse."

"Well, you were good at pretending," I said, and then we were quiet for a moment. And I wondered maybe if motherhood wouldn't have felt like such a struggle if I'd been more open about how tough it was. Maybe I would have found that it wasn't some fatal flaw in me after all. "Thank you for not asking specifically what I'm worried about with Cleo tonight."

Janine smiled, her eyes going a little glassy. "The 'what' never really matters, does it? Only the 'who.' You're Cleo's mother. She's your daughter. And you love her. You're going to do what you have to, to protect her—no matter what . . ." She reached over and gave my hand a quick squeeze. "Anyway, I wanted to apologize, for the other night in the restaurant."

"What do you mean?"

"I shouldn't have said that about Kyle. I'd like to claim that I didn't mean to upset you, but . . . I've been so worried about Annie lately. I don't know what's going on, but she's so distant. When I'm worried, some mean little part of me feels better pointing to other people's problems. There's no excuse. I'm sorry. But I did want to ask you if you knew anything about where—"

My phone rang just then. A cell number I didn't recognize. "Janine, I'm sorry, do you mind?" I gestured toward Cleo's light. "I have to take this."

Janine looked a little taken aback, but then she nodded. "I'll watch her like a hawk," she said.

I stepped toward the street to answer.

"This is Tim Lyall," the voice on the other end announced. Like he was calling me back. I drew a complete blank. Who the hell was *Tim Lyall*? And then it came to me—a junior corporate partner at the firm. Sat around the corner; his assistant shared the pool with Jules. But we'd never worked together. He had no reason to be contacting me. "Jules told me to call you about Darden?" He sounded distracted, maybe irritated. It was hard to tell.

"Oh, yes. Thank you. I was hoping to match notes." My voice sounded tight, but I hoped Tim Lyall would have no way of knowing that.

"Of course," he said, his tone still unreadable. But then he hesitated for just a beat too long. I had a feeling I'd lost him. "Listen, I'm racing to catch a plane to Zurich. And need to get on a conference call. Why don't I call you once I land, when I'll have a solid window to talk."

"That's fine," I said as matter-of-factly as I could, given that I had no clue why Jules had told him to call me. "I'd appreciate it."

"Perfect. Talk soon."

I felt sure Tim Lyall planned never to call me back. And when I tried Jules again in search of an explanation, it went straight to voice mail. My next call was to the office.

"This is Kat McHugh," I said to the weekend operator. "I need to get some documents to Tim Lyall at home. Could you get me his home address?"

Janine stood up as I walked back to the bench. "Is everything okay?"

"Not really," I said. "I'm so sorry to do this, but I need to run up to the Upper East Side to pick something up. Work-related. Do you think you could wait here until I get back? I know you're supposed to meet Annie and that it's a lot to ask, but—"

"I can do it." Janine put a warm hand on my forearm. "I see how worried you are. I can absolutely do it."

"Thank you. I need to know if Cleo leaves, or"—I scrolled through my phone until I located the photo of Kyle I'd used with Jimmy—"if this person goes in?"

Her forehead scrunched as she peered at the photo. "I'll stay as long as you need me to, of course. I'll text Annie. But can you . . . Kat, what is going on? Who is that?"

"It's Kyle," I said. I hesitated, then plunged ahead. "You should probably ask Annie about him, too, Janine. I think she may know him . . . better than she should. Better than you'd want her to."

TRANSCRIPT OF RECORDED SESSION

DR. EVELYN BAUER
SESSION #4

CLEO McHUGH: I almost texted my mom after our last session. I don't know—to say hi. It's not like I suddenly forgive her or something. But I did miss her for the first time in a long time.

EVELYN BAUER: It sounds like you had a very special relationship when you were younger. Not everyone has that.

CM: I thought we did. Or she was special to me. But that was when I was little, before Charlie. As soon as I went to middle school, it was like . . . she, like, started slowly shutting off, disappearing. I used to have dreams sometimes of her getting sucked into a black hole in outer space. I didn't remember that until the other day . . .

EB: Do you know what her own childhood was like? Sometimes there can be a connection between how someone parents and how they were parented.

CM: She was adopted, but by a woman she really loved. I don't know a lot of the details. She didn't like to talk about it.

EB: I expect her own childhood isn't unrelated to the way she's acting now.

CM: I don't see how.

EB: These things don't always connect in a straight
    line. I'm guessing you didn't end up texting her
    the other day?

CM: No. Because then I was thinking about Will.
    And how she might make me feel bad about that
    situation. I just want to be happy about it, you
    know? Before anything ruins it.

EB: I do. But how exactly do you think she'd ruin it?

CM: My mom sees the world in this one rigid,
    traditional way. Things are all good or all bad.

EB: Will is untraditional?

CM: No, no that's not what I mean. He's a regular
    person.

EB: I see. And you said you two met on campus?

CM: Mmm. My mom has all these arbitrary rules about
    when you should lose your virginity or all that
    stuff about what I wear—she's uptight. That's
    what I mean. And this thing with Will is the
    opposite of that.

EB: Are you at risk again in this situation with
    Will, Cleo?

CM: No, God, it's nothing like that. Why would you
    say that?

EB: You seem a little tense when you speak about
    him, quite honestly.

CM: I'm afraid of losing something that matters to
    me. Will is kind and sweet—he's nothing like
    Kyle. You know Charlie and I broke up after I
    had that fight with her. I couldn't shake the bad
    feeling. I want the chance to love Will without
    my mom messing it up.

EB: That makes sense.

CM: Why do I feel like you mean the opposite?

EB: I promise that's not the case. But I do think a more helpful question to ask yourself might be whether your focus on what other people think—me, your mom—has more to do with how *you're* really feeling deep down.

CM: That I'm the one who thinks there's a problem with Will?

EB: I think, Cleo, that is a distinct possibility.

CLEO

I'm painfully aware of the weight of my mom's laptop in my bag as I get out of the car and say good-bye to Detective Wilson. After she tells me *again* not to interfere and also to be careful, "about everything else I've got going on." Whatever that means. I'm not about to stick around and ask.

I want out of the car before the guilt overwhelms me. I had plenty of time to tell her about the laptop as she drove me home to Park Slope. But it feels like the very last thread connecting me to my mom, and if I give it away, I worry that I'll be handing away the last of my hope. There's no way I'm letting go of my mom. Not when I feel like I'm finally seeing her for the first time.

I pause at the bottom of our steps, filled with dread again. The way I had been when I came home to see my mom.

My dad might be inside already. I texted and asked for him to meet me at the house. It's one thing to tell Detective Wilson about the money and his affairs; it's another thing not to admit that I have. Then I'd be a liar, no better than he is.

"Oh, there you are," a voice calls out as I start up our brownstone steps. When I turn, George is standing at his gate next door, an old Yankees hat pulled low over his eyes. There's something accusatory about his tone. Like he feels put out.

He must have seen the commotion, the police cars. I know that

Wilson interviewed him. George has a soft spot for my mom, but he's also . . . George.

"Sorry about all the . . . fuss," I say, though I feel annoyed.

"That's one way of putting it," he says, gesturing behind him to his front stoop, where he so often sits. I wonder if he's under the impression that he's now some kind of official neighborhood watch. As with his obsession with making sure everyone's trash cans are brought in right away after the garbage collection, it's a responsibility he does not seem at all happy about.

"Um, okay?" I say, because he's still glaring at me.

"Kids," he mutters, then charges away toward Seventh Avenue, newspaper tucked under his arm.

Inside the dark house, I lock our front door and lean back against it, eyes closed. Bracing myself. The smell, the blood, the screech of the fire alarm, the terrible details rush back. Luckily, when I finally do take a deep breath, it smells, so sweetly, of home—that gardenia scent my mom loved, *loves*.

I open my eyes slowly, squinting at first, still a little afraid of what I might see.

Relief—the house is immaculate. The kitchen has been cleaned up, along with the blood and the broken glass. Like nothing ever happened.

My dad must have taken care of it or, more likely, paid someone to. It's a little creepy, come to think of it. Like maybe he was so on top of it because he wanted to be sure any evidence of his guilt was washed away.

I sit on one of the stools at the island, smooth my hands over that porous marble, think of the place mat or coaster or newspaper my mom always insists goes under every plate or cup or bowl. Then I close my eyes and I'm seven or eight, watching her in the soft morning light as she races around making me eggs on toast, packing my lunch, and answering emails, all while smiling and chatting, like she doesn't have a care in the world. That was the way she was most mornings. But I wonder now, knowing the sort of cases she was working on, the kinds of people she was dealing with, whether she was more stressed than I knew. She hid so much; maybe she was even afraid that something might happen to her.

But I never felt it. She never made me feel like anything less than the most important thing.

"Don't go to work, Mommy," I'd said that morning. "Stay with me. And then you can relax."

And she'd smiled and said, "I'd love to, baby, but you have to go to school."

"No, I don't."

"Well, Mommy has to go to work, baby."

But I wasn't angry at her or resentful about her work. Not on that morning. Not on any other back then. Because I never had a need that wasn't fulfilled. When I was little like that, my mom was always where I needed her to be when it mattered. And I always, always knew that I was loved.

Where the hell are you, Mom?

I pull the complaint with the handwritten notes I found in Jules's apartment out of my bag and begin to read. It's the one document I didn't hand over to Wilson, which seems a reasonable compromise. *DRAFT* is stamped in the upper right-hand corner. The first few paragraphs are all formalities: identifying the parties, the law allegedly violated (negligence, product liability), and a section on jurisdiction. The second page is a summary of the charges in question, where the summary of what allegedly happened to Jane Doe begins.

The summary continues onto the third page, though after a few lines the handwritten notes stop and computerized Track Changes start—all attributed to Jules Kovacis. Except it's a document written by the *plaintiffs'* attorney, and Jules worked for Blair, Stevenson, so how could she be making changes to it? Wait, is this Jules's story? Some of the details about her daughter sound familiar. *She's* a plaintiff in this huge lawsuit? Because Blair, Stevenson couldn't have been okay with that. Is the lawsuit why Jules got fired? Why she's so scared? Did my mom do something to try to protect Jules and got hurt in the process?

I open my mom's laptop and type in "Xytek and Jules Kovacis," but nothing comes up. It's her personal computer, though, so nothing would. I'm staring at the screen when a notification pops up from her messaging app—a missed dentist appointment. A text dated yesterday. I didn't realize she had her texts linked to her laptop. *Holy shit.*

I hear the front door open and slam the laptop shut. *Protect my mom*—it's instinct now.

"Yikes," my dad says almost playfully as he steps into view. Because why not? This is all a game, right? "Hope I'm not interrupting anything."

"You scared me!" I shout. "What are you doing?"

"Meeting you!"

"I know that! I mean, why didn't you knock?"

"It's still *my* house, remember?" He puffs up his chest when he says it.

It was never your house. She paid for everything.

"If you say so." I tuck the laptop into my tote bag.

"You still have that, huh?" he asks, gesturing to it. "Detective Wilson is not going to be happy."

"You and Wilson are tight now, huh?"

"Whoa, Cleo." I can tell he's trying for a joking tone, but he sounds annoyed. "What's with the hostility?"

"Nothing," I say, then look away. I think of demanding an explanation for why he's lied about so much. But what's the point when I'm not going to believe him anyway?

"Detective Wilson actually just called." I prepare myself for what's next: *How could you tell her those things about me, Cleo?* But I'm ready to own it. I told her the truth, that's all.

"Oh, yeah," I say noncommittally.

"She said you told her something about Mom having some kind of special role at her law firm?"

I shrug, feeling like I dodged a bullet. "She's some kind of fixer, apparently. I talked to one of the people she was helping . . . a client, or whatever you want to call it."

"A client?"

"It's a long story." I have no intention of getting into a discussion about how I found Vivienne through Randy. As far as I'm concerned, that's my mom's business. "But this one client, this woman, she . . . she sort of threatened to kill Mom. That's why I thought I should talk to her."

"She threatened to kill Mom and so you *went* to see her? Cleo, what were you thinking!"

"That I actually want to find Mom!" I yell back at him.

"And I don't?"

"I don't know, Dad," I say. "I don't feel sure about anything anymore."

He looks like he's about to tell me off. But instead he blinks and looks away. Like even he isn't willing to come to his own defense anymore. The silence is unbearable.

"Anyway, I went to see her in front of the *Dakota,*" I go on. "What was she going to do, attack me in front of a bunch of moms pushing thousand-dollar strollers? Also, she threatens to kill people all the time . . . it's, like, her thing."

"Cleo, what are you doing?" my dad asks quietly. And he does look concerned now for real.

"What am *I* doing?" I say. "*Something.* Somebody has to."

"This is all really dangerous—Cleo, I'm worried."

"You want to know what I'm worried about?"

"What's that, Cleo?" he asks in this aggravating, extra-patient dad voice that I've never in my life heard him use before.

"I'm worried about the fact that you were cheating on Mom," I say.

His face is freakishly still. It looks like a mask. "What are you talking about?"

"I *know,* Dad. Mom told Lauren about Bella. It's creepy."

He shakes his head. "It's not what you think . . . I'm not dating Bella."

"Okay, fucking." My face feels hot. "It's pretty creepy for you to be *fucking* somebody who's only a few years older than I am."

"Jesus, Cleo." He looks disgusted. Like *I'm* the disgusting one. "I *did* . . . I made a mistake," he admits. "It wasn't with Bella, though. It's still not good, I know. I'm not making excuses. But it's not that . . . bad."

I'm surprised by how tight my throat feels. "What about the money, Dad? Lauren told me that Mom didn't want to give you some loan. When I was in your office, I saw the emails that show you have it now."

My dad opens his mouth, then closes it like a big dumb fish. Then he gets up to pace, energy turned manic. He's scrambling now.

"The situation with money, between your mom and me, it's complicated," he says, rubbing his forehead.

"What does that mean?"

"It means maybe because this movie is so important, and so close to being done, it pushed me to make some bold choices."

"So instead of figuring out how to, like, raise the money yourself, you took Mom's money?"

He closes his eyes for a moment. "Yes," he says, finally looking at me. "But I have a line on some new financing, and my plan was to get the money back before your mom even knew it was gone." He grimaces as he rubs his forehead with a hand. "Or maybe I was hoping she'd change her mind. There's always a first time, right?" And then he kind of half laughs, like *Come on, you know how she is.*

"This isn't funny." I start gathering up my stuff. "None of it is."

"Cleo, please," he says, a sharper edge creeping into his voice. "No one's saying it's funny."

"But you're also not exactly devastated that she's gone, are you?"

"Cleo, your mom *left* me," he says. "I'm not at the peak of my warm feelings toward her. But I will always love her, of course. I want her to come home safely, and as soon as possible."

"You love her?" I cross my arms. "Was that before *and* after you were having an affair?"

My dad's eyes have gone cold in a way I've never seen before. It's like he can tell he's lost control of me. "I've admitted that, Cleo. And I take full responsibility. Obviously, it would be very bad if the police found out about any of this. That detective already seems to suspect me of something. But you know as well as I do that your mom wasn't exactly warm and emotionally available. She had her reasons for being a little closed off, sure. But it didn't make her the easiest person to be married to."

And the look on his face, eyebrows lifted, head tilted slightly: *Come on, cave.* Because I always do in the end. But this time I only stare back at him.

"Well, at least she didn't pretend to be something she wasn't." I hop off the stool and gather my things.

"And I do?"

"No, you're just a liar." I turn away from him and start for the front door. "If I were you, I'd figure out what to tell Detective Wilson about the affair, though. And the money."

"Why would I tell her anything?" he asks.

"Because she already knows. I told her. And for the record, that wasn't a 'mistake.' I did it on purpose. Because I'm not covering for you anymore."

I cry on the subway back to Manhattan. I can't help it. And I'm not even sure what I'm crying about—except everything. When

I'm back at my dorm, I text Will—even though it's late, even though I know it will make me seem needy. Even though, all the rest. *Could you come over?*

Now?

I don't do this—ask him to come over in the middle of the night. But I need Will here now. I need him to put his arms around me and tell me that everything is going to be okay. I need to be able to believe him.

Yes, now. Please.

Will also doesn't usually come to my dorm. But I need for tonight to be an exception.

Of course. Be there in a few.

As I wait for Will, I return to my mom's laptop, to the text messages I didn't have time to read before my dad interrupted me. Sure enough, this is where her dating back-and-forths are, at least with that one guy Lauren mentioned, the one who died. There are lots of texts with my dad, too, but what catches my eye is a reply to an unknown number, a few down from the top. *I SAID I WOULD PAY.*

I tap on it—my stomach dropping when I see how far back the chain goes. There are at least ten messages. One of the last ones from my mom was in response to a photo of a bunch of parked cars. I scan the other messages. They're all pretty much the same—some person, whoever it is, going on about "some terrible thing" my mom had supposedly done a long time ago. And my mom repeating some version of *I don't know what you're talking about.*

No matter how many fancy degrees you get or how perfect you make your house, we both know you'll never be anything more than a white-trash slut.

What the fuck? And then another:

*I bet your own daughter doesn't have any idea who you really
are. What you're capable of. But I do—I know everything. And
pretty soon, I'm going to make sure everybody else knows what
you did, too. You'll spend the rest of your life in jail.*

Jail? My mom?

I click back through the messages, but I can't focus on reading
them in a coherent way. My eyes keep jumping around from one
to the next. I think of that last journal entry I'd read of my mom's,
about her having some kind of explosion. What did she do?

I startle when there's a knock on the door.

I hurry over to open it and Will slips inside, wearing a casual
blue button-down and jeans, a loose kind of canvas jacket. Cool,
easy. His cheeks are a little flushed from the chill in the air, which
makes his blue eyes glow even more than usual.

He smiles gently and tilts his head to the side. "Are you okay?"

Instead of answering, I reach for him. I want to disappear
inside him—safe and hopeful and free. I need to. I press my lips
hard against his. Feel the burn of his stubble against my cheek as
I slide my tongue into his mouth. Will hesitates for a second—
I'm not usually so aggressive. But then he moves toward me.
Because he knows this is what I need right now. A second later
he's tugging off my shirt and pushing me back toward my bed.
We don't make it that far, only to the wall nearby. I tug at his
shirt and then at my own jeans. When he pushes inside me, my
back is up against the wall. And I am lost to the heat of our bodies
becoming one.

I gasp when it's over. Will is breathing even more heavily than
I am. He laughs. "You may be the death of me, Cleo. Literally."

I force out a laugh, too. But what we have feels serious. Right
now it feels like my one good thing.

"Want to tell me what's going on?" Will asks once we're curved around each other under the covers. He wraps an arm around my waist and presses his mouth gently against the back of my neck.

"Yes," I say, pulling his arm tighter. "But not right now. Right now, all I want is this."

The Wall Street Journal

TROUBLED EMPLOYEE LINKED TO DARDEN PHARMACEUTICALS' DRUG WOES

A review of an internal Darden Pharmaceuticals investigation suggests that errors may have been made by a Darden employee tasked with oversight of Xytek, an antiseizure medication now the subject of a potentially billion-dollar multidistrict litigation. According to the company's own investigation, in his capacity as vice president of Risk Assessment, Doug Sinclair, now deceased, ignored physicians' warnings about unexpected and adverse side effects in pregnant patients and failed to file the required Adverse Event Report with the FDA. These findings are yet to be confirmed by an independent investigative body, though the matter has been referred to the FDA. A company spokesman says that Darden is prepared to cooperate fully. According to fellow employees, who spoke on condition of anonymity, Doug Sinclair was generally respected, but there were recent reports of performance issues. The matter has also been referred to the FBI for investigation.

KATRINA

A search of the Blair, Stevenson database revealed that Tim Lyall wasn't just any corporate partner at the firm. It appeared he handled special projects, too. It's not the kind of thing that would have been obvious to anybody *but* me—I knew the telltale signs, the cryptic matter names, the expense billing to "general office." But it seemed that, unlike me, Tim Lyall was a true corporate fixer—acting on behalf of the companies themselves, not their rogue employees. Mark had never mentioned there being more than one of us, but I'm not sure I would have wanted to know. My Uber was pulling off the FDR at Sixty-first Street, only a few blocks from Tim Lyall's apartment, when I got a text from Mark.

A heads-up that the Journal *went live with a story for tomorrow's paper about Sinclair and Darden.*

He followed it with a link.

It was bound to come out. Anonymous sources are definitely other employees doing a CYA. Doesn't change the work that remains to be done.

Bound to come out? Darden had clearly gone to the *Journal* themselves. Mark could try to act blind, but he wasn't an idiot. I began to type something to that effect, then deleted it. I wanted to see these documents Tim Lyall had before I did anything else. And maybe I was a little afraid of how Mark was going to respond. I had a bad feeling about all of it.

Okay, I wrote back instead. *Thanks for letting me know.*

"I work for Tim Lyall," I said to the doorman crouched behind the small reception desk in the clearly pricey but also very generic Upper East Side apartment building. I flashed my work ID.

"He's not—"

"Here. I know. He's on his way to Zurich. He left some client documents in his apartment. He needs me to take them to him at the airport."

"Residents have to leave permission in writing and their keys if they want to let somebody in," he said, taking a step back. "Those are the rules."

"Well, my boss needs the documents. We can call him if you want. But he was yelling at everybody before he left the office." I dug out my phone and extended it to him. "Maybe if you want to be the one to tell him . . ."

Tim Lyall's apartment was a postmodern box with parquet floors and neutral mid-century furniture, utterly devoid of not only personality but any trace of a person. Like a corporate Airbnb. There was not a single photograph or birthday card or piece of evidence that a Tim Lyall existed.

It took me only a couple minutes to find the file cabinet tucked away in a mostly empty closet. It turned out what Tim Lyall lacked in knickknacks, he made up for in client files kept at home—way more than even the most conscientious partner should ever have. His own little insurance policy, perhaps. The documents touched on a whole range of matters, but all of them had to do with some kind of corporate hiccup: an agency violation, expedited approval needed, an accounting error excused. Tim had retained only a few documents in each case, probably enough to use as leverage in a cover-your-ass fashion. But at the back of the cabinet there was a thicker hanging folder labeled *Darden.*

Inside were dozens of folders containing a range of documents—studies, data, FDA correspondence, and internal documents related to the FDA approval process for Xytek years ago. There were research results and test studies, internal memos and emails.

At the back I spotted a sealed envelope, unmarked.

Inside the envelope were printouts of more recent emails, sent from Doug to Phil Beaumont, Darden in-house counsel, six months ago. And they made Doug's position crystal clear in very formal, on-the-record fashion:

Phil,

To reiterate what I stated in our discussion earlier today: We need to discuss this phone call. Dr. D'Angelo is the head of obstetrics and gynecology at Vanderbilt University Hospital. He's highly respected. He claims he spoke with people at Darden YEARS ago. An adverse event report was never made, Phil. I'm sure that whatever happened was an oversight. But we need to at least look into it.

Sincerely,
Doug Sinclair

Phil,

I understand the company's position that D'Angelo was being sued for malpractice and maybe he was indeed trying to put the blame on Xytek. Regardless, these claims need to be reported now. An adverse event report needs to be made to the FDA that reflects when Dr. D'Angelo made his first call to Darden, which was long before the lawsuit. There was an oversight. It happens. The only path forward is transparency.

Sincerely,
Doug Sinclair

And then one from only a month or so ago. After the filing of the multidistrict litigation complaint.

Phil,

I'm not going to stay quiet about this. I'll come forward myself if need be. I'll go to the press and I'm going to tell the truth.

Sincerely,
Doug Sinclair

There was one last page. A draft email addressed to me only a week ago: *Dear Kat, Where to start . . .*

That was all. But there was my email address, clear as day in the "To" line. An email I never received. I stared at it for a long time, the page trembling in my hand. Darden had known about Doug and me and, evidently, so had Tim Lyall. Was this why they'd wanted me on the case? It wasn't insignificant that the email had been saved, and sent on to Tim Lyall, though presumably not to Mark. If Tim operated anything like I did, Mark wouldn't know any of these details, which was starting to feel a little convenient. Had Darden counted on me to do what they wanted, and quickly, in order to make sure that my relationship with Doug didn't come out? Had they been signaling to Tim Lyall that Blair, Stevenson was mixed up in this already in more ways than one?

I was still staring at the message when my phone pinged in my pocket. *Shit—Janine.* How long had I been in Tim Lyall's apartment?

But the text wasn't from Janine. It was from the same unknown number as the other anonymous threats. Except this message didn't have any words at all.

It consisted of a single photo. Of Cleo.

It had been taken across the street from her dorm, only her profile as she went inside. At twilight. And then a second message:

Three million. That's what it will cost for me to keep your secrets. You have 24 hours, or she's the one who'll pay.

Yes. Tell me where. Please leave her alone. Just like that, all the advice I'd given to clients over the years—taking their time, not responding, patience, reserve—went right out the window.

I gripped the phone, praying for an answer that never came. It was possible they would send detailed instructions later. Unless whoever was messaging me didn't actually care that much about the money. That the messages blackmailing me were some kind of ruse, like the ones that had been sent to Doug. These were different from the ones sent to him. But it was possible that, too, was a ploy.

I texted Sergeant McKinney. *Can you call me? ASAP.*

My phone rang almost instantly. "What is it?"

"I need you to watch Cleo. Can you go to her dorm, follow her if she leaves? Make sure she's okay?"

"This because of that kid again?"

"I'm not sure," I said. Because I couldn't risk mentioning Darden, not yet. "But I'm worried. Very worried."

CLEO

It's early when I slide carefully out of bed, not even 6:00 a.m. But I've already been lying there with my eyes open for what feels like forever. I don't want to wake Will, don't want him to leave, not yet. I feel so much better with him here.

But it is light now, reality creeping slowly back. The disturbing texts I stumbled upon on my mom's laptop last night are all I can think about. I'm trying to wrap my head around the idea of my mom doing something terrible. Because between her journal and the texts and her eventually agreeing to turn over the money, it seems like she definitely did something.

It was the picture of the cars that got my mom to agree to pay up. But why? I reach for the laptop, lean back against the bed, and prop it open on my knees. I click back on the thumbnail photo near the top to take a closer look. When I expand it, I recognize my dorm in the background. And there in the back of the frame, that's me, isn't it? Headed through the front doors at a distance. After that came the first demand for money. They hadn't only been threatening my mom. They'd been threatening me.

I close my mom's texts and start searching for information about Haven House and an incident years ago, something bad. I try every variation of my mom's name and then only "female" and "girl." But there are no reports of specific incidents involving any kind of violence or crime and a teenaged girl back then.

What I do find, though, is a rabbit hole of information about Haven House. It's still up and running, seemingly well funded now—thanks to a generous grant from the Gladys Greene Foundation. It has a decent-looking website and even a virtual tour. But then I find the exposé, published in *Connecticut Magazine* five years ago: "Horror House: Rampant Abuse of Girls by Doctors and Staff Persisted for Years at Haven House." Apparently, a director, Robert Daitch, who ran the facility from the early eighties through the end of the nineties, failed to supervise staff, and buried complaints of sexual and verbal harassment of female "residents"—as if any of the girls had chosen to live there—in order to preserve Haven House's "stellar reputation" and procure a lucrative position for himself at a private boarding school. He served as a beloved headmaster at Sloan Prep until his death in 2012. Daitch was dead by the time the story was published and even more victims' stories started flooding in, so there could be no criminal prosecution.

"Hey," Will murmurs sleepily. "What are you doing on the floor?"

"Reading my mom's texts," I say. "Somebody was threatening her."

"Threatening?"

"Well, asking for money," I say. "Blackmail."

"You saw this, just now?"

"I didn't realize they were on her computer."

"Blackmailing her about what?"

Will raises himself up in bed, leaning back against my wall with all my favorite quotes taped up—about love and hope and freedom. I think of my mom all those years ago, so young, doing something bad enough that she could be blackmailed for it. There must have been a reason. I've learned a lot about her that I never would have thought was true, but she's not a bad person. I know she isn't.

Will snaps his fingers in front of my face. "Hey, you okay?"

"Oh, sorry, yeah," I say, feeling irritated by the snapping, overly so. I'm wound so tight. "Blackmail about something she did. But it doesn't say what."

"Who are the texts from?"

"I don't know. My mom didn't know, either, I don't think. Somebody who knew her in that place she grew up in." I try to ignore the heavy feeling in my chest. "I think I need to go up there and ask around."

"Are you sure?" Will looks worried. "That sounds . . . kind of dangerous."

Do I want him to offer to go with me? I don't know; maybe. But that's not a good idea.

"I'll be careful."

He laughs. "Cleo, come on. How can you be careful? You have no idea what you're walking into."

This isn't untrue, unfortunately. But that doesn't make it any less annoying.

"I don't really have a choice."

"Of course you have a choice, Cleo," he says, his voice softer. He reaches out a hand and lays it on my cheek.

He's bare-chested and beautiful as always in the pale morning light. But—and I don't know if it's his being in my little bed or maybe the way I am looking up at him from below—all those quotes I have taped up look so young now. And naive.

"There was something that happened back there to my mom, or with my mom. Something *she* did," I say. "I need to find out what it was before I can involve the police. Otherwise, my mom could get in trouble herself."

"But none of that will matter if something happens to you, Cleo. And I care about that," Will says. "I care about you. Don't go, please."

Will's tone is still sweet, his hand warm as I gently remove it and close the laptop. And maybe he's right that going up to Haven House is a crazy idea. But my shoulders feel tight. I need him on my side.

"I know, I get it," I say. "But I have to go. I should, um, get ready. It's a long train ride."

"Ah, okay. I can take a hint." He looks wounded as he gets out of bed and starts pulling on his clothes.

"I'm sorry, I'm . . ." And maybe it's only because I know he's right, but I really do want him to go.

"It's okay," he says. But he seems a little pissed off. "I *am* only trying to help, Cleo. Because I care about you."

When the door closes behind him, I brace myself for a wave of regret, for the urge to race after him. But there's only me, alone again in my quiet, empty room.

The Uber driver is full of questions on the ride from the train station to Haven House: Where am I from? What am I doing in New Haven? What do I think about this new thing where they want to charge you for bags at the grocery store? Why does no one in New York City say hello on the sidewalk?

"Because there are too many people," I offer as I stare out the window at the bleak downtown. "You'd be saying hi all the time."

I'm trying not to think about the text I got from Wilson on the train. *I think we should talk, Cleo. I've got some concerns—about you.*

I didn't reply. I don't want to know about her concerns, not when I've got so many of my own. Starting with the decision to go to New Haven by myself. I do feel I need to be there—like I said to Will. But that doesn't mean I'm not nervous, or that I haven't had second thoughts about not telling Wilson. I did take screen shots of those threatening texts my mom got. And I did *think* about sending them to her.

We're a world away from Yale's stone and ivy as we sail down empty streets past boarded-up houses and abandoned cars. The area around Haven House is even more grim. I can't imagine a place like this exists still, but growing up there? I've taken so much for granted.

"Never too many people on a sidewalk to say a simple hello," the driver goes on. I don't jump to the city's defense like I ordinarily would. He can criticize, as long as he keeps talking. I can almost pretend everything is normal so long as I'm not alone with my thoughts.

But when Haven House finally comes into view, I nearly tell the driver to turn around and take me back to the station. The faded brick building is massive and menacing against the gray sky. Angry-looking fencing rings the roof. A prison. My mom grew up in a prison.

And for the first time, I feel more than nervous. I feel scared. Really scared. I send Wilson the screen shots of the anonymous texts my mom has been getting. It's not the same as telling her I'm up here and might need help—but it's not nothing, either.

I regret not asking the Uber driver to wait as I enter the building. It's cool inside and cavernous, with stone floors and tall arched windows, not unlike an old church. It even has that church cardboard smell. Except it's steeped in foreboding.

"Forget about it!" an angry voice calls out from behind me as the doors close with a menacing thud.

When I turn, there's a woman with curly red hair and a full round face seated at a small desk on the far side of the doors. She's wearing a turtleneck under a light blue cardigan that makes her seem at least two decades older than she is.

I hold up my hands. "Oh, I just—"

"Let me guess: You're here to see our girl Claudia, aren't you?" She crosses her short arms and pushes out her lower lip, which makes her look like an unhappy toddler. "You look like her type."

"I don't think—"

"Claudia doesn't think, either. She goes into town and finds somebody she likes and convinces herself that she can invite a girlfriend over, like this is her own private bachelorette pad." She shakes her head. "That girl's got a bunch of screws loose. If I were you, I'd steer clear."

"I'm not here to see Claudia," I say.

"Well, whoever . . . it's none of my business. I'm not trying to *intrude* on anyone's sexuality. There's a whole mess of people here who *do* think that way, but not me. He, her, them, they. What do I—"

"I'm here about my mother," I say, cutting her off. "She lived here years ago."

The woman's eyes narrow. "What about her?"

"She's missing," I say.

"Well, she's not here." She snorts. "We don't house adults. And we don't have, like, reunion weekends."

"I know. But I think maybe whatever happened to her now could have something to do with when she lived here," I say. "It was back, you know, when there were all those problems?"

"Well, don't look at me." She holds up her palms. "That was way before my time."

"I have a few questions. Is there someone who might be able to answer them?"

She stares at me for a long moment, like she's trying to see if I'll take it back. Finally, she sighs dramatically. "Go down the hall to the registration office and ask them if you want. But I wouldn't get your hopes up."

I brace myself for another unwelcome reception, but when the very, very old lady inside the registration office looks up from her desk, her face lights up. Like she's been waiting all day for me to walk through that door.

"Do I know you from somewhere?" She is stooped and frail; I try not to stare at her bony arms beneath her floral-print dress as she makes her way over to the counter. She leans in closer, squints. "You look so familiar."

"My mom used to live here. We kind of look alike."

"Oh my." She brings a hand to her mouth. "You look exactly like her! It's uncanny."

And for the first time in my entire life, the suggestion doesn't flood me with resentment.

"Her name was—" My voice catches.

"I know, Katrina Horning. She came here when she was nine and left when she was fourteen. I remember exactly. Of course I do." She smiles. "She was adopted by Gladys Greene, I believe. I'm Rose, by the way, and I haven't been here quite as long as this place has, but nearly."

"Cleo," I say, pointing to myself.

"Well, I have been surprised by *a lot* of things in my time here, but Gladys . . ." She rolls her eyes good-naturedly. "That one . . . she was very sweet. But a few cards short of a full deck, if you know what I mean. For years she came up here every Saturday. Like clockwork. Had a driver who would bring her. She'd spend some time with the girls, read to the younger ones, bring games and books and clothes. Like she was visiting grandchildren, or maybe more like puppies at the pound. But she got real fixated on your mom, kept saying how she reminded her of her little sister, who'd died young. You ask me, Gladys thought your mom *was* her sister. Anyway, I didn't think they'd ever let her actually adopt anyone, but shows what I know. And Gladys did give money to the school afterward. I always did wonder . . . worried a little, even, about what became of your mom. But hard to see how staying here would have been much better. Things aren't necessarily perfect now, but back then . . ." She makes a clucking noise, then forces a smile. "Anyway, I guess it must have all worked out. Because here you are, beautiful as your mom."

"Yeah—I mean, thank you—except . . . my mom is missing now. And I think it might have something to do with her time here."

"Missing?" She blanches. "What do you mean?"

I press my lips together until I feel steady enough to speak. "She's gone, and the police think something bad happened to her. They don't know what yet. But someone from her past—from here, I think—has been threatening her."

Rose charges with surprising force from behind the tall counter through a little swinging door. She grabs one of my hands in hers, a tiny, bony vise. "Come sit down here and tell me what is going on." She motions to a bench along the wall, where we go and sit side by side.

"That's just it: I don't know. I found some texts. They mentioned something bad that had happened while my mom was here. Do you know what that might have been?"

"I'm afraid there were *a lot* of bad things that went on here once upon a time."

"It sounded like this was something *she* did . . ."

"*Your* mom? Do something bad?" she asks. "Oh, I can't imagine that . . . I have sympathy for any girl who finds herself here, but we have had plenty of troublemakers. Your mom was never one of them. Let me check her file. If there was an incident, it would be in there." She stands and heads to a long row of wooden file cabinets on the opposite side of the room. "Ten years ago, we put everything online. But the older files are still here."

"Thank you," I say as she pulls open a drawer.

"Horning, Horning. Looks like someone decided the *H*s came after the *I*s. Here it is. Oh, that's . . ." Her voice drifts as she turns around, flipping open an empty folder. "The records must have been . . . misplaced."

"Misplaced?" I ask, stepping closer, even though there's nothing to see. "Does that happen a lot?"

She stares down at the empty folder for a long time. "No. But

Director Daitch . . . there were things he wanted to go away. And so away they went."

"What about someone named Silas who used to work here?" I ask. "I know that it was a long time ago, but his name is kind of—"

"I know Silas." She lifts her gaze to mine, holds it for a moment before looking away. "There were times I worried that working here might be, in a way, condoning the things that went on. But then I thought maybe leaving would be worse. At least if I was here, there'd be one person the girls could go to . . . I did make an anonymous report to the police more than once. Nothing was ever done. They'd call, ask some questions, decide everything was okay . . . Daitch was friends with everyone who was anyone—police chief, mayor, head of the hospital. Gave him way too much power, you ask me."

"Do you maybe have a phone number or a forwarding address for Silas? I need to try to find him."

"Oh, you don't need an address," she says. "Silas is here. Upstairs right now, as a matter of fact. The new director is better. He did clean house, fired a whole bunch of the old-timers. But Silas and a few others threatened to sue for wrongful termination. I guess the lawyers must have decided he had a case, because here he still is."

Outside the second-floor community room, where Rose has determined that Silas should be supervising the art club, I stare at the closed doors for a moment, listening to the voices on the other side. I think of what Detective Wilson said: *You think this person will be happy if and when you do find them?* I didn't in a million years think I would; I guess that's the bottom line. But now Silas is right there.

The room on the other side of the doors is nearly the size of my high school cafeteria, with the same linoleum floor, high ceilings, and institutional chill. But it's way dingier here—dull lighting, a grayish film covering everything. Two dozen teenage girls are seated at the round tables at the far end of the room, the low couches nearest the doors empty. Standing at a set of doors opposite are a grim-faced man and woman, mid-twenties maybe, only distinguishable from the teenagers because of their gray uniforms. They glance my way, then go back to talking. There's a much older man seated at a table with the girls, chatting as he draws. He's a grandfatherly hipster type, wearing one of those cable-knit fisherman's sweaters, jeans cuffed high, stylish slip-on sneakers, and a plaid scarf tied expertly at his neck. The girls with him are laughing, seemingly hanging on his every word.

Silas? Not at all what I expected. But he's the only person who seems old enough.

"Who the hell are you?" The voice behind me is deep and unfriendly. *Shit.*

"Oh, hi," I say as I turn. "I'm sorry, I'm a friend of Silas's." I gesture in the direction of the art table.

I'm now facing a much older, much more intimidating man, also in a gray uniform. He's taller than my dad—six foot three, maybe even four—and heavy with muscle. His face has a weathered, beaten quality, including a noticeable scar on his right cheek, and he's older than his body would suggest—sixties maybe.

"A friend of Silas's, huh?" He looks me up and down, eyes lingering inappropriately in a way that makes my skin crawl.

I glance in the direction of the woman in the gray uniform by the doors. She's looking right at me, her face tight, and I think, *Phew, she's going to help.* But then she turns away; I'm on my own here.

"Yes," I say. He's close enough now that I can feel the heat of him. He smells medicinal, like menthol. He definitely could be Silas. He's old enough. "Unless . . . I'm guessing you're . . ."

"What do you want?"

"I know about your texts," I manage to say. This is my chance, my only one.

"What texts?"

"To Kat McHugh—you were blackmailing her, and now she's missing."

He glares at me. "Kat *who*? What the fuck are you even talking about?"

"I mean Katrina Horning—that was her name when she used to live here. Like thirty years ago. She was adopted away by a rich lady, Gladys Greene, *after* she reported you like a dozen times for messing with her? And then, all these years later, she starts getting angry texts looking for money. She's my mom. She looked *just* like me?"

He squints at me, then grunts in recognition.

"I didn't send any fucking text. But I should have gotten paid for keeping my mouth shut after what she did."

"And what's that?" I ask, like I don't believe him.

"I don't know exactly. I didn't *want* to fucking know." He laughs. "Daitch was freaking out and so I did as I was told. Because I wanted to keep my job. Tossed a bunch of bloody clothes. And Katrina Horning walked out of here a couple days later, safe and sound. So, wasn't *her* blood . . . Wait, why am I even talking to you?" He motions to the doors. "Get the hell out of here before I throw you out."

"Okay, but then I'll go to the police. Tell them you sent the texts."

"Search my phone if you want," he says, digging it out of his pocket and holding it out to me. "You aren't going to find any fucking texts."

"What does that prove? Come on, you'd use one of those secrecy apps to send them or a burner or something," I say. "What if I tell the police you admitted it? Who do you think they're going to believe?"

The anger in his eyes is frightening. "What the hell do you want from me?"

"I want to know what happened that night. Where did the blood come from?"

"I. Don't. Know."

"I'm not kidding about going to the police. You must know something. Did she get into it with another kid here? Sounds like the girls were pretty rough."

He glares at me. "All I know is it was *a lot* of blood. Somebody else would have shown up hurt. Besides, she snuck out, that's what Daitch said."

"Snuck out where?"

"Fuck if I know, probably to see that college prick. Did tutoring here. You ask me, those two spent way too much fucking time together."

THE DAY OF

Did you get it?

Nope. It's a no-go. Sorry.

"A no-go. Sorry"? Seriously?
Now what am I going to do?

I think you should stop worrying.
Forget about it. Really.

Easy for you to say.

What does that mean?

You don't have to worry about anything.
Because no one is counting on you to fix
anything!
What a fucking luxury that must be!

Whoa! I don't think I deserve that!

Hello? Janine. Come on. Where did
you go?

Are you going to answer me?

Hellllloooooo.

KATRINA

I stood on the sidewalk outside of Mark's beautiful limestone town house on West Seventy-fifth, staring up at the huge gleaming windows. It was midnight, the house dark and still apart from one small lamp left on downstairs—the kind that signaled people at home and asleep inside, poor burglary opportunities. I was putting off ringing the bell.

Surely Mark didn't personally know about Doug's emails, not the down and dirty details of what Tim had seen. And even Tim surely didn't know he was helping to cover up a murder, though he'd be an idiot not to suspect it now. Perhaps his sudden trip out of the country was even a response. I could easily imagine Tim being enlisted to help handle Doug's threat of blowing the whistle about Xytek, and then Darden getting impatient and handling the problem themselves. And Mark would have made sure to remain in the dark, as he always did when it came to the matters I handled. Certainly Mark didn't know that Darden appeared to have targeted me. Doug's draft email to me would have been enough to clue them in to our connection, and with a little digging they'd have uncovered our relationship. Who better to enlist in helping throw Doug under the bus than me: somebody with something to lose?

But I had to lay it all out for Mark now: that Darden had *killed* Doug to scapegoat him for knowingly leaving a drug on the market that they knew was hurting *babies,* when Doug had, in fact, tried to hold them accountable. And that Blair, Stevenson might be implicated in helping them cover up Doug's death.

My phone vibrated in my hand. Sergeant McKinney—who was watching Cleo. *Fuck.* I fumbled to answer it. "Is Cleo—"

"She's fine, she's fine." He didn't even let me get all the way there—a person accustomed to handling panicked people. "But she went out. To some house. She seemed happy enough going inside. Appeared completely voluntary. So I think it's all fine. I mean, within reason. I don't know whose house it is."

"Okay," I said, but I didn't like the sound of that. "Can you text me the address? I'll meet you as soon as I can."

This conversation with Mark would be uncomfortable but brief. Because I planned on getting right to the point. Mark would probably be defensive at first—it was only human not to want to be responsible, even tangentially, for something bad that had happened. But the facts were the facts. And they were not good. Darden had done something monstrous and the firm had helped them do it. The fact that Mark had kept his eyes shut the whole time wouldn't protect him from the fallout.

Mark looked wary when he peered out his living room window. I'd had to ring the bell a couple times when I arrived and then texted to wake him. When he finally opened the door, he was in a robe, gray hair sticking up in a bunch of different directions. He looked much older and smaller than he ever did in the office, like glimpsing Oz out from behind his mighty curtain.

"Kat?" he asked. "What are you . . ." He looked past me to the street, like the answer might lie over my head. "What's wrong?"

"I'm sorry," I said. "I know it's the middle of the night. I wouldn't have come if it wasn't important."

"Is Cleo okay?"

"Yes, yes—she's fine. At least for the moment."

Mark reached for my arm. "Come in, come in."

As I stepped inside, Mark's wife, Ruth, appeared on the stairs in a matching robe, looking equally sleepy and even more concerned. Very frail, too, noticeably ill, worse than the last time I'd seen her.

"Oh, Kat," she said, pausing halfway down the staircase. "Is everything okay? What's wrong?"

"Kat is having an issue with a case," Mark said. With the state of Ruth's health, he didn't like to worry her. "Nothing's wrong. Go back to bed, honey. I'll be right up."

Ruth scowled, looking from Mark to me and back again. She wasn't the kind of woman to be sent away easily. "Kat shouldn't be working in the middle of the night, Mark. People need sleep. No case or client is worth making yourself sick."

Mark adjusted his glasses on his nose. "I know, Ruth. Now, please go back to bed," he said, calm but firm. "We can't talk about a client matter with you down here. And we can't get Kat on her way back home to bed until we've spoken."

She shook her head and sighed heavily before turning back up the steps. "Fine, fine, fine. But quickly, please."

Mark put a hand on my shoulder and motioned with the other toward the living room.

"What's happening, Kat?" Mark asked when we were seated. "Tell me everything."

"It's Darden," I began, pulling out my phone. I had taken photos of Tim Lyall's documents.

"Darden?" He made a face. "They're absolutely delighted at the moment. Perhaps that's the wrong word, but didn't you see the article?"

"I didn't have a chance to read it yet. I saw your text, though."

"The *Journal* somehow got ahold of the information about Doug Sinclair."

"You mean that Darden intentionally leaked it to them."

"Oh, no." Mark shook his head. "I'm sure not." He was quiet

for a moment. "Someone *at* Darden may have leaked it. I'm sure there are employees anxious not to be thrown under the bus themselves, or to be sure Darden isn't going to go under because of this lawsuit. People are human. They're worried about their—"

"They *knew,* Mark."

"Who knew what?"

"Darden knew there was a problem with Xytek. Right after approval, they had calls from doctors reporting issues with pregnant patients." I gathered myself. "The same doctors called more recently and spoke to Doug, relatively new to Darden at the time, and yet Darden still didn't notify the FDA. Doug Sinclair was threatening to go public."

Mark went still for a moment, then rubbed a hand over the top of his head, smoothing his rumpled hair. "Okay, explain to me how you know this?"

"There are emails from Doug *to* Phil Beaumont, warning him of the report from the doctor six months ago. And the first calls from doctors came right after the drug went on the market. Darden knew about the potential risks to pregnant women and yet didn't even warn patients or doctors. You and I both know what that could mean in terms of punitive damages. Tim Lyall knew about these emails and about Doug's threats." My eyes locked on his—*I know about the other fixer.* "It's possible that we've been helping Darden cover all of this up."

Mark closed his eyes, then dropped his head into his hands. A few seconds passed before he looked up at me. "Shit."

Thank God. "I know."

Mark crossed and uncrossed his legs. "You know my policy about not getting into details," he said. "As you can imagine, that applies to Tim's work, as well." His eyes were imploring. Imploring *me.* It was all out in the open now—what I knew, what Mark knew, what had been done—and he wanted me to let him off the hook. To let his willful blindness win the day. After all, that's what I'd always done before.

But I couldn't do that now. Not this time.

"Darden killed Doug, Mark," I said. "Phil Beaumont summoned him to a meeting that night and probably that same car that's been following me drove him off the road."

"Ha!" Mark's laugh sounded more like a bark. But when I didn't respond, his face slowly fell. "You cannot be serious."

I nodded. "I believe they got rid of Doug to keep him quiet about the problems with Xytek. It's a bonus that they can now blame those problems on Doug, who's not around to defend himself. Or they can try to. At a certain point, those doctors are going to speak up."

"You really believe . . ." Mark didn't finish the thought.

"I *know,* Mark. I wouldn't be here otherwise."

"You've already spoken to the police?" he asked. "Or were they the ones you heard it from?"

"I haven't done anything yet," I said. "I came here to speak with you first."

"Okay," Mark said. He got up to pour himself a glass of water from the wet bar. Took several swallows, then turned back to face me. "I appreciate that." His tone was grave. "What are you proposing we do?"

"Go to the U.S. attorney's office," I said. "I don't think we have much choice."

Mark exhaled. "That would be an ethical breach," he said. "I mean, we can argue that any wrongdoing with Xytek is ongoing and so the privilege is pierced . . . But we are definitely in a gray zone here."

"They've threatened Cleo, Mark. To get to me," I said, trying to tamp down my alarm at hearing the words out loud. "I know you're friends with Phil, but—"

"Kat, come on." Mark waved the suggestion away. "I know the guy, that's all. That doesn't mean . . ." An angry flush rose in his cheeks. "Wait . . . And Cleo? What do you mean they threatened her? You're absolutely sure?"

He was looking for an out. I swallowed back my irritation. "They sent a photograph of her and a demand for money," I said. "An implied threat." I didn't plan to tell Mark any more than that—Cleo was what mattered, not what I'd done at Haven House.

"Oh . . . Well, a demand for money? Sounds vague. And you're assuming this came from Darden because . . ."

"And you're assuming it's a coincidence? Mark, you know I've been getting to the bottom of situations like this for a very long time. The car that's been following me is the same, or similar, to the car that drove Doug Sinclair off the road. The kind of threat they made against Cleo is similar to the one that was made against Doug—essentially faux blackmail that could be used to establish alternate suspects should something happen to me. Just like Darden hoped that Doug Sinclair's involvement in some college scandal might insulate them from suspicion."

Mark lifted his eyebrows. "Darden got what they wanted: the article in the *Journal*. Why would they threaten Cleo now?"

"Because I'm a secondary liability. I've spoken to Tim Lyall. I know about Doug," I said, my voice catching the slightest bit.

"I am sorry about that, Kat." And he really did look sorry. "I know that you and Doug were . . ." He let the words drift. And I might not have even noticed, had his face not twitched. For only a split second. But long enough. "Well, the whole thing is upsetting."

I know that you and Doug were . . . It felt like I'd been slapped. Mark knew about Doug and me—our relationship. Even though I hadn't told him. Even though he'd *just* pretended that he'd never seen the emails in Tim Lyall's possession, including the one that proved a secret connection between Doug and me. The truth was, Mark had known all along. He'd helped Darden use me.

I needed to get out of that house, right now.

"Listen, I should get back to Cleo." I stood calmly. Calm seemed absolutely critical.

"Are you sure it's even safe for you to be going back to Cleo? I mean, alone?"

I avoided looking at Mark, afraid his expression would belie the implied threat. I worried I might be sick.

"Oh, I'm not alone. I've got the NYPD watching her. Close friend of mine, very close." I could only hope Mark would pass along the warning to Darden. "So, she's safe for now—completely. But thank you. You should look out for yourself, though. Right now, Darden seems willing to cast a very wide net."

I waited until I was safely around the corner before I dialed Emily Trachtenberg, the intrepid *New York Times* reporter who'd been dogging Vivienne Voxhall. She answered on the first ring.

"Who is this?" Her voice was hoarse.

"It's Katrina McHugh," I said. "I'm sorry to be calling so late, but I've got something for you. And it's much, much better than Vivienne."

I opened the car door and slid in next to McKinney, who was parked across the street from a row of immaculate brownstones. He was sipping coffee out of a paper cup. Handsome as usual, though visibly tired. I felt especially bad for dragging him out of bed at that hour. His wife, a nurse in the NYU NICU, was pregnant and they didn't get much time together. Not to mention that McKinney could get in trouble for helping me. Getting fired by the NYPD certainly wouldn't help with bar admission once he graduated from Fordham's night school—no matter how glowing my recommendation had been.

"Thank you," I said, waiting until he met my eyes. "Really, I know, this is not ideal . . ."

He nodded. McKinney never could stay mad for long. "It's

number two thirty-four. I can't tell which apartment, haven't gotten a visual."

"Thank you again for coming, McKinney. I'm so sorry that I had to bother you."

He looked toward the brownstone. "You going to be okay?"

"Yeah—yes. You should get to your shift."

I could feel McKinney staring at the side of my face. "You want to tell me what is really going on?"

As much as I wanted to tell McKinney about Darden, I couldn't risk involving the police yet. Darden might see that as a reason to move more quickly or intensify the pressure. "It's that same kid you helped me with before. I know it's ridiculous that it's come to this: staking out my own daughter. That's why I didn't want to say anything."

McKinney's eyes didn't leave my face. "Okay, then," he said. He did not sound like he believed me. Only that he had decided not to press. "You want me to get someone else on standby?"

I closed my eyes for a second. I hated having to ask McKinney for more help, but I did need it. "That would really help."

He reached for his phone. "Consider it done."

CLEO

The woman seated at a desk behind the counter in the Yale registrar's office peers at me over her reading glasses, eyebrows lifted. I've worked myself into tears, a play for sympathy. She does not appear the least bit moved.

Thanks to Rose, I have a name for the tutor: Reed Harding. But that's all I have. I'm probably chasing a dead end. But if I go home now, I'm going to have to face the fact that what Detective Wilson said is true: When bad things like this happen, it's almost always someone close to the victim who is responsible. Someone with a motive, like money or an affair.

The woman in the registrar's office stands reluctantly, then lopes her way over. She folds her hands in front of her on the counter that separates us.

"And how can I help you?"

"I'm sorry," I say, wiping at my eyes. "My mom is missing."

She leans against the counter. "The security office is out the front door and on the left. They can help you."

"No, that's not—" My voice cuts out. I take a breath. "She didn't disappear from here. We live in New York."

"Uh-huh . . ." She draws it out.

"But I need help finding a student who went here a long time ago. He knows something and we need his help. I thought you'd have an address in your alumni files. His name is Reed—"

"No, no, no."

"But it's a—"

"No." She wags a finger in my face. "I can't even tell you if he went to school here," she says. "That's all private information. Legally. And these days people take all that legality *very* seriously. I can't go around giving out people's home addresses."

"But my mom—"

"And I'm sorry for you. That sounds real upsetting." She walks away from the counter and returns to her desk. "If I were you, I'd go to the police. If the police tell me I've got to give you that info, then I'll hand it right over. But I won't be breaking the law in the meantime."

The Yale campus is beautiful, not only because of the Gothic architecture but also because, unlike NYU, it's so *green*. The students even look more relaxed. I sit for a while on the grass, facing a huge library. I think of the last time I was in the NYU library. The smug look on Kyle's face when he told me he'd gotten the money I'd left for him in his gym locker. That we were square. And then he'd gone and sent Geoff anyway. What a waste of time.

My phone buzzes. I see the message first. *I'm sorry*. I feel a sharp pang of relief: my dad, trying to make things right. But the apology isn't from my dad; it's from Will. I darken the screen. And I feel annoyed. I'm not even sure exactly why. When I look out instead across campus, I notice several people stopping to simultaneously take random selfies. These days, it's a familiar sight. UNow photos being taken in the precise two-minute window and paired with a curated song. *Vivienne*. Maybe I'm not at a dead end after all.

To my surprise, Vivienne picks up right away. "Did you find her?" she asks without saying hello.

"No. But now I also need to find someone else." I feel a twinge of guilt. This is the kind of call I could be making to Wilson.

Except I know she'd refuse to help me freelance this way. In fact, she might even send someone to get me. "He might know something about what happened to my mom. Can you get into Yale's alumni records? I know he went there like thirty years ago. I need a current address, so I can try to talk to him."

"Yale? *Please,* in my sleep. Give me his name and a five-year window of his graduation. Shouldn't take long."

Vivienne calls me back in less than ten minutes. "They don't have *any* current records on this guy. He didn't graduate, never came back after the holidays his sophomore year. From what I could see in his academic file, there wasn't any obvious reason. Good grades, no disciplinary issues, tuition paid in full. You want his last address in New Haven? It was off campus. Maybe they know something there. But, I mean, this was thirty years ago . . ."

"I'll take it—thanks."

Half an hour later, I'm standing across the street from a run-down house about a mile east of the campus. It's small and cream-colored, with a sloped front porch that gives the impression that the house is slowly melting into the ground. The neighborhood is deserted, the house next door boarded up, another one nearby partially destroyed by fire.

I jump when a dog barks behind me, hurling its enormous, angry, white-spotted body against the flimsy chain-link fence separating us.

"Jesus," I mutter as I run across the street. The front stairs are so lopsided, I lose my footing, and the railing nearly gives way when I grab on to it to steady myself.

"Who the fuck's there?" There's a huge bald man standing at one of the porch windows. I can't see his face through the torn screen, but it's clear he's not happy.

I dig out one of the twenties I specifically brought for this purpose and wave it in the air, like a dog treat. I already have the sense I am doing this wrong.

"I'm trying to find somebody who used to live here."

"Who?" he shouts, but his tone has softened the tiniest bit. It's got to be the money.

"Reed Harding? It was, um, a long time ago. Maybe before you—"

"I've lived in this house my whole life and I was born in '81. Before that, my parents lived here, and before that, my grandparents."

The man disappears for a minute, and I think maybe I've lost him. But then he appears at the front door. He's even bigger than I realized. He motions me to approach with his massive mittlike hands. I inch closer. Not near enough that he could easily grab me, but still way too close for comfort.

"Yes?" I do a pretty good job keeping my voice steady.

"Give me the damn money," he says, like I'm the total idiot I appear to be.

"Oh, okay." I toss the twenty at the door and spring away.

He opens the door, picks the money up off the ground, inspects it.

"Now who is it you're looking for?"

"He was a Yale student and he—"

"Oh, you mean the apartment. We rented that out to students. Still do."

"Reed Harding was a student at Yale in 1992," I offer tentatively. "The school records say he was living here in this house and then left school around Christmas of 1992."

"*Christmas* of 1992?" he asks. "Wait a fucking second. I remember that asswipe. He screwed us out of half our presents, including my Reggie Jackson baseball card! I'd been waiting a hundred years for that thing."

"I need to find out where he is now. I need to talk to him."

"That's not going to happen."

"I know it was a long time—"

"He's fucking dead."

"Dead?"

"Yup—that's how he killed Christmas. The asshole bled out on our steps middle of the night on Christmas Eve. So there my mom was all freaking about that, and my dad worried about losing a tenant and the money and all that crap. Us kids were the real ones that got screwed."

"Bled out?"

"Yup. Stabbed." He gestures to the back of his neck. "There was blood fucking everywhere. I guess he tried to get himself out to a doctor. Collapsed on the steps. My mom was screaming her head off when she found him."

"What happened?"

Although I already have a theory, don't I? The same Christmas Eve my mom had some kind of explosion, the writing teacher she was a little "too close" with gets stabbed?

"Who the fuck knows." He shrugs, gestures at the street. "Believe it or not, this is a lot safer than it used to be. Anyway, an ambulance took him away. Police came later. I don't remember the details. My parents were so freaked about the whole thing, they wouldn't let any of us talk about it ever again."

It isn't until the train ride back that I text Will: *Thank you for checking on me. I'm sorry, too.* None of this was his fault, but I'm feeling jittery and needy again. *I think I just really, really need some sleep.*

Then I reread the *Connecticut Magazine* exposé about Haven House. There's a mention of Daitch's connections with local officials that allowed him to cover up all kinds of violations and bad behavior, exactly like Rose had said. The last thing Daitch would have wanted was for Haven House to be on the hook for a murder—and he had the means to make any evidence of such an incident vanish.

Wilson texts then—as I knew she would eventually—to ask about the screen shots I sent.

Cleo, what the hell is this? And then a second message comes through. *And we need to talk about that boyfriend of yours, Cleo. It's important.*

Kyle—great. I knew Wilson was going to fixate on him. But there's no way I'm answering her right now. She'll definitely ask where I am.

As I tuck my phone away, the bad thought that's been working its way to the front of my mind finally reaches its destination: What if my mom did run away? What if this person from her past was threatening to tell the world that she murdered Reed Harding, and she ran so that no one would ever find out what she'd done? Maybe finding her is the exact opposite of what she wants right now. I wonder if I love her enough to leave it at that. I'm not sure. Leaving well enough alone is a lot harder than it looks.

The four blocks from the West Fourth Street station to my dorm feel endless, as if I'm walking through wet sand. I've turned onto my street, when someone rams me from behind. I stumble sideways into the corner of my building. My head knocks against the stone and I see stars. *Wow. Actual stars.* Then there's a forearm against my neck. My brain tries to piece it together—a person, on me. A face jammed in front of mine.

Kyle.

There's a cut over his right eye, and the left one is purple and swollen shut. He bares his teeth at me and I can see that one of them is missing. There is a huge gap. And holy shit, does he look pissed.

"You fucking sicced the police on me?"

His arm is pressing so hard against my neck, it's hard to talk.

Wilson *already* went to talk to him?

"What?" I gasp.

"That fucking cop your mom brought to my apartment beat the shit out of me."

"My mom . . . what?"

"The cop she brought to my apartment!" Spit sprays into my eyes as he shouts.

"What cop, when?"

"Fucking months ago, before we broke up," he says. And suddenly it all makes sense, how willing he was to let me go. Not that I thought he loved me, but he sure didn't like to lose.

"I didn't know."

"Well, tonight he fucking showed up again, grabbed me out of nowhere, and did fucking this to me—said I did something to your mom. Did you tell him that?"

"No!" I'm starting to feel light-headed. "I don't even know who he is."

"Then who fucking sent him?"

"Kyle, stop." I'm going to black out.

"Hey!" An old woman smacks Kyle in the side of the head with her handbag. "You let her go, or I'll call the cops!"

And then I am free. The blows stun Kyle long enough that he releases me. "Mind your own fucking business, bitch!"

As I run toward my dorm, the security guard appears outside. Tyler—the sweet nighttime one.

"Hey, asshole!" he shouts at Kyle, heading right for him. He's nearly twice his size. "What the fuck do you think you're doing?"

"Please don't let him come in." I realize I'm limping as I make my way to the entrance. "He tried to choke me."

Tyler nods as he continues toward Kyle. "Hey, why don't you and I have a conversation, friend?"

"This isn't over, Cleo!" Kyle shouts after me. "I'm getting my fucking phone back!"

KATRINA

When Cleo emerged from the brownstone a half hour later, enough time for sex maybe but not much else, I felt only angry—at her, then at myself. Especially because I had no idea who she'd seen, much less if sex had anything to do with it. I followed her back to her dorm, watched her go inside, waited until her light went on and then off.

And then I got another text. My phone shook as I read the message.

Tonight. Three million dollars. Routing info below. There was a row of numbers. *If it's not there by midnight, she'll be the one who pays.*

Darden was *still* making threats? Was Mark really not going to make them stop? Or had he tried and been unable to? Both felt like terrible options.

The text was followed by a new picture—this one of Cleo going into her dorm from a different angle. In the corner of the photo was a guy in a red baseball hat, a guy I realized I'd seen walking past me only moments ago. Whoever sent the picture must be very close.

This was escalating, quickly. I couldn't wait for Darden to make the next move, couldn't trust that Mark would protect us. Couldn't trust that I even knew who Mark was. I was going to have to deliver a preemptive strike, and hope it landed.

* * *

I stayed on the bench, watching Cleo's room until dawn, then called McKinney's friend to take over and sent a message to Ahmed at Digitas asking him to trace the anonymous texts. I'd held off asking him to trace the messages earlier, because the last thing I wanted was anyone I worked with knowing about them, even someone outside the firm. I wasn't the only lawyer from Blair, Stevenson that Digitas helped with research. But given the threats to Cleo, I'd no longer felt I had any choice. I also texted Mark, who suggested we meet at the office right away.

Even with Cleo in safe hands, I couldn't quell the nauseating worry in my gut as I got off the elevator on my floor at Blair, Stevenson. There was no one there that early on a Sunday. I expected Mark picking the deserted location was not an accident.

As soon as I was out of the elevator, I could see the door to my office was wide open. I hadn't left it that way. I was sure of it.

The ransacking had been thorough. Drawers gaped open; papers and files were strewn all over the floor. Even my locked desk drawer had been pried open and emptied. No one had bothered to clean up, either, because that's where we were—in a place where pretenses were no longer required.

Down the hall I found Mark behind his desk, facing his computer. There was another man, leaning against the windowsill—gray pinstripe suit, well-coiffed salt-and-pepper hair, artsy black eyeglass frames. Phil Beaumont, Darden's general counsel. I recognized him immediately. I'd seen him on TV—Xytek wasn't the first scandal Darden had weathered.

"Is someone going to put my office back together?"

They both looked at me standing in the doorway. And for a long moment, the only sound was my pulse pounding in my ears.

"Kat. So good you're here," Mark said with forced brightness. But it was too late for him to act like this was all some unfortunate accident he was trying to help them weather. People were *dead.* Cleo was in danger. And Mark's getting whatever it was he really wanted out of this Darden situation—billables, prestige, power—was certainly no excuse for his continued participation in this fiasco.

"Get them away from Cleo, right now," I said, keeping my eyes on Mark while jabbing a finger in Phil's direction. "They are *still* threatening her."

Mark offered a weak smile. "Kat. Please. We are going to get this all figured out."

Phil turned to me, expressionless. "Those documents you have in your possession are privileged, and they are the property of Darden Pharmaceuticals. Turn them over or you'll be disbarred."

I whipped around to face him. "You threatened my *daughter,*" I shot back. "*You'll* go to jail."

"What are you talking about?" Phil made a face, like he had just tasted something sour, then turned to Mark. "What is she talking about?"

"I told you she mentioned this," Mark said, aiming an accusatory look Phil's way. "I warned you about doing anything extreme."

"No one threatened anybody's daughter," Phil said to Mark. Then he turned back to me. "I have no idea what you're talking about. That never happened."

I dug out my phone and clicked on one of the two photographs of Cleo. "*This.* This is what I'm talking about." I held the phone up at eye level, making sure both men got a good look. "There were also men in a car, watching me. I saw them more than once. They took this picture. They're threatening my daughter, and it needs to stop."

"We didn't have anything to do with that photo." Phil almost sounded amused. "That looks like the work of an amateur."

"I *saw* your men." I was nearly shouting at this point. "They were following me."

"I don't deny we did surveillance," he said. "That's standard procedure in high-profile matters."

Mark reached out to put a hand on my arm, but I moved out of reach. "Kat, if a threat was made, I apologize—"

"*What* are you apologizing for? It didn't happen!" Phil hissed at Mark. "What did happen is that your employee screwed *my* employee and lied to you about it. And now she's trying to use privileged information to destroy us, *your* client. It's unethical *and* illegal."

"Maybe we can dispense with the hysterics and stick to the facts," I snapped back. "Those facts are the following: I have the documents that were in Tim Lyall's possession, or rather, I have photographs of them. And before you get any ideas about quick fixes, you should know that they are safely and securely uploaded to several places, including the cloud. The good news about using someone as careful as Tim is that he keeps extremely thorough records. And the bad news about threatening somebody like me is that I am always prepared."

"You should keep in mind where those documents got Doug Sinclair."

I felt an uncomfortable prickle across my skin. They would try to kill me, too. But I was well versed in men thinking they were entitled to take what they wanted from me. I knew how to navigate my way around them. I knew how to survive.

"What's actually going to happen right now is the following: I'm going to walk out that door." I kept my voice low and even. "Then I'm going to leave this building, unimpeded. Once I'm gone, you've got twelve hours to call off the dogs *and* get me the phone that sent the threats about Cleo, as a show of good faith. If you don't comply, I'll see to it that the emails Doug Sinclair wrote, warning you personally about Xytek, are published in *The New York Times.* And before you think about trying to remove me as a threat—it's too late. It's already in motion. If something happens to me and I'm not there to stop it, the story will run in the *Times.*"

"You'll be disbarred." Phil's face was beet red. But his voice had lost some of its strength.

"You think I care?" I asked. "You threatened my daughter. She's the only thing that matters to me."

"Kat, they didn't threaten Cleo," Mark said softly. "I would know. Which means they don't have that phone. They can't deliver what they don't have."

"And *why* should I believe you?"

"I know you're disappointed with me, Kat. That's fair. There are things . . . I wanted to stay in business, in part so Ruth could be taken care of. I'm not trying to use that as an excuse. But it is the truth. It's also the truth that if Cleo is being threatened, it's coming from someone else."

Mark wasn't stupid; he had to know I was recording this meeting. Why carve out the threat to Cleo as the one thing he wouldn't admit to—unless it was true?

"Don't send those documents, Kat. Please," Phil went on. His tone was imploring now. "Mistakes were made with this particular drug, obviously. But Darden is committed to making that right. We're settling with the plaintiffs and we'd be happy to follow your specific guidance with respect to fair compensation."

"For the babies you knowingly injured? The ones who died?" I asked. "You think there's a dollar value for that?"

"Come on," Phil said quietly. "You and I both know there's a price for everything. And everyone."

I turned to leave. "Why don't we see how tonight goes—get me that phone, like I asked, and we'll see." A few more steps and I was at the door. "But if I get another threat about Cleo, I promise you, you'll have your answer."

December 24, 1992

I'm going to do it! Sneak out. *It's a risk. You can lose your weekend privileges permanently. But like Reed said, are those privileges really worth anything anyway?*

He's right that you only live once. I have to start determining my own future. And I am brave enough to do that. Reed believes it. And I believe it, too.

As for tonight, all I need to do is slip out the front door when the attendant isn't looking. She's hardly ever at that desk lately. I think maybe she's dating one of the orderlies.

Because I deserve to be a regular teenager. To have fun. To live a little. To sneak out to see a boy I have a crush on.

Anyway, what's the worst thing that could happen? It's Christmas Eve.

CLEO

Vivienne is already there, sitting in a red booth at the back of the narrow diner when I arrive an hour later. She summoned me with a text that was light on explanation. She has her hair back in a wide white headband, huge red reading glasses perched at the end of her patrician nose. And she's smoking. Inside. She's focused on her phone, punching out a text, gives no indication that she's even noticed me as I slide into the booth and sit across from her.

"Fucking idiots. Think an MBA from Harvard makes them God."

"You can't smoke in here," I say, looking around for the employee who is surely about to charge over to scold her. "Obviously."

She gestures to the cooks in the open kitchen, the waitress standing nearby. "Do they look like they care? It's late." She peers at me through her reading glasses. "Our offices are around the corner. They always let me smoke when it's empty. That's why I come here." She takes another long drag as the waitress appears, grim-faced, with a little saucer for her to flick her ashes in. "They don't mind."

"Pretty sure they do . . . What's up?"

"I got a call from that *New York Times* reporter." Her voice is quiet and serious now. "But this time she said she was looking for your mom, too. She wouldn't tell me why, but she sounded . . . worried. Genuinely." She hesitates and looks up at me. "I thought you should know."

"What did she say, exactly?"

"She wouldn't tell me much." Vivienne stubs out the cigarette in the saucer. "But apparently your mom gave her documents related to something, something that wasn't me. But your mom was stressed at the time, according to the reporter. And then she vanished."

"Why did she call you and not my mom's law firm? Or the police?"

"That's what I asked . . . She wouldn't tell me that, either. Practically hung up on me instead."

"Oh," I said. "That doesn't sound good."

"It's like I said from the beginning. I think her job might be the point after all," Vivienne says. "It's not new information."

But for some reason, this feels like terrible news. I look down at the table. I can feel Vivienne staring at me.

"Hey, what about that Reed Harding guy?" she offers. "You have any luck finding him?"

There's no way I want Vivienne sniffing out Reed Harding's trail; not when I have a pretty good idea where it leads. "No, that was a dead end," I say, convincingly, too, I'm pretty sure.

"I can keep looking," she offers. "There's always something, somewhere."

I shake my head. I need to divert her attention. "It would be a waste of time. There was someone blackmailing her, though. I think we should figure out who."

"Blackmailing her about what?"

"I have no idea." I keep my eyes focused on the sticky sugar dispenser on the table between us. "They said they knew something about her past. Anyway, I have the phone number the texts were coming from. Do you think you can find out who it belongs to?"

"Maybe," she says. "It'll depend if it's a prepay or on a service, for starters. But I can—I *will*—do the best I can. I can probably find out something."

"Thank you," I say. "Can I ask you something else?" It's something I've been wondering ever since Vivienne started helping me.

She lights another cigarette, takes a long drag, and eyes me through the cloud of smoke as she exhales. "Sure, why not?"

"If you can do all this stuff—hack in anywhere and all that— why did you even need my mom? Why not fix your situation yourself?"

Vivienne finally notices the waitress shoot a look her way. With a small rueful smile, she stubs out the cigarette. She carefully swipes up a few rogue ashes with the palm of her hand, then looks up at me.

"Because computers, information, *data*—it only gets you so far. You can figure out what happened, you can follow a trail to what's next, but you can't really *fix* anything, not usually. A problem that starts with people usually has to end that way, too. And your mom is good with people. Very good. Just like you."

"Hey!" someone shouts as I pass a brownstone stoop on my way home from the diner. It's dark, the street mostly empty, and it's the kind of outsize New York City shout that makes you want to speed up. "Hey! Cleo!"

I turn warily. Annie. She's marching toward me, crooked but determined. Like she's concentrating hard to accomplish her mission. She's definitely wasted. There is nothing good about seeing Annie at this hour, looking that angry and out of it. But I suspect that taking off will only make things worse.

"What's up?" I ask as she stops in front of me.

"Tell your dad to leave my mom alone."

"What do you mean?"

"*Your dad.*" She draws it out, stepping close enough that I can smell the alcohol on her—sour and stale—like she was drunk yesterday before she was drunk today.

"I have no idea what you're talking about."

"Right," she says. "Your dad won't stop texting her. And she wants him to *stop*. Obsessive freak," she mutters.

"That's not true." But my heart is hammering in my chest. The affair. The affair.

"You McHughs are *all* alike. You come in and use people and ruin shit and do whatever you want. All you care about is yourselves." She's waving her arms around wildly as she talks. "Look at what you did to me," she says, jabbing a finger into her own chest.

"What *I* did to you?" I ask, though I immediately wish I hadn't.

"Yes! We were best friends—you totally ditched me!"

"We were *twelve years old*! Annie, my mom is missing. And I'm really upset. I just—I can't do this now. I need to go." I start to step around her, but she blocks my path.

"Well, my mom is *freaking out*! So tell your dad to leave her the hell alone, the sloppy-haired fuck. Or maybe *I'll* tell him myself." As she wobbles triumphantly away, she calls back, "Because maybe that's what he needs, someone to make him back off—for good. I mean, look how well it worked with your mom."

TRANSCRIPT OF RECORDED SESSION

DR. EVELYN BAUER
SESSION #5

CLEO McHUGH: Kyle has started sending customers to mess with me. He says I owe him two thousand dollars. That it cost him that much money when I stopped working for him, which isn't true. And anyway, Kyle doesn't care about money. He has so much already. The drugs, the dealing—it's all a game to him, something to piss his parents off. His dad is a total monster.

EVELYN BAUER: That sounds upsetting. But you seem pretty matter-of-fact about it.

CM: That's funny. That's exactly what Will said when I told him. He said that I was "disassociating" from the situation and that wasn't good.

EB: That's a smart observation . . . By the way, how did you and Will meet again, exactly? At last week's session, you said on campus; then we got off on other things.

CM: We met in class. Is this two thousand dollars even going to be enough? . . . Maybe I'm done disassociating, because right now I am starting to freak out about it a little bit.

EB: You know, what Kyle is doing is illegal. You

could call the police, or report him to the
school—he is a student, after all.

CM: But then wouldn't I end up getting in trouble,
too? I helped him sell drugs.

EB: I suppose that is possible. What about your
parents? I think you need to tell someone, Cleo.
You have good reason to be concerned about
your safety. Kyle has already proved that he's
willing to get physical.

CM: I asked my dad for the money.

EB: Okay, but that's not exactly what I meant. You
need to tell someone about Kyle's threats, the
situation in general. What did your dad say?

CM: That he'd get me the money.

EB: Did you tell him what it was for?

CM: No, he's not like that. He trusts me.

EB: That's good that he trusts you, of course. But
that doesn't solve the problem that no adults
have been alerted to this situation. He needs to
know the details. Maybe you could send a text to
your mom and let her know. It might also be a
way of reopening that door of communication.

CM: You've been alerted.

EB: Yes, but I'm bound by rules of confidentiality.
I don't like the idea of your being in this
situation alone, Cleo.

CM: Will knows.

EB: Again, another student isn't exactly what I—

CM: Will's not a student.

EB: I'm sorry, I'm confused. Didn't you say that you
met in class?

CM: Yeah. Modern poetry . . . It's um . . . I know
what this is going to seem like, so I don't
think I want to . . .

EB: Cleo, you know I don't like to push you to talk
    about things before you're ready. But your
    obvious hesitation to get into details about
    Will is raising concerns for me.

CM: It's not like that. It's just . . .

EB: Just what, Cleo?

CM: It's Will's class.

EB: I don't understand.

CM: Will isn't *in* my class. He's . . . he's the
    professor.

KATRINA

It took a couple hours for Ahmed to get back to me. If he'd noticed the texts' content, he didn't say a word.

It's an actual burner phone. Not an app.

Ok. That's a dead end, then?

Not necessarily. I can do a little more "digging." I think I've got someone who might have better access. If I can get a point of purchase, will send ASAP . . . You're welcome. And you owe me.

An actual burner phone purchased in an electronics store with security cameras? Darden security would never make such an amateurish mistake. Phil Beaumont had made this point back in Mark's office and it had stuck with me. Darden would surely use some kind of app, which would be far harder to crack than a physical phone, even a disposable one.

What if Phil had been telling the truth? If Darden hadn't been sending me those messages, then who—Kyle? He was furious, but he didn't have the savvy or the commitment to dig that deep into my past. Which left . . . whoever was in the hall that night at Haven House. Silas presumably. What I'd suspected from the start. But why now, after all this time? Something about the timing didn't make sense.

Or maybe the timing *did* make sense—but not for Silas.

Aidan. I'd been trying to avoid even considering the possibility. Quite a coincidence that the amount the blackmailer was demanding was almost exactly the amount Aidan needed. And while I'd never told him the details, I'd alluded to how they'd shuttled me out of Haven House like smuggled contraband. It wasn't all that difficult to imagine a scenario in which a desperate and frustrated Aidan could have gone poking around, and eventually tracked down Silas or whoever had been on the scene that night and found out the whole story, or enough to threaten me with it. He was lazy, but he could be surprisingly resourceful when it came to getting the things he wanted. But threatening Cleo, even as a ruse? That would be a new low.

I could barely contain my relief as I looked down at the old-school burner Jimmy handed me when he showed up in Park Slope unannounced a few hours later. A burner meant no cloud, no Find My iPhone app. Just as I'd hoped. "Thank you. And thanks for the house call. I really appreciate it."

"There's something you should know, though," he said, pausing halfway back down the steps.

"I feel like I probably would rather not."

"Guy woke up on my way out," Jimmy said, ignoring me. "I had a mask on, but he saw me. He said, 'I'll fucking kill that bitch.'"

"Shit." Did he mean—me or Cleo? She was a much easier target.

"Listen, who knows who or what he was talking about. He was half asleep," Jimmy went on. "And I did grab a couple other things—some cash, gold chain on his nightstand. It's possible that when he notices that, he'll think it was a robbery. But I got to be honest; my feeling was he knew it was you."

* * *

I spent the afternoon at the Central Park Precinct, trying to convince them to let Ben Bleyer, wayward CMO of Play Up, go. He'd broken out of rehab in the Hamptons and made his way back to the city. He'd been arrested for public intoxication (and urination) near the John Lennon memorial in Central Park— all before 11:00 a.m. He was so different this time when I saw him—exhausted and disheveled and also sad. His eyes were red-rimmed as we stood on the sidewalk outside the police station, listening to kids playing raucously in the park nearby.

"Thank you." Bleyer sounded so sincerely remorseful that I had a hard time making eye contact. I needed to extricate myself.

"No, problem," I said.

"That's the thing," he said. "I think I finally see how big a problem this is, how big a problem *I* am. I always thought if I got worse, I would stop drinking. No one warns you that when you feel ashamed enough of the things you've done, the opposite can be true."

"You know what, Ben? I think you may be right," I said, not liking how dry my own mouth felt as I turned to go. "Absolutely right."

The late-afternoon sun cast a warm gold light over the rooftops as I turned down our block. It made me feel safe, almost hopeful for a moment. But when I reached the house, my feet were rooted in place. We had a security system, a good one—I would have received an alert if someone had gone in. But I couldn't shake a feeling of unease.

I shaded my eyes—was that a figure in Cleo's bedroom window? But no, it was only the sun. I started at a sound behind me, turned around quickly. It was George, angrily dragging his neighbor's trash cans up to their gate. I felt a surge of relief. George might not be the most reliable watchdog, but he was much better than nothing. And despite his prickly exterior, I had a soft spot for poor George, especially these days. I knew what it was like to be lonely, how it changed you.

"Hi, George," I said brightly.

He squinted, like he was trying to place me. It wasn't clear whether he'd been successful. "Hello," he said warily as he came to a stop at his own gate.

"I'm worried there might be something of a situation inside my house. I'm sure it's nothing, but it could be . . . dangerous." I needed to keep my request simple enough for George to understand but sufficiently serious to trigger a moment of clarity. But George's face was still a total blank—neither alarmed nor intrigued. "Could you keep an ear out?"

George pointed at my house. "If this is some kind of danger to the rest of the neighborhood," he said a little aggressively, "then we should get the police out here right now."

Alerting the police would be a very bad idea. Amateurs were even more dangerous when they panicked.

"No, no," I snapped nervously. "No police. Please. They can't be trusted in this situation." I felt guilty for preying on George's paranoid tendencies. But I wasn't sure what else to do.

"Hmm." He nodded, eyes narrowed conspiratorially. "I see. Okay. Okay."

But wait. I *did* want him to call the police if there was somebody inside waiting for me, didn't I?

"How about don't call the police *unless* I scream 'Fire!' Okay?"

"Fire," he repeated, then looked up toward the house.

"Yes, then *do* call the police."

"I suppose I can do that."

"And if you hear something else . . . maybe check it out?" I added, and then immediately regretted confusing the issue.

"Mmm," George grunted, decidedly less committal.

"Oh, also, please don't mention this to anyone, okay?" I added.

"Even Cleo or Aidan. I don't want to scare them." The last thing I needed was to give Aidan more ammunition in a divorce proceeding. Or for Cleo to have another reason to be angry.

George gave me another blank look. I smiled as I started up the stairs to the house, not wanting to muddy the waters any further. "Okay, great. Thanks, George. I really appreciate it."

George stayed there watching as I made my way up to the door. I decided to take this as a good sign.

Inside, I flipped on the lights and headed straight for the butcher block on the kitchen counter. Pulled out the largest carving knife. I felt oddly more vulnerable with the knife in my hand as I moved quickly, checking the rooms downstairs first—in the closets, behind doors, under the desk. All clear. I relaxed a tiny bit as I looked up the steps, only two more floors to go.

Upstairs, I checked under our bed—my bed—and in the walk-in closet, then up to the rooms on the third floor, including Cleo's, my chest loosening a little with each place I cleared. Nothing was out of place anywhere.

Are you on your way? I texted Cleo when I was back downstairs.
OMFG! I'm headed to the train! CALM. DOWN.

I'd never been so happy to be told off. Almost home. Almost safe and sound. Everything might be fine if Cleo could just get here in one piece.

Okay! See you soon!

I quickly texted McKinney, back on Cleo watch himself, who confirmed that he would stay on her until she arrived at the house.

Shit, food. Cleo was supposed to be coming for dinner. It would make what I had to tell her seem less alarming: *Look, I cooked dinner. How bad can it really be that someone is threatening to kill you unless I pay them off because once upon a time I murdered someone?*

A quick rummage in the refrigerator turned up a roasting chicken and some green beans. I set the water to boil and grabbed a box of couscous. As I ripped open the top, the doorbell rang. Too soon for Cleo, I was pretty sure. I put down the box and made my way over to the living room window. Janine was standing on the stoop.

"I was beginning to worry you weren't home," she said when I opened the door.

"Oh, hi," I said. "Thank you again for the other night. That was really above and beyond."

"No problem," she said. But she looked stressed.

"Is everything okay?" I asked, though whatever this was, I had no time for it now.

"Do you have—could I come in?"

"Cleo is actually coming home for dinner. She should be here any second." I was hoping she'd take the hint.

"Only until she gets here, then?" Janine's tone was a little manic. "I sort of need to avoid going home myself."

"What's wrong?"

"It's kind of a long story . . ." Her eyes were brimming. "I really won't stay long, I promise. I'll vanish as soon as Cleo shows up."

Crap.

"Sure," I said, forcing a smile. She'd spent hours sitting in the dark, helping me watch Cleo. "Come in and have a seat." I gestured toward the kitchen counter. "I'm glad for the company. But if you could maybe kind of slip out as soon as Cleo gets here? I barely got her to come. I don't want to set her off." I also couldn't run the risk of Janine mentioning our little dorm-side vigil to Cleo.

"Say no more," Janine said, snapping her fingers. "I'll vanish. And don't worry, I will not breathe a word about the other night." She made a locking motion near her lips. "As far as I'm concerned, that never happened."

I exhaled louder than I'd intended to. "Thank you," I said. "Can I get you anything?"

"A glass of water would be great," she said, looking around.

"God, your house is always so spotless. *And* you work. I don't know how you do it all."

"You should see my office," I said, which would have been funny were it not for the mess Darden's men had left behind.

"I find that hard to believe, but okay," Janine said, a tightness to her voice. Like I'd stuck my foot in my mouth somehow.

Janine still looked uneasy as she sat on the edge of one of the stools. Like maybe she regretted coming, that bond we'd formed in Washington Square Park dissipating in the light of day. Friendships grounded solely in motherhood did tend to be extremely fragile. I grabbed two glasses from the cabinet and filled them from the spout in the refrigerator. I couldn't remember the last time I'd had anything to eat or drink.

"I'm sorry. I'm really on edge," Janine said as I handed her one of the waters. The prickly edge was gone again from her voice, like some kind of storm had blown through. She sounded sad now, and vulnerable. "Things at home are just . . . Liam and I got into this huge argument a second ago—like out-of-control explosive." She shifted uncomfortably on the stool. "He's got a temper. People don't realize that about him. Anyway, I confronted him about something and . . . He completely flew off the handle."

"I'm sorry," I said, and I was. I was also aware this might not be a throw-someone-out-when-Cleo-gets-here kind of situation. "Do you want to talk about it?"

"Liam has been having an affair, for *years*. I just found out. I told him that I want a divorce." I stared at her in shock. Liam may have been a cold fish, but he had always seemed so devoted. "And, you know, he had the nerve to refuse to leave? So there he is, over there at the house . . . And there's . . . Well, I guess there's nothing I can do about it. It's his house."

"Did you buy the house while you were married?"

Janine nodded. "Yes. But he earns all the money."

"It's still half your house," I said. "Half of everything is yours.

It doesn't matter if you contributed financially . . . Half of everything I have is Aidan's."

She looked at me quizzically.

"Aidan and I are getting a divorce," I said. And what a relief it was to tell someone. "He cheated on me, too."

"What?" It was Janine's turn to look stunned. "Why would he do that?" Like she genuinely couldn't imagine.

I laughed. "Well, the sex, I'm guessing . . . And the wide-eyed admiration."

Janine laughed, too. "Men are so ridiculous. Funny how you can see the absurdity of it so clearly when it's somebody else." She gestured to me. "Aidan is insane." She set her glass down on the counter. "You know what? I think I need to call my lawyer. Could I use your office? I raced out without my cell phone."

"Of course." Letting Janine use my office for a few minutes to call a lawyer was something that I could absolutely do. I wanted to. I led her down the hall and pointed to the open door. "Let me know if you need anything."

"Is it okay if I close this—so you don't have to hear me. I'm a phone shrieker, according to Annie."

I could indeed hear Janine as I quickly prepared Cleo's favorite chicken recipe from memory—rosemary and olive oil. The familiar repetition was profoundly comforting in this moment: one thing done right, done so many times, for so many years. Maybe in the end that was the most important part of being a mother: being there to do the expected thing again and again. I had gotten some of that right at least. I thought of Janine back in my office, on the phone with a divorce lawyer. Annie, the daughter she was so close to, using the same drugs that Cleo had sold. Maybe no relationship was perfect. Maybe nothing was what it seemed.

Janine's voice was still echoing down the hall as I turned toward the stove with the chicken. She *was* shrill—Annie was right about that. It made me like Janine a little more, this awk-wardness in her otherwise flawless façade.

The wave of heat unexpectedly hit me full in the face as I slid the chicken into the oven. "Shit." I reached for a paper towel, dampening it and pressing it to my eyes.

When I tossed it in the garbage, I noticed a crumpled piece of paper on the floor next to the trash. It hadn't been there that morning—you noticed such things once you lived alone.

I picked up the paper and uncrumpled it. *KM*. It had been torn from the monogrammed pad in my office. There were two long rows of numbers in Aidan's handwriting. He'd been in the house? In my office? He still had keys—I'd been avoiding a con-frontation about getting them back. But we'd agreed he wouldn't come in without letting me know first.

I walked down the hall toward my office, listening to see if Janine was nearly done. I didn't want to interrupt her, but I needed to see if Aidan had left any other evidence behind of what he'd been up to.

It was quiet on the other side of the door. I pushed it open very slowly, ducking my head apologetically in case I had misinter-preted the silence and Janine was still listening to someone talk on the other end.

It took me a minute to process what I was seeing.

Janine was seated at my desk, bent toward a drawer on the right-hand side as she rifled through it. There were other draw-ers open, too. Lots of them. No headphones or earbuds anywhere in sight. Then I spotted Janine's cell phone sticking out of her bag on the floor.

"Yes, yes, I understand," she said quite loudly—as though she was on the phone, instead of looking through my things.

Then she froze. She'd noticed me, finally. Her mouth lifted slightly as she looked up. Her stare was cool as she slid closed the open drawers, one at a time. I waited for her embarrassment to surface—*I was only looking for a pen; I was curious; I'm so sorry.* For her to seem flustered or contrite. Something. Instead, she leaned back in my chair and crossed her arms.

"I need that phone, Kat," she said.

"What are you talking about?" I asked. But it hit me fast: Kyle's phone.

"Look, Annie was arrested the other night. Obviously, it's all some kind of misunderstanding. The lawyer I've got on the case says they'll have to dismiss all the charges—unless they come up with some kind of corroborating evidence. Like the photos on Kyle's phone."

"Why would I have Kyle's phone?" Denial: always the best first line of defense.

"I need to be able to protect Annie, Kat," she pressed on, undeterred. "And, of course, I'll make sure Cleo is protected, too. But I need that phone."

Luckily, the phone was now on a high shelf in the closet in my bedroom, inside my Mark Cross pocketbook. The small blue square one that Cleo had always loved as a little girl.

"I don't know what you're talking about," I said.

But Janine had been about to ask about something when we'd been at Washington Square Park, hadn't she? Right before we'd been interrupted by Tim Lyall's call. She'd been about to ask about the phone.

"I *know* you have it, Kat." Janine's voice was trembling now with rage. "Aidan told me."

Aidan? I'd only *just* told him. As I stared at her, a not-quite smile played on Janine's lips. *Aidan. Aidan and Janine.* All that time they'd spent together over the years when Aidan was home in the middle of the day. The way they loved to make fun of Liam and me and our corporate selling out to pay the bills they ran up—all their inside jokes. God, I was so stupid.

"You're *Her,*" I said. "You're with Aidan."

"*With* is an overstatement," she said, smirking. "*That* was never true."

The texts I'd read—about the feel of Aidan's mouth, the one that said I was ruining Cleo—had been from Janine. I gripped the doorframe as anger flooded me. But I needed to stay focused. Janine was not today's problem.

"Get out of my house, Janine," I said calmly, then turned for the doorway. "Right now."

In the kitchen, I began chopping the beans. I was going to give all my attention to what mattered, the hard conversation I needed to have with Cleo. I was going to make dinner.

Janine appeared a moment later. She came to stand alongside me at the sink. I kept my eyes on the beans. Kept chopping.

"What do you think you're doing, Kat?" she asked. "I mean, you're a mother. You know as well as I do: I'm going to do whatever it takes to protect Annie." Chopping, still chopping. I was hoping if I kept ignoring Janine, she would go. If she didn't, things were going to escalate—I wasn't giving her the phone, and I *was* angry about Aidan. It was an insulting, disrespectful betrayal. "Hello, Kat? I know you're going to do the right thing. That you're a good person, despite where you came from."

I stopped chopping. Turned to look at Janine.

"Where I came from, huh?" I asked quietly. I'd never told Janine about Haven House. Aidan must have. "You need to leave, Janine. Right now. I am not giving you that phone. Not now. Not ever."

"Kat!" she shouted, smacking a palm down on the counter. "If you don't give it to me, I'll go looking." She gestured toward the stairs. "I bet it's upstairs in your bedroom."

My eyes flashed up in that direction before I could think better of it. "Leave, Janine. Now."

She'd caught the tell—Janine was not stupid. "You know, if I were you, I'd probably put it *in* something. Like a pocket of some kind . . ." She started for the stairs.

I moved fast, heading her off, the knife still in my hand, gripped at my side. I raised it an inch. "Get out now, Janine." She looked down at the knife for a long moment. Finally, she met my eyes again, and shook her head.

"Seriously?" But she'd taken a small step back, lifted her hands.

I crossed my arms so that the knife rested menacingly against my forearm. "Maybe you were right—what you texted to Aidan . . . Maybe what I need is a really good therapist. Until then, you should leave. While you still can."

CLEO

As I wait for my father in the dimly lit, very quiet, impeccably clean kitchen, I picture Janine's face when she swung open the door the night my mom disappeared. Eyes so wide, mouth in a big O. Was it all a bit too much? Her hand to her chest, a damsel in distress in her teenage clothes—the low-rise jeans, the white cap-sleeve T-shirt . . . I was wearing almost the same thing that night. And then it occurs to me: Maybe that's why George said he saw me going into the house earlier. It was actually Janine. Mistresses kill wives all the time.

And yet, I'm still hoping somehow my dad and I won't have to get into details about whatever has gone on between Janine and him. We all spent so much time together over the years—dinners and sleepovers and family vacations. Were they together the whole time? I look around, as if there might be an answer that has nothing to do with my dad floating in the air. Because even now, I'm holding out hope.

My dad is late, as usual. I check my phone. Nothing from him, but there are four texts from Wilson of increasing intensity. She wants to talk to me *now*. She wants to *see* me. Whatever. Maybe that's even fine. She can come out to Brooklyn and cross-examine me about my drug-dealing "boyfriend," as she keeps insisting on calling him. It doesn't seem like I've got much choice when Wilson's last message is essentially an outright threat. *Tell me where you are, Cleo. Or I'm issuing a warrant for your arrest.*

At home in Park Slope, I finally write back.

I send the call that follows straight to voice mail.

Stay there. I'm up in Washington Heights but I'm on the way. An hour, hour ten. I'm not getting into it here in case you're not alone, but don't move, Cleo. I'm serious.

Ok, ok

Then I text my dad: *Where r u?* It'll serve him right if Wilson shows up while he's here. Maybe he'd like to explain Janine to both of us.

Almost there! comes his quick reply.

Maybe he's at Janine's right now. I feel like he might actually have the gall to do that.

I head over to the windows, careful to stay out of sight as I look across the street. I see Janine—I think it's Janine—pass in front of her bedroom window. I swear she looks toward our house. But then I see my dad, rushing down the block on our side of the street. *Thank God.* I return to my spot at the island. A second later, I hear his keys in the lock.

"Hey." He calls out, then comes from the vestibule into the kitchen, tossing his keys back and forth between his hands. He smiles stiffly. He's nervous. He should be. "What's the emergency?"

I want to stall, to delay the many terrible ways this conversation could go. All of which involve my dad adding to his pile of lies. But I know I need to get to the point and get this over with.

"It's Janine you've been having an affair with, right?" I ask—before he's even sat down.

"What?" My dad laughs awkwardly. He's avoiding my eyes.

"Annie told me you guys were together, Dad," I say. "Please don't lie to me any more than you already have."

I see the moment he reconsiders denying it. He sighs as he

drops himself onto the stool next to me. He rests his elbows on the counter, hands linked together. He presses his mouth to them as if he's keeping the words inside, before finally reaching down to grip the edge of the counter.

"You know the craziest thing about being an adult?" he asks, though it's not really a question. "You still manage to surprise yourself in all these ways. And some of those ways aren't good. They are not good at all." He smiles sadly. "I would have sworn I'd never cheat on your mom. Not because our marriage was so great—it wasn't. And I'm sure your mom would agree. Maybe we're too different. But I would have been sure that I was a better person than that." He gestures across the street, toward Janine's house.

"So it's true?"

He nods, eyes on the floor. "I'm sorry, Cleo," he says. "I am really sorry."

"Holy shit." My face feels hot as I grip the counter. I could have sworn that I'd already accepted the reality—my dad and Janine. But all these years, all this time?

"It was a mistake, obviously." My dad looks up at me, and I see that while he wants me not to be angry, he doesn't actually feel bad. There's something so flat about his expression. Calculating.

"What if Janine had something to do with what happened to Mom?" I ask.

"She didn't," he says. "I know that she didn't."

"But George saw somebody that night—I think it might have been Janine."

My dad shakes his head.

"Why, Dad? Because you think she's so great?"

"Because I know she didn't. She *was* actually mad at your mom, though," he says. "I'm telling you that because I don't want you to think I'm hiding anything anymore. Angry or not, it wasn't Janine, though. I know it wasn't."

"She was jealous, that's why she was angry?"

"No, your mom had Kyle's phone. Because he had pictures of you on there, I guess. She took it to protect you." Kyle showing up at my dorm, some cop going after him—that all makes a little more sense now. "Well, apparently, there are also pictures of Annie on there . . . So Janine wanted the phone. Your mom said no. They argued . . . And then Janine left."

"And then Mom just happened to end up . . ." *End up what?* I still can't bring myself to think dead is a possibility. Even though I know, at this point, it's the most likely one. "So you think it's a coincidence that Janine, who you were cheating with, was mad at your *wife* and now your wife . . . Are you fucking *kidding* me?"

"It wasn't Janine, Cleo."

"I get that having sex with Janine has made you delusional, apparently, but—"

"I was with her," he says, cutting me off. "I was *with* Janine, across the street, when something happened to your mom here."

"You were at the airport," I say stupidly. But my hands have tightened into fists. *His lost time. There was lost time.*

He shakes his head. "I was across the street," he says, looking me in the eye, and now it's with . . . self-righteousness? "I landed at four-thirty and went to Janine's. I got there around five-thirty, right after Janine left your mom. There wouldn't have been enough time for Janine to do what you're suggesting. To do something to your mom and then, you know . . . move her."

"Wait, was Annie there . . ."

"She came home at one point," he says. "She's known about us. You know how Janine and Annie are—more like friends than mother and daughter."

"How long has it been going on?" My voice is icy as I glare at him.

"Cleo," he says, with a shake of his head. "Come on, you—"

"How long?"

He's quiet again. "Years," he says. "Since you were little."

And I think of the beach that day, my dad not being there to make sure I didn't drown—not because he was off somewhere. But because he was off with Janine.

I might be sick, right there on the island. "Can you please go?" I manage. "I just—I need to be alone."

For a moment it looks like he's about to argue. But then he stares up at the ceiling, like an answer is written there.

"I'm sorry, Cleo," he says again as he gets up to leave. "I really am."

This time I know what I'm looking for as I search my mom's bedroom—Kyle's burner. It's small, a flip phone. It's possible that I missed it tucked somewhere, that the police did, if my mom was hiding it on purpose. I look again under her bed and in the drawers. Nothing.

But when I open the closet, my eyes snag on the top shelf. The small collection of fancy handbags—the only luxury I ever saw her allow herself. Maybe that's why I was obsessed with playing with them when I was little, because they seemed like a window into some secret frivolous side to her. I grab a stool and reach for the blue box-shaped bag that I'd always loved the most because it looked like an adorable little suitcase. I used to carry it around the house when I was seven or eight, pretending that I was "going on a trip."

As I'm stepping down from the stool, sure enough something shifts inside the purse. When I snap it open, a phone tumbles out. Kyle's phone. I sit down on the bed, clutching the square box to my chest. What if whatever happened, happened because of this? Because of me and my stupid choices?

The doorbell rings downstairs—Wilson made way better time than she said. I get up and make my way slowly down the stairs.

I know that I need to turn Kyle's phone over to her, no matter what might be on it.

But when I finally look out, I see Will standing on the stoop. I jerk open the door.

He can't return my aggressive hug because his hands are full, a book in one, Whole Foods bag in the other. "I saw your dad leave, thought maybe you could use some company."

"I'm so glad to see you," I say. The rush of relief knocks the wind from me. I can't even remember why I'd felt so irritated at him earlier.

He lifts the bag of groceries as he steps inside. "I thought I could cook."

I take a seat on a stool at the island as Will unpacks the groceries—tomato, garlic, onion, pasta—on the counter. While he begins to chop, I consider the fact that he'll be here when Wilson arrives. But who cares? She can judge if she wants. It's not like we're committing a crime. Kyle is a *much* bigger problem.

As Will cooks, I tell him about what happened in New Haven. And then without really planning to, I tell him that I think my mom killed someone all those years ago. That she must have had a reason, but still . . . That maybe she's been kidnapped by someone blackmailing her. Or killed. That is possible, too. "So, in the end, it seems like you found more questions up there than answers?"

"Only what my mom apparently did," I say. "And that place she lived in was . . . horrible. I had no idea how bad. It's amazing she's as normal as she is, given what she's been through. Maybe I should tell the police about the blackmail at least. What if it really does have to do with what happened to her? If she did kill somebody, I know she must have had a reason—self-defense maybe. Whatever happened, I'm sure he deserved it."

"I don't know—as you said, the last thing you want to do is have your mom come back, only to get arrested . . . I mean, the reality is, you don't know what happened that night. It was a long time ago. What if that person deserved it but your mom is still somehow guilty of murder?"

He's right. Why is Will the only person in the world who seems to be able to be honest with me and not make me feel worse?

"I want to do something."

"Of course you do. How about a glass of wine?" he asks. "I think what you need most is a second to collect your thoughts."

He checks in a couple cabinets before he finds two wineglasses. Like we're a married couple. Like this is our home. I imagine myself older—at a place where the years between us no longer matter—Will cooking, me watching from the couch, feet tucked beneath me. And I feel so safe and calm. This is right. It wouldn't feel this good if it wasn't.

"A glass of wine would be great, thank you."

"Oh, and that's for you," he says, pointing at the book he left facedown on the island as he pours from an already opened bottle tucked in a corner of the counter.

I turn it over. Mary Oliver's *A Poetry Handbook*.

"Obviously, your mind is elsewhere right now. But I thought it could be a reminder. Despite all this, there are still good things in your life, things to feel hopeful about. You have a future, Cleo, that will extend beyond this chaos. You are a truly gifted writer. I believe that will light your way."

How, exactly, am I supposed to *not* be in love with him?

"Thank you," I say, and my eyes fill with tears that I don't try to hide. "Really."

As Will pours, some wine sloshes onto the marble counter. "Oh, shoot," he says. There are red flecks on his white shirt. "Ah, I'll be right back. Let me go take a look in the mirror." He gestures down the hall.

He disappears toward the bathroom and I flip the book open to the title page. There is a note from Will. *Please promise me you'll be a writer. God gives the gift to few.*

KATRINA

I hadn't gone back to lock the door after Janine left. Otherwise, Cleo would have had to ring the bell—she never remembers her keys.

"Hey!" I called out when I heard the front door open. "Perfect timing!"

Cleo didn't answer. And I couldn't see her from where I was on the far side of the kitchen island. Taking off her shoes in the vestibule, headphones on probably—they'd been surgically implanted in her ears since she turned twelve. All the times I yelled at her to take them off. I worried about her hearing going; I worried about her getting hit in a crosswalk; I worried about her being one of those rude and obnoxious teens. What a waste of time. I'd worried so much, about all the wrong things.

I put the knife down and wiped my hands on a towel. As excited as I was to see Cleo, I knew we had a hard conversation in front of us.

I headed around the island and toward the door.

"Cleo, what's taking you so—"

I froze. Not Cleo. A tall figure. A man. An unfamiliar man.

"Hey!" I shouted, backing up. "Get out! This is my house!"

But the man didn't move. Not toward me. And not toward the door. He was turned to the side and the vestibule light was off. I couldn't see his face clearly. I didn't recognize him.

But then I did.

My phone. On the island. I lunged for it with shaking hands.

"Put down the phone, Katrina," the man said calmly. "If I have to hurt you, when Cleo gets here, I'll have to hurt her, too."

I ended the call as the 911 operator picked up. My whole body was trembling.

"It is a very beautiful house," he said. *His* voice. It was like fire in my bones. "You have good taste, especially considering where you came from. But then I guess all the money you were given helps. Not all of us got so lucky."

And with that he stepped forward, so that I could see him more clearly: longish salt-and-pepper hair, square jaw, and his bright blue eyes. Electric. That's what they were. And I knew them. I did. All these years later, those eyes were exactly the same. Impossibly blue. And now utterly dead.

But Reed was *dead.* I had killed him. I'd stabbed him in the neck. Not intentionally maybe, but I'd done it. I'd seen his lifeless body on the stairs when he'd collapsed chasing after me. And yet here he was, standing in my house.

Run, I thought. *He's going to kill you.*

But I couldn't move. And there was no way out anyway. I was trapped.

"You thought I was dead, I know," Reed said, smirking. He was still very attractive in that way he had always been, beautiful really—those eyes. And all that confidence. "I lost a lot of blood, so much blood, right? The lady who owned the house would not stop screaming. That's the last thing I remember before I lost consciousness." His laugh had a bitter tinge to it. "Anyway, it was touch and go there for a while, but in the end no permanent damage. Apart from this—" He lifts his hair to reveal the back of his neck. "Nasty scar. But I'm lucky with the hair. It's made it easy to hide."

The texts had been from him. Reed. The boy I killed. Still alive after all this time.

And Cleo. Now he was threatening Cleo.

"Stay away from my daughter." I didn't recognize my own voice, it was so deep and fierce.

"Bit late for that," he said with a lopsided grin. "Cleo and Professor William Butler—I so wanted to go with the Yeats also, but, you know, there was no way . . . Anyway, Cleo and Professor Butler have been having a very good time together."

The new boyfriend. Breathe. I had to keep breathing. I had to stay focused—Cleo would be here any minute.

"What do you want?"

"Well, let's see," he spat out. "I want my fucking future back. I'm a fifty-one-year-old assistant professor at NYU. I'd have been tenured at Harvard fifteen years ago if it weren't for you. You cost me everything—money, success, happiness. You cost me everything I deserved. You owe me."

"I defended myself."

"You know, it's funny how similar you and Cleo are," he went on, smiling suggestively. "In nearly every way."

Kill him. I am going to kill him.

The knife. I glanced toward the island. But Reed snatched it up, inspected the blade, then pointed it in my direction.

"Can't have this getting into the wrong hands, can we?" He held the knife, point down, grinding it into the marble. Then he motioned for my phone. "Give that to me, too." I handed it over, and he tucked it into his jacket pocket. "I ended up having to leave Yale, you know. After I got out of the hospital, Director Daitch made that *very* clear to me. My choices were leave New Haven or get sent to jail. Even though you and I both know you wanted it that night."

"You drugged me. You *raped* me." The words burned coming out of my mouth. I'd never said them out loud.

"Right, rape, sure," he said. "What, exactly, did you think was going to happen coming over that night? You knew. You knew exactly. And you wanted it. You just felt bad about it after so you attacked me like some kind of insane animal."

I hated the way it felt. Like he was right. Like I was to blame. For liking a boy who was that much older. For wanting so desperately for him to like me back. For someone to. Even though all I'd done was sneak out and go over to his house. I drank a cup of peppermint tea at eight o'clock at night.

Then blackness. The rest was only flashes. Like the lights going on and off. Or the scenes of a relived nightmare. My body being yanked this way and that—arms, legs. Like a rag doll. Panting in my ear. Sweat. The sound of my one "no"—only one, but loud and clear. Like a punch into the air.

Some days it felt like that sound still lived inside me—an endless primal howl.

And then, when I woke up hours later, my mouth so dry, it felt like my skin was tearing when I opened my lips to drink from the bathroom sink. The pain between my legs. The dried blood on my thighs. I was naked except for my gauzy pink top.

Back in Reed's room, I tried not to wake him as I tugged on my underwear and my jeans next to the bed. It was late, past midnight. He opened his eyes as I was lacing up my first sneaker.

"Where you going?" he'd asked, sleepy, playful.

"Just . . . home."

"What's the matter?" He sounded grumpy now.

"Nothing, I need to go." But my voice sounded like something was very wrong. I couldn't help it. "They'll notice I'm gone."

Reed sat up as I focused on tying my sneakers. Then he reached out and grabbed my thigh, hard.

"Don't get confused here," he'd said. "About what happened."

I'd tried to pull my leg away, but he squeezed it tighter. "You're hurting me."

"Tell me you understand."

"Let me go."

"I will when you say you understand: We were having fun."

And then I saw the little knife next to the lime on his night-stand. The one he must have sliced up for a drink, or maybe to stick in the top of a beer. Maybe to celebrate while I was passed out cold.

"Let me go."

And he did. His hand dropped from my leg. Maybe I could have even run then. Maybe I could have gotten away. Maybe.

"Stop being such a fucking bitch and—"

I grabbed the knife. Reed laughed and reached to grab it back. I swung for his arm. To stop him from touching me again. But when he lunged toward me, the knife ended up in the back of his neck. There was this slow-motion moment when we both realized what I'd done. I watched his face fall. And then all that blood.

But now here he was all these years later, in my kitchen. Furious. *Cleo.* Reed was still ranting about something. It seemed like he had been ranting for a while.

"My parents cut me off. Completely. No money. No contact. Nothing. Because they wanted an explanation for my dropping out of Yale, and I couldn't give one. Even wrote me out of their will. I mean, they were always assholes—they went away to Paris for Christmas that last year, *alone.* Left me to fend for myself for the holiday, when I was only a sophomore in college. Without their money, I had to get a job waiting tables and finish up at Fairfield University—at night," he said. "*Fairfield University.* Do you have any idea how long it took for me to claw my way back?" He was pointing the knife at my face now.

He was going to kill me. I felt sure he was going to try. I needed to get him talking, distracted. I needed to buy myself time.

"You seem like you're doing all right," I said. "Professor at NYU?"

He began to pace, gesticulating with the knife in his hand. "*Assistant* professor." The cords in his neck strained. His face was flushed. "Do you know where I'd be right now if it weren't for you? I was derailed for *years*. I killed it at Fairfield University, obviously. Eventually, got my master's at a piece of shit state school that was basically free—but not my Ph.D., at Rutgers. That was on me, *again*. Then it was years and years of crap adjunct positions at Dumbass Community College and Blue-Collar State. And God forbid some girl makes some shit up about you at one of those places—you're out, no questions asked. In the Ivy League, no one cares who you fuck!" He stopped pacing and turned to look at me. He was smiling now. "But I guess there was one big consolation prize. Who would have thought I'd look up during my very first lecture at NYU, my first *real* job, and see . . . *you*? The person who ruined my life. God, for a minute I thought I was going crazy. That Cleo really *was* you. You two look exactly the same. Exactly. And to be clear, it's not like I was obsessing about you all these years or something. Don't flatter yourself. I've had far better things to do with my time. I looked you up, once or twice over the years, sure. But there was nothing. You were a ghost. Then when I looked *her* up, Cleo McHugh . . . boom, there you were with your good-looking husband and your fancy job and your brand-new married name."

"What do you want, Reed?"

"What do I *want*?" He laughed. "I want you to make me whole. Give me the money. Three million dollars."

"Three million dollars?"

"I know you have it. The court filings? When those relatives contested Gladys Greene's will? They laid out all the details. Like I said, I spent some time googling you after I recognized Cleo. It was all right there," he said. "I'm willing to bet you still have most of it. Somebody like you, coming from where you did—you've probably got it all squirreled away."

He wasn't wrong. And money was easy. Money I could do.

"You want money?"

"Sure," Reed said, but the hatred in his eyes told me this wasn't going to be that simple. "And I want you to know how much I enjoyed fucking your daughter. She was very . . . enthusiastic."

I closed my eyes. It took everything in me not to lunge at him. But he'd use that knife on me. Happily. Maybe that was what he really wanted—an excuse.

"Fine, I'll give you the money right now. I'll wire it to you. The whole three million. But then you'll go. Never talk to Cleo again. Never come near me."

"You think you're really in a position to negotiate?"

I wasn't, of course.

"You want the money?" I asked. "Then you need me."

Reed walked the perimeter of my office, inspecting my books and our family photographs like he was gathering ammunition, as I stood behind my desk and typed as quickly as I could on my work laptop, not easy with my hands shaking. It was 6:15 p.m. Cleo could be there any minute. Reed could be planning on killing me, after I gave him the money. But I needed to at least try to get him out of there before Cleo arrived.

When my account finally opened on the screen, I could only stare. The balance read $53,297. I clicked back to the home page, hoping that I'd missed something. I considered firing up the desktop to see if it would give me a different result.

"There a problem?" Reed asked.

"There is . . . Money is missing from my account," I said. "I don't know what's going on. But you can see for yourself." I gestured to the computer.

He stayed where he was. "Find that fucking money right now. Or this is not going to end well."

I thought then of the crumpled piece of paper on the floor. Aidan. He went in and took the money, leaving me standing here as usual, holding the bag.

"I can't find it." I pointed at the screen again. "It's gone. My ex-husband must have emptied the account. We're in the middle of a divorce."

"Find it," he repeated, turning the knife in his hand as he stepped closer. There was something like delight in his eyes. Of course, *this* was why he was really here. For revenge, not money. But he wanted an excuse, a struggle. He wanted to hurt me and to be able to tell himself I asked for it.

Run. I have to run.

But he was blocking the path to the door. "I'll talk to Aidan. I'll get the money back and give it to you."

"Sure. Maybe we can talk to Cleo about it when she gets here." He changed his grip and raised the knife.

Cleo. All I could think about was all the little things I'd done to make her feel safe over the years. How pointless they were now. I thought of her small—two or three—new to a big-girl bed. How I'd snuggle in next to her when I got home from work. If she was still awake, I would read to her—*Goodnight Moon* always. If she was asleep, I'd sing quietly, "Momma's gonna buy you a mockingbird," hoping she could hear me in her sleep. And always when I was done, she would reach over and squeeze my hand and say, "Stay, Mommy. Stay until it's light."

In one quick motion, I slammed my laptop shut, flipped it on its side, and cracked it down against his elbow.

"Fuck!" he shouted, bending over in pain.

I sprinted past him and for the door. Ran as fast I could down the hall, blood pumping in my ears. *Don't look back. Almost there. Run out and scream "Fire!"* Before Reed's pounding feet could catch up to me.

But at the kitchen island, I was jerked back. An arm around my neck. Windmilled my arms through space. Trying to stop myself. But there was nothing.

Only air.

Through my fingers. Emptiness in my closed fists. The sound

of shattering glass. Then my head. Cracking down hard. The soft part of my temple, against stone. My brain vibrating. A giant bell inside my skull. There was something warm and wet on my face, burning in my eyes. But no pain.

I'm okay. I'm going to be—

CLEO

The book is shaking in my hands as I stare down at the inscription—the looping handwriting, the slant of the words. *God gives the gift to few.* It's like an echo from very far away. A ghost. And then I remember: the inscribed copy of *Leaves of Grass* that was given to my mom all those years ago. I look up from the book, down the hallway. The hall bathroom door is ajar, but the light is off. I can hear water running, though, from farther away—the little bathroom . . . way back in my mom's office. A bathroom you'd never—

I jump when my phone rings . . . Vivienne.

"Hello." My voice sounds like it's underwater.

"I haven't had any luck with the blackmail yet. That number you gave me is a burner and to trace those you need a contact in law enforcement willing to cross some shady lines." She's talking fast. "But I did end up closing the loop on that Reed Harding guy. I know you said it wasn't relevant anymore, but it was bothering me. People don't usually up and vanish. Guess where he ended up?"

"Dead." I'm still staring down toward my mom's office and the little bathroom: *God gives the gift to few . . .*

"Nope. I mean, he did change his name more than once, which for some reason none of the half dozen colleges he worked for seemed to care about. But Reed Harding is Will Butler these days—an assistant professor of English at NYU. Poetry. That seems like an awfully big coincidence."

The ground shifts underfoot. I grab the counter.

The boy my mom tried to kill isn't dead after all. He's a grown man now. A man in my house. He was in my bed.

I cared for him. I trusted him. This is my fault.

I look toward our front door. A way out—to safety, the police. I need to run out that front door while Will—Reed, whoever he is—is still back down the hall.

My mom would want me to do that. To save myself.

But if I run, that will be the last I'll see of Will. He'll know that I've figured him out. What if he's holding my mom somewhere right now? She could be running out of time.

I see her face that day on the beach when she taught me how to swim. Afterward when I was racing back toward my dad and Janine and Annie up on the sand.

"Cleo," she'd called out, and when I turned, she was smiling in the late-day sun. "You did it," she said, holding a thumb up in the air. "You did it all on your own."

But so much of it had been her. It always had been. I know that now.

And so I open my eyes, drop my phone. And run.

Toward him.

Run. Keep running.

The hallway telescopes in my vision as I race down it, like the bathroom is getting farther and farther away the faster I run. I can hear the water running, louder and louder as I get closer.

Will is at the sink, washing his shirt. Time slows to a stop as I lunge for the door. He turns. Eyes wide. Mouth open.

"Cleo, wha—"

I slam the door closed and turn the key, yank it out and back away as he tries the knob again and again, slowly realizing that he is trapped inside.

As I back out of the room, the pounding starts. "Cleo! What's going on? Open the door!"

I turn and run down the hall. This time toward the front door, the way out. I don't look back, not once. Even as I hear Will start to yell. Especially not then.

"Cleo, what the fuck!"

I can't feel my legs as I reach the front door. Can't feel my hand on the knob. But then a gush of fresh air and I'm outside, headed down the front steps.

"What's going on?" someone shouts.

It's George, looking alarmed. It's only then that I realize I've left my phone inside, dropped it with Vivienne on the other end. "George, I need you to call the police."

George scowls at me, looks up the steps toward my front door. "No," he says, then starts to head back inside his house. "No police."

"George!" I scream. "What the hell are you— I need to use your phone! It's an emergency."

"No. I gave my word."

"To who?" Did Will see George on his way in and say something? Threaten him? "Who told you not to call the police, George?"

He shakes his head and backs toward his door protectively. "No."

"Is there somebody in your house?"

"No, no—no one," he stammers. "She's not in there."

She.

"George, let me come in."

"No," he says. "You can't do that."

George is an old man, but quite large and not all that frail. I need to get past him, though. I need to see for myself what he's hiding. Then I notice George's trash can. His empty trash can. George has got a thing about those cans. I reach over, grab the handle, and throw it as hard as I can over his fence and into his neighbor's yard, where it smashes into the shrubs and sends dirt flying.

"What are you doing!" George shouts as he rushes out of his gate and toward the neighbor's front yard.

And just like that, I am at the door. And then inside George's house.

"Hello!" I yell as I run through the labyrinth of long halls and small rooms. "Hello!" It smells vaguely of mildew, and orange-scented air freshener. The ancient kitchen appliances were once a bright yellow, the linoleum black-and-white-checked. There isn't a dirty dish in sight. I startle at a sound in the corner, but when I look, it's only a cat with bright blue eyes.

I hear the front door open. George is coming. I race to check upstairs.

I freeze on the landing at the top of the steps. Through a doorway, I see the end of a bed. And feet. They're not moving. I hurry down the hall, stop short in the doorway.

She's there. My mom is right there, laid out in George's bed.

Her eyes are closed. But there is color in her face and a bandage on her head.

"Mom?" I move closer. Reach out. Put a hand on her arm. She's warm to the touch.

George is behind me in the doorway now. "Why didn't you tell someone she was here?" I ask him. "It's been three days."

"No, I don't think— One day. It's been one day . . ." George says, squinting toward the windows like he's checking to see if it's day or night. He shakes his head a little. "And she asked me not to. Every time she woke up she said it: *Don't tell anyone*." he says. "Over and over again. She kept saying that. And so I did what she wanted. But I said thirty-six hours was the limit. Then I was calling an ambulance. And only because there were no signs of internal bleeding. I checked. I did the best I could."

The doorbell rings. Blue and red lights strobing down the hall. Wilson. It must be.

"George, can you go let the police in? Tell them we need an ambulance."

"But I don't—"

"George, please! It's been *three* days. She needs to go to a hospital."

"Mom?" I ask again as George disappears downstairs. I shake her leg a little.

Her eyes flutter open. She stares at me for a moment. I can't tell whether she's even seeing me. But then her lips curve into a smile.

"You're here," she says finally. "You came."

The New York Times

EMILY TRACHTENBERG

DARDEN PHARMACEUTICALS WAS NOTIFIED OF ADVERSE DRUG REACTIONS

A months-long investigation has revealed that Darden Pharmaceuticals may have known of potentially lethal risks of Xytek to fetuses in utero. A review of internal documents provided by an anonymous whistle-blower has revealed that several OB-GYNs contacted Darden about these potential adverse side effects. Specifically, Dr. Frederick D'Angelo of Vanderbilt University Hospital has stated that he personally contacted Darden twice to warn them. First, shortly after the drug was introduced to the market, then again after the first lawsuits were filed. This group of OB-GYNs requested that the drug be removed from the market until further investigation. In neither instance was an adverse event report filed with the FDA.

There is currently multidistrict litigation against Darden Pharmaceuticals for alleged damages resulting from Xytek's impact on infants, including disabilities, injury, and death. Some of the most catastrophic consequences are alleged to have been sustained by fetuses during gestation.

One previously anonymous, now named, bellwether plaintiff in the lawsuit, Jules Kovacis, alleges that taking Xytek caused her daughter, now nearly three, life-long debilitating injury. Ms. Kovacis was, until recently, employed by Blair, Stevenson, but she resigned when that firm took over as lead counsel for Darden. When reached for comment, Darden said that it looks forward to fully cooperating with any investigations and defending itself in court.

Sources say that the FBI is investigating the procedures with respect to Xytek's sale and marketing, as well as its possible connection to the death of Doug Sinclair, a former Darden employee.

EPILOGUE

I run my hand across the books on the shelf in Cleo's childhood bedroom. The poetry is from high school: Mary Oliver, Adrienne Rich, Sylvia Plath, Emily Dickinson, Maya Angelou. Up above are a handful of books she saved from earlier childhood: *Out of My Mind, From the Mixed-Up Files of Mrs. Basil E. Frankweiler, The Giver, Little Women*. Tucked at the far end is a single board book—a battered copy of *Goodnight Moon*. It's the one I used to read to Cleo every night, long past when it was age-appropriate. I pull it out now and sit down in the deep windowsill to thumb through the thick pages. It turns out I still know the words by heart. I will have to ask Cleo if she remembers when she arrives.

She's coming home for the summer, instead of attending the writing program at Middlebury she got into. Cleo wants to be around to help as I work my way through the rest of rehab. I did try to talk her out of it—told her I had someone lined up from a service to stay with me—but she insisted, saying the college would hold her spot for next summer. Despite my protests, I am so glad she'll be here.

I spent a few days in the hospital after Cleo found me, but, surprisingly, I wasn't in terrible shape. Official diagnosis: a TBI, traumatic brain injury, which was confirmed by an MRI, but luckily there were no signs of any bleeding on the CT scan, as George had surmised. He had indeed lost track of time, which—combined with my repeated post-traumatic amnesia-fueled demands for his silence—had resulted in him keeping my whereabouts to himself for far longer than he realized.

Gradually, many of the details of what happened have come back to me. Still, I have no memory of anything after Reed grabbed me by the back of the hair, except the awful thud as my head made contact with the counter. Apparently, I did yell, loud enough to scare off Reed and bring George running. But since I didn't yell "Fire," George hadn't called the police, and instead did what I asked by not telling anyone.

My prognosis is good, though it will take time to heal. It always does—so much more time than you think. And recovery often does not progress in a straight line. So I'm learning to focus instead on one small step at a time. And I'm trying hard to see everything that has happened as an opportunity, a second chance. For so much of my life I wanted to believe that I was fine because I had survived. But surviving, I have come to realize, is not the same as being alive.

Even once I have recovered physically, there will still be a lot to rebuild. My job, for one. I have the excuse of my injury for now, but there remains the possibility that I will be disbarred for disclosing the Darden documents, not that Darden has expressed any interest in participating in an ethics probe. At the moment, they have their hands full with dueling FBI and FDA investigations, not to mention the ongoing multidistrict litigation. That's on top of the forthcoming indictment of former general counsel Phil Beaumont and his henchmen for Doug's murder—which Lauren's friends in the Manhattan DA's office have assured me is imminent.

According to Jules, they were following Cleo, like she'd warned—no one was more confused or worried than Darden when I disappeared with Doug's damning emails. It was thanks to Tim Lyall's secretary leaving them out in plain sight in the workplace she shared with Jules—only for a few minutes, but long enough—that they came to be included in the lawsuit. And no one is happier than Jules that Darden has a spotlight on it these days. It's allowed her to feel safe focusing on Daniela and getting settled into the position at UNow that Vivienne found her.

Tim Lyall has wisely remained in Zurich on an extended sabbatical, teaching at the Center for Security Studies. In any case, Blair, Stevenson has, thus far, not been held accountable for its role. Because so much of the firm's help was clandestine, there's simply no proof of wrongdoing. Mark continues on as managing partner at the firm, and I hear that billables are up—proving once again that all publicity is good publicity. I'm learning to accept the fact that maybe some people—some men especially—will forever emerge from disasters unscathed. Anyway, I choose to believe that, deep down, Mark knows what he did was wrong, and the true punishment will be having to live with that guilt.

I've already resigned from Blair, Stevenson, which means that for the first time in my professional life, I have no idea what comes next. I'm thinking of starting my own firm. There is room in the world for people who fix the right kinds of problems, second chances for people who make mistakes.

Other things have had a way of working themselves out, too. Like Aidan and Janine, whom Lauren saw arguing on the street when she came to visit the other day. I, for one, hope they share a very, very long life together. They deserve each other.

And Reed. He's being held at Rikers Island as a flight risk, denied bail as he awaits trial. Attempted murder, extortion, and assault. It's unclear if he'll face any charges for the string of young women he abused before Cleo and after me, but there's reason to hope he will. Vivienne was hugely helpful in locating these women and making sure they were aware of his arrest, in case they wanted to testify. But it was Wilson who'd known the second she laid eyes on fifty-one-year-old Reed and Cleo together, walking along the Hudson, that she needed to get her away from him. Of course, even once she had looked into him, all Wilson discovered was his checkered work history and changed names—not the connection to me.

At long last, my past has also been exhumed, my ugly mistakes dug up and dragged to the surface. As part of his defense, Reed has already revealed that I stabbed him years ago, and eventually, the whole sordid story will come out. The blood on my hands.

But that doesn't feel so terrifying anymore—or at least, it doesn't feel only terrifying. A part of me knows it will be a relief.

Cleo has had questions, of course, about my past, my job, Aidan, who did return the money, for now. It remains to be seen how it will be divided once our divorce is finalized. Aidan's misappropriation of the funds might work in my favor in arguing that all of it should go into a trust for Cleo. And I've been as honest as I can be with Cleo, about everything. I don't always have the answers, but I'm finding that's what she appreciates most—my willingness to inhabit a space of uncertainty, with her.

And while it is true I did many things wrong as a mother, I know now that I did enough right, too. If I ever doubt that, all I need to do is look at Cleo, in all her Technicolor wonder. She isn't perfect. But she is everything that is good in me, and, more important, she's herself. And that's the only thing I've ever wanted her to be.

"Hey." When I turn, Cleo is standing in the doorway. "Shouldn't you be somewhere lying down or something?"

"I was just making sure everything was ready for you. No one's been in here for a while." I hold up *Goodnight Moon*. "Remember this?"

"Of course. Be careful with it."

She crosses the room to where I'm perched in the windowsill, her face lit up by the midday sun streaming in. She takes the book from me and slides it back into its place.

"I'm so glad you're home," I say, opening my arms for a hug.

As she leans over and I wrap my arms around her, Cleo feels at once small and so completely, fully grown.

"I'm glad I'm home, too," she says.

I loosen my embrace, but she doesn't let go—and so neither do I. Instead, I bury my face in her neck and breathe deep, the way she always used to when she was a little girl. She smells of violets, and hope.

ACKNOWLEDGMENTS

Endless thanks to my incredible editor, Jennifer Barth, who worked so tirelessly on this novel from its inception. Your insight, wisdom, and patience were absolutely critical at every stage of the process. I'm so thrilled that we are continuing on this wild, creative journey together. Thank you to my equally fierce and kind literary agent, Dorian Karchmar, for your keen editorial eye, your faith in me, and your boundless empathy. I feel profoundly lucky to have you in my life.

Thank you to Reagan Arthur for giving me a new home.

Thanks to Alison Rich, Stephanie Bowen, Zehra Kayi, and Rachel Perriello Henry for your creativity, enthusiasm, and guidance. Thank you to my incredible marketing and publicity team at Knopf, especially Erinn Hartman, Laura Keefe, Abby Endler, and Elora Weil. Thanks also to Jenny Carrow for my beautiful cover, to the incredibly patient Kathleen Cook, and to Brian Etling and Isabel Meyers.

Deepest thanks to very early, very generous readers and brilliant friends Motoko Rich, Megan Crane, Susan Berfield, and Nicole Kear. Bless you for not admitting that the rough state of the manuscript back then made your eyeballs ache. Gratitude also to my favorite beta readers and beloved friends, Tara Pometti and Heather Weiss. Thank you, thank you to the ever-fabulous Victoria Cook—early reader, entertainment lawyer extraordinaire, and most wonderful friend. I am so grateful to have you in every one of my corners. Thanks also to Per Saari.

Thank you to Julie Mosow for your early heavy lifting and to my miraculous assistant, Katherine Faw, who I am just grateful continues to tolerate me. Thanks also to the wonderful Christina Cerio and my dedicated, talented, and hilarious publishing lawyer Mark Merriman. Thank you to my team at WME, especially Hilary Zaitz Michael, James Munro, and Lucy Balfour, for all your tireless efforts on my behalf. Thank you to Sophia Bark, Erin Bradshaw, and Robby Thaler. Thanks also to Andrea Blatt.

Thank you to the generous experts who shared their wisdom with me or helped me find someone who could: Roshma Azeem, Eric Franz (always!), Hallie Levin, retired detective Richard Reyes, retired detective Peter Frederick, Yalkin Demirkaya (NYPD, retired), and Dr. Kristen Dams-O'Connor.

Last, and most certainly not least, I am grateful to my daughters, Emerson and Harper. Thank you, Emerson, for so patiently allowing space for my art, which I know has a tendency to gobble up more than its fair share of the oxygen. I am so lucky that you fill my days with so much laughter and love. Thank you, Harper, for always inspiring me with your passion and joy, for making me feel seen no matter how far away you are, and for reminding me that you are proud of me, invariably when I need it the most.

This book never could have been written without you both. And not simply because it is a novel about mothers and daughters, but because the current of love that runs through these pages exists in me only because of you.

A NOTE ABOUT THE AUTHOR

Kimberly McCreight is the *New York Times* best-selling author of *Reconstructing Amelia, Where They Found Her, A Good Marriage,* and *Friends Like These,* and a young adult trilogy, the Outliers. She's been nominated for the Edgar, Anthony, and Alex Awards, and her books have been translated into more than twenty languages. She lives in Brooklyn with her two daughters.

A NOTE ON THE TYPE

This book was set in Granjon, a type named in compliment to Robert Granjon, a type cutter and printer active in Antwerp, Lyons, Rome, and Paris from 1523 to 1590. Granjon, the boldest and most original designer of his time, was one of the first to practice the trade of typefounder apart from that of printer.

Linotype Granjon was designed by George W. Jones, who based his drawings on a face used by Claude Garamond (ca. 1480–1561) in his beautiful French books. Granjon more closely resembles Garamond's own type than do any of the various modern faces that bear his name.

Typeset by Scribe
Philadelphia, Pennsylvania

Printed and bound by Lakeside Book Company
Harrisonburg, Virginia